I0818363

THE
STONE
CURSE

DEBBIE CASSIDY

Page & Vine
An Imprint of Meredith Wild LLC

Cover by Covers by Christian

Paperback ISBN: 978-1-964264-76-9

CHAPTER 1

CAMERON

THE AFTERMATH

The graynite took to the air with Serath dangling, limp and lifeless, from its talons.

A roar filled my head, and the world vanished.

"Cam! Cam, come back. Come back, please," someone cried.

"Hold her, hold her down," another voice, familiar yet distant, ordered.

A scream. A wail of anguish, and fire raced over my skin.

Bands circled my wrists as sobs rose in the distance.

"Oh, God. Oh, God. Please help her. Help her."

"I've got her. Cam, I've got you."

Serath? No. Not Serath. Serath was gone. Serath was dead.

No, no, no.

I allowed darkness to take me back under.

"CAMERON, CAN YOU hear me?"

I knew this voice, even though I hadn't heard it often.

"Cameron, you should have come to me. You should have told

me. I would have helped you. Protected you."

Fuck off, Lionel. I'm happy here. Safe here. It's dark, cozy, and warm, and I want to stay.

"You need to come back. You need to surface. I'm your sire, and I *will* protect you."

I wanted to remind him how he'd never done anything for me before, but that meant speaking; it meant surfacing, something I wasn't eager to do.

But even if you do say those things, they'd be a lie.

I squeezed my eyes shut against Derek's voice in my head. I didn't want to follow this train of thought.

He do something for you. He give you Romi.

Romi.

My brother was in danger.

But Serath was dead.

The darkness hugged me tighter. Desperate to keep me.

Romi alive. He alive and he need you.

No, no, no.

Time for us to wake up, my Cameron.

I hate you.

I hate me too.

No, that wasn't what I meant. Derek, I'm sorry.

I sorry, Cam. I so sorry.

As much as I wanted to hide, as much as I needed to block out the world, Derek was right: it was time to wake up.

"You're healing well," Levi said. "You'll be good as new by the morning."

I stared back at him from my bed in the infirmary, my thoughts numb.

His throat bobbed. "You should have told me you'd found your fated mate."

He knew. Everyone knew now. "Your father is on the council."

His brows knitted. "And you thought I'd sell you out? So, you fake dated the Mason boy to throw me off the scent?" He shook his head in exasperation. "I knew it, that day outside Stone Comfort when you protected Serath, just before Derek showed up and—"

"Go away, Levi." I didn't want to remember. I didn't want to see *him* in my head while speaking to Levi. His face, his beautiful face, now gone. I was done with the conversation. Done with anything that made me think or feel. I was awake, and that was enough.

"No, Cam. I need to know. To understand how you could *ever* have thought I'd rat you out."

"Can you honestly say that you wouldn't have told your father? In the name of protecting me from myself?"

He opened his mouth to reply, then snapped it shut again.

"Yeah, I thought as much." I turned my head away, wanting to fall into dreams. Into a place where everything was like before. A place where Serath was alive. "Go away, Levi. I want to be alone."

"No."

The first flicker of anger since I'd woken flared inside me. "Go. Away."

"I'm not leaving you."

Something ugly and twisted surged to life inside me. "Why? Because you think you have a chance with me now that Serath is gone? You think I'll fall into your arms, all weepy and desperate for comfort?" I sat up, eyes burning with indignant wrath and the vicious need to hurt someone, anyone. Him. "I will *never* love you. I will *never ever* love *anyone* again. I might be breathing, but I'm dead. You understand me? Cameron is fucking dead. Now get the fuck out!"

Levi met my rage with calm assurance. "I'll go. But I need you to know that I'm here for you. I care about you, Cameron, and I'll always be your friend."

I turned my head away and closed my eyes, battling the heat of frustrated rage, and after a few moments, I heard the door open and close.

He was gone, and I was finally alone. I sniffed and wiped at my wet eyes. Fucking stupid tears. Stupid world.

I hurt. I hurt all the fucking time.

The door opened again. Fucksake! "What is your problem?"

Sharniza stepped into the room, trailed by Curi, Touron, Ginia, and Palia. "My problem is that my best friend is in pain," she said, "and I can't do a damn thing to fix it."

My vision blurred as the people I loved the most in the world entered the room and surrounded my bed. Derek materialized beside me, his huge, solid mass dwarfing us all.

"I don't know if I can do this." My words were a whispered confession. "I don't think I'm strong enough."

"Then we'll be strong enough for you," Curi said. "You're not alone."

"We fight," Derek said. "We fight, and we get Romi."

I squeezed my eyes shut, dislodging tears. "It hurts. It hurts like it will never stop."

Derek put his arm around me. "Then we share the hurt. We bear it together."

"We love you," Ginia said.

"So much," Palia added.

"But you need to get out of that bed and on your feet," Sharniza said, her tone hard and unforgiving. "You owe it to Serath and to Romi, but most of all, you owe it to yourself."

Romi...How the fuck would I save him now? How would I avenge Serath? "The elite team is gone. No Prasan, no Serath and Selas..." Selas was injured so badly she'd had to be taken back to Arcadia for treatment.

"Selas is strong," Touron said. "She'll heal. But we need to make the motherfuckers who did this pay."

I looked up at his determined face. "Without an elite team?"

They exchanged glances. "No," Sharniza said finally. "You'll have a team. Elite trials are in less than three weeks, and you won't be taking them alone."

CHAPTER 2

CAMERON

ONE WEEK LATER

Serath was dead.

I'd lost count of how often that thought stopped me in my tracks.

But if I closed my eyes and pretended hard, then I could imagine him here with me, standing behind me, the heat of his body brushing mine. Sometimes, I could even feel the weight of his hands on my shoulders. And in that moment before waking, when the world was soft, fuzzy, and unreal, his gruff, rumbling voice would tease my senses.

But reality always seeped in, and the tiny voice inside me that refused to allow me to succumb to delusion would remind me of the bitter truth.

Serath was dead.

He was gone.

But I was here, and I couldn't stop. I couldn't curl up and die. I didn't have the luxury of crawling into the bosom of my grief and staying there. So, I ate and walked and talked. Trained and breathed, all the while carrying an empty place inside me where my heart had once nestled.

Serath was gone, and I would never be whole again.

The only thing that kept me going was Romi. My brother was alive. I'd save him. I'd use everything that Serath had taught me and make him proud.

The tentative knock on my door made my teeth ache. Everything was eggshells and hushed voices. Everything was cotton wool and care, and although part of me understood that my friends were trying to help, that they cared about me, loved me even, the other part, the beast inside was enraged by it.

We were not weak.

We would not fall.

We would find Romi and kill the alpha, avenging our mate.

"Cam?" Curi called through the door. "The meeting starts in thirty minutes. We should leave."

I closed my eyes and breathed to center myself before pulling open the door.

Curi was in full lastonflex initiate uniform, blue hair pulled back in a knot so that his brutal features were highlighted to their best advantage. To someone who didn't know him, he could come across as intimidating, frightening even, but not to me. Not when his dark eyes were brimming with concern. My agitation ebbed. For some reason, it was impossible to stay angry around Curi.

"You good?" he asked.

No. My mate was dead, but I was still breathing. "I'm good."

He exhaled and nodded. "We just need to get through this meeting, and then we can focus on the mission."

They'd made us wait one week before calling for a meeting to determine what exactly had happened the night of the cadet exams.

One whole fucking week!

My blood simmered, and it took every ounce of will to soothe it. "Where are the others?"

"Headed to the main building. I volunteered to come get you." We headed down the stairs. "Any news on Selas?"

"I spoke to my uncle last night. She's stable, thanks to the antivenom that Willowman brewed up, but she's badly wounded. They're not sure if and when she'll be able to return to active duty."

Which left Orix as the only active elite. There was only one way forward, and we'd waited a week for it to be confirmed.

This meeting was more than just about rehashing the events of the attack. This meeting was about rebuilding the only team that could take down the monster who'd ripped out my heart.

"Are you ready for this, Curi?"

"I've never been more ready in my life."

Good, because if all went to plan, I wouldn't be the only one taking the elite exam in two weeks. Curi, Sharniza, and the next Halle in line, whoever that was, would be taking it with me.

THE MAIN BUILDING was buzzing with goyles, all here to hover, to get a listen in on the proceedings that were about to take place. Personally, I thought this meeting was a waste of time. Everyone involved had given their statements. The goyles who'd come to our rescue had seen what happened. This...this was a waste of time, but it was protocol. An informal face-to-face fact-finding exercise was what they called it, but there was nothing informal about the cloaked and hooded alchemists that crawled over campus.

They'd arrived the day after the attack, and it was now clear that they had no immediate plans to leave. Our security had been upgraded by mind readers, a precaution to ensure that any other moles were rooted out quickly.

Goyles stopped talking to look our way as we passed, then the whispers began. Curi's grip on my hand tightened, not the grip of a lover like we'd faked the past few weeks, but of a friend loaning support in the face of controversy. Because my secret was out.

My reaction to Serath's death on the battlefield had been witnessed by all. I'd blacked out, and the moments after were a blur, but I'd heard the accounts whispered on campus and relayed to me by a stone-faced Sharniza.

According to them, I'd torn off my clothes and gouged welts into my arms and face. I'd been incoherent. Crazed.

The actions of a grieving mate.

My secret was out, but Serath was dead, and my sire had been true to his word, reminding all that would listen that they needed me.

I was still here.

Unpunished by them but ruined by fate.

"Can't believe they hid it all this time..."

"A mercy he's dead—"

A low growl rumbled up my throat, head whipping around to face the speaker.

The goyle recoiled, holding up his hands, but my beast was awake, pushing against my skin, incensed, because how fucking dare he? How fucking—

Shadows bloomed in my path, coalescing into a familiar form. "No," Derek said. "We not do this, Cam."

The rage bled out of me, and my shoulders slumped. I was tired. So fucking tired.

Derek put his arm around me and drew me close. "We get through this. Together."

I looked up into his beautiful diamond eyes filled with love, compassion, and regret, and couldn't help but wonder *what if*. What if I hadn't made Yarrow promise to keep Derek away from the cadet exams? Would it have made a difference if he'd been able to get to me?

Would Serath still be alive?

But these thoughts were redundant.

The past couldn't be altered.

All we could do now was move forward. One moment to lean into Derek, to squeeze Curi's hand, to draw strength, then I was standing on my own two feet, untethered, chin up as we walked past all the prying eyes and whispering mouths, up the stairs and down a long corridor to the assembly chamber.

Shar, Touron, Ginia, and Palia waited by the assembly room doors, along with several other cadets who'd survived the attack. Waxen and Hawke were among them.

We exchanged nods before my attention was drawn to Orix standing by a side door, deep in conversation with a dark-haired woman. There was something familiar about her—something in the curve of her mouth and her almond-shaped eyes.

She must have felt me staring because she looked over. Her mouth turned down as she said something to Orix before breaking away from him to stride toward me.

I wasn't sure why, but I braced myself.

"Cameron Basque, my name is Nandini Aziza. I hear you killed my son."

My stomach went rock hard. This was Prasan's mother. "I didn't kill him, but I wish I had."

Her jaw flexed. "You misunderstand me. I'm grateful to you. What he did..." She swallowed hard. "He has brought shame on our family, and I assure you that I will personally stop at nothing to uncover the full extent of his duplicity. I'm...I'm sorry for your loss."

Serath...

I pressed my lips together because there was nothing more to say. Her son had been a murderer. He might not have struck the killing blow, but he'd orchestrated the attack that had. I was not sorry for her loss. Not one bit.

She inclined her head and slipped away through a set of side doors that led fuck knows where.

"Haven't seen her in years," Sharniza said, joining us.

It was odd to think that Shar could be related to Prasan, the traitor, but they were blood. Distant cousins on her sire's side.

"The woman is married to the Stone council," Shar continued. "One of the few omegas to take a post outside of Arcadia's nest. She practically lives at HQ from what I've heard. Azizas value their reputation above anything else, and her mate will blame her for Prasan's defection. Any negative traits or fallacies are always blamed on the mother, and any triumphs are attributed to the sire."

I didn't have it in me to feel sorry for Nandini. Emotions had been running a little dry as of late; the only ones that seemed to come unbidden and easy were anger or rage. They seemed to traipse about hand in hand, waiting for any small fracture in my emotional shields to seep through.

But tonight was about poise and calm. Tonight, I'd get what I needed by using logic and clean-cut argument.

"We should be called in soon," Orix said. "Once this is over, we can focus on the mission."

"They'll address the elite issue?" Shar asked.

"I'll make sure they do," Orix said.

There were dark circles beneath his eyes. Lack of sleep had caught up to him. The loss of his team—one friend's betrayal and another's death...

I'd been so caught up in my own loss that I'd failed in acknowledging the pain of those around me. Grief was indeed a selfish beast.

Guilt settled heavily on my shoulders as I looked, really looked, at my friends and fellow cadets—the slump of their shoulders, the smudges beneath their eyes. The loss...so much loss.

"Any more news on Selas?" Touron asked Curi.

"Not since last night," Curi replied. He looked like he wanted to say more but then pressed his lips together and shook his head slightly.

"What?" Touron demanded. "What aren't you telling us?"

Curi sighed. "I'm wondering what *you* aren't telling *us*."

Touron's expression shuttered. "I don't know what you mean."

"Yeah? Well, when you figure it out, know that we're here and...I'm pretty sure she's allowed visitors."

Wait, who...Selas? The look on Touron's face was pure devastation and longing and—Oh God...Did he have a thing for Selas?

"Everyone," Orix said. "We're being summoned."

There was no time to press Touron on it now, because the doors to the assembly hall were swinging open.

It was time to give testimony.

CHAPTER 3

CAMERON

The assembly room was designed for graduations and special events. But tonight, the stage at the back of the room was taken up by a row of seats, each occupied by a goyle that I didn't recognize.

No, wait, there were six goyles and a human. *The* human representative, no doubt.

More seats had been set in a row, backs against the base of the steps, taken up by more goyles, one of which was my sire.

Lionel Basque fixed his attention on me, assessing, probably checking to ensure I didn't fall apart.

He'd been there for me after, and even though it didn't make up for the years of radio silence, it mattered.

"No one will touch you, Cameron. You're a Basque, and I won't allow it." He hadn't held me. Hadn't comforted me with physical touch, but his words had shown his support.

And he was here now. To speak for me, if needed, and *that* mattered.

A side door opened, and Prasan's mother entered, followed by two cloaked alchemists.

"What are they doing here?" Touron whispered.

"Lie detectors, no doubt," Shar said.

"They'll probably be scanning our thoughts during this

whole thing," Curi said.

I had nothing to hide. Not any longer.

Prasan's mother took a seat at the base of the stage while the alchemists flanked it, their faces hidden inside their hoods, hands clasped so they were hidden by the bell sleeves of their cloaks.

The door opened again, and Levi slipped into the room. He stayed in the shadows, looking up at the stage. Of course, Ulrickson would be up there somewhere. Which one was he?

The one in the middle with the stunning sapphire eyes like Levi? Yes, he had the same straight nose, too, but that was where the similarities ended. Where Levi's mouth was full and generous, this goyle's mouth was a thin slash of a line. Where Levi's eyes held warmth and compassion, this goyle's gaze was cold and calculating.

He was a Halle. Serath's uncle. But I saw nothing of my mate in him.

He spoke, his mouth barely moving with the words. "You have been called to give oral testimony on the events of..." He looked down the stage toward the drapes that covered the side exits, where a small man was huddled over a notepad.

The man looked up, a startled expression on his face, pushed his spectacles up his nose, and recited the date of the cadet exam. A date etched into my memory but obviously not important enough for Ulrickson to remember.

Ulrickson nodded curtly at the man before continuing. "We have studied your written accounts of the evening in question and spoken to the goyles who witnessed, or were part of, the awful events, and we're confident that we have a good understanding of what transpired; however, memory is a complicated beast, and there may be details buried in your subconscious minds. We will wish to view those." View? What did he mean? "We'd also like to discuss the graynite behavior witnessed."

Another goyle sat forward. "You say that there were five graynites to begin with. That they attacked you with the goal of eliminating Miss Basque. This makes sense as she is our only viable Basque at present. Eliminating her would give the graynites an advantage. But your statements also assert that several more graynites joined the fray toward the end of the battle and attacked the first troop of graynites?" He swept his gaze over us. "Is that correct?"

We all nodded and mumbled, "Yes."

"This is unusual behavior for graynites," the goyle said. "Our history of conflict with them shows that their strength lies in their unity."

"Maybe there are fractures in their camp," another one of the council members said.

"Yes, Iram. It wouldn't explain why they would want to save our cadets."

"Who says they were saving them?" Iram asked. "Maybe the second troop was simply taking the opportunity to eliminate the first. The cadets could merely have been a distraction."

I'd been thinking about this over the past few days, and it didn't make sense. Ignus saving me didn't make sense. He'd tried to kidnap me once; if anything, I'd have thought he would have been on the side of the graynites trying to kill me...unless...Unless he wanted me alive and was working with the *second* troop to take me, but then why *hadn't* he taken me? It had been the perfect opportunity.

"Miss Basque? Are you listening?" Iram asked.

Shit. "Sorry?"

The goyle pursed his lips, clearly irritated with my lack of attention. "You say that this Ignus creature saved your life?"

"Yes."

"The same creature who attempted to kidnap you a few weeks ago?"

"That's correct."

"And why would he spare you? Why not take you with him?"

"Do I look like a mind reader?" Had I said that out loud? The stunned silence in the room said that yes, yes, I fucking had.

"No, Miss Basque, I do not think that you're a mind reader."

His tone was clipped. "But I think it's time we employed the mind readers we do have to do our fact-finding. Who knows...you may learn something."

Two more alchemists entered, each carrying a large glass ball. They came to stand in the center of the room, putting them between us and the council. I met Lionel's gaze and saw my confusion echoed on his face. He was just as out of the loop as I was.

"What's going on?" Curi said under his breath.

"No clue," Sharniza replied.

The other two alchemists took a step forward, and the air crackled with strange energy. Gooseflesh pricked my skin. Sharniza sucked in a sharp breath, and Curi groaned softly, but before I could look at either of them, the center of the room was filled with images. Cadets running in battle against...graynites. Oh...oh God, this was that night. A projection of that fucking night. I spotted myself running one moment, evading the next, and then from a different angle, held captive by Prasan. My pulse raced, blood galloping through my veins, rushing to my head and filling it with a buzz of a thousand bees as Serath came into view with his back to me. The angle of viewing changed, sweeping round so we could see his profile, but beyond that, I'd been saved by Ignus, his form a shadowy figure at my back for barely a moment. I remembered what happened next...I knew what happened next, and I didn't want to see it. I didn't want to relive this.

My head was suddenly tight, as if someone was pressing on it, gripping it. Squeezing.

I cried out and clutched my head.

"Basque is resisting," a male voice said.

"Miss Basque, you will allow the alchemists to do their job."

I didn't want to see this. I didn't want to watch him die again, but what if there was something in my memory that could help? What if I'd subconsciously picked up on something that could be vital?

"Miss Basque!" Ulrickson snapped.

I exhaled and relaxed, allowing the alchemist into my mind. But the pressure remained, a resistance that I wasn't in control of.

"Miss Basque, you will stop this at once!" Iram ordered.

But I wasn't doing anything.

The projection stuttered and froze on the image of Serath's profile, and a fist squeezed my heart. The vise around my head tightened as the alchemist tried to get in.

My vision blurred, and the pressure on my mind increased.

"What are you doing?" Lionel asked. "Two alchemists? You'll hurt her."

"We must know what she's hiding," Iram insisted.

A fiery blade lanced through my head, and I cried out, knees buckling. They were crushing me. Crushing my head, and the pain was so intense I couldn't draw breath to cry out.

"Stop it!"

"Let her go!"

"Oh God, she's bleeding."

"*No!*"

The pain cut out, leaving me clearheaded, on my knees, palms kissing cool wood. A droplet of blood hit the floor. My blood. I wiped at my nose with the back of my hand, leaving a crimson smear across my skin. Across the room, Derek's large menacing form loomed over the two unconscious alchemists who'd tried to crack open my brain.

"Cameron..." Sharniza gently grabbed my arm. "You okay?"

I allowed her and Curi to help me up as the room broke into a cacophony of exclamations.

"What is it?"

"Surround it!"

"Extinguish it."

Like hell. I broke free of my friends and rushed forward to place myself between Derek and the alchemists, my back to my buddy's chest. "Don't you *dare* touch him."

The council was on its feet, wary and...fearful.

I wasn't ashamed of the stab of satisfaction that gave me.

These fuckers needed to know they weren't all-powerful. That we *gave* them power with our compliance.

Lionel pinched the bridge of his nose and stepped away from the stage so he could look up at the council.

"This is my fault," he said. "I neglected to mention that Cameron has a unique shield. This is Derek." He aimed a closed-lipped smile over my head. "Say hello, Derek."

"He's not a puppet." I turned away from them, dismissing them in favor of my friend. "It's all right, buddy. I'm fine." He continued to stare at the council, his body vibrating with rage. I placed a hand on his chest. "I'm okay. Honestly."

He exhaled and slowly dropped his gaze to my face. "Are you sure, my Cameron?"

I forced a smile. "Positive."

A muscle feathered along his jaw as he looked back at the stage. "If you try and hurt my Cameron, I *will* hurt you." His diamond eyes narrowed, chest rumbling in a low-grade growl. "Do. Not. Touch." He misted into shadow and melted away.

Nandini rushed over to the alchemists and crouched to take each one's pulse. "Their pulses are strong."

"That *thing* can't be permitted," another council member said. "It's dangerous."

"No more dangerous than any goyle's shield." Yarrow strode into view. I hadn't seen him come into the room. "Derek is a part of Cameron. He is her shield made sentient."

"How is this possible?" Ulrickson asked.

"We don't know, but there is much we don't know about halfbloods."

"It hardly matters," Lionel said. "Cameron felt threatened, and her shield protected her. It's a natural response."

One of the alchemists sat up with a groan, and his hood fell back to reveal a young man with closely cropped dark hair and lean features. He looked up at Nandini with a dazed expression. "What happened?" His gaze cleared, expression hardening. "Wait...she ejected me."

"Her shield protected her," Lionel said.

"Shields don't work that way against alchemist intervention," the alchemist said.

He was right. It hadn't been Derek stopping them getting into my mind. It had been something else. Something innate. But they didn't need to know that.

I looked down my nose at him. "Mine does."

The alchemist stood up. "No shield should. We're trained to bypass any blocks."

"Maybe you require more training," Lionel said dryly.

"Are you questioning my ability?"

"I wouldn't dream of it," Lionel drawled.

"I can prove it. I can look in your mind."

"Raffe!" Ulrickson barked the name, and the alchemist's head whipped up. "You know the rules. The council and supporting council's minds are not to be probed."

Raffe's jaw flexed, eyes flashing, and for a moment I thought he was going to argue, but then he pulled up his hood. "Apologies, Master Halle."

The second alchemist woke, and Nandini helped him to his feet.

"I think we've seen enough," Ulrickson said. "Alchemists, you may leave the room."

All four robed figures glided out, and my gaze flicked to Lionel in time to see his shoulders relax. He caught my eye and dropped me a slight nod before reclaiming his seat.

Around me, my fellow cadets were subdued. The council had torn open a wound that had barely begun to heal. Seeing the events play out before us like a movie had shaken us all. The alchemists had somehow infiltrated all our thoughts at the same time to create a full picture of events, all angles, all the tiny details. Everyone's memories except mine.

"The graynites are obviously divided for some reason," Ulrickson said. "We can use that to our advantage. Attack the alpha while their forces are weakened."

Lionel sighed. "For that, we must assume that the second troop in this scenario had no interest in the cadets."

"The fact that they attacked the first troop, then left, rather than finishing off the cadets, indicates just that," Ulrickson said.

"Or maybe they were protecting us?" The words were out before I could stop them, and the room fell silent.

"What is this academy teaching its cadets?" Ulrickson looked about as if searching for a tutor to hold accountable. "A graynite is a gargoyle's mortal enemy. They seek to wipe us out so that they can claim this world as their own. That is their *only* purpose. Their only goal." His eyes bore into me. "To entertain anything else is to weaken our defense." I pressed my lips together to hold back my arguments. "Besides, can any of you say with certainty that it wasn't one of the second troop that murdered Serath Halle?"

My heart dropped into my stomach.

He held my gaze. "I believe it happened right before your eyes, Miss Basque. Although we were unable to view it." He let the dig settle before continuing. "We are forced to rely on your oral and written account of the incident. So, can you say for certain that the killer *wasn't* a graynite from the second wave?"

The hollow pit inside me expanded, and the room melted away, and despite my desperate bid at blocking it out, the memory bloomed in my mind. For a moment, I was back in the field with Serath the instant before talons exploded from his chest. I didn't want to see this. Didn't want to remember.

There was movement in the periphery of my vision from where Levi had been standing, but my focus was wholly on Ulrickson—the bastard intent on poking at my wound. "What possible benefit would killing Serath have for them? You have other Halles to take his place on the elite team."

"But no other Basques," Ulrickson said. "Prasan Aziza must have known about your fated pairing." He waited for me to confirm or deny, but I kept my mouth shut because saying anything would call into question who else had known. There was no way I was getting my friends into trouble over this. Ulrickson must have realized I wasn't going to give him anything because he continued. "We all know that losing a fated mate can break even the strongest gargoyle, and you, Miss Basque, are a halfblood."

"If that was the case, then why come in two troops?" Sharniza said. "If they had the same goal, then why not attack together?"

Silence greeted her question, and it was Lionel who finally broke it. "With all due respect, council, I don't think there is anything further that we can glean from our cadets. We should simply consider the facts. Fact one, there were two troops of graynites, one which attacked our cadets, and one which attacked the first troop. This suggests a conflict within the graynite camp, which, yes, we should exploit. Fact two, the first wave of graynites wanted my daughter dead."

His daughter? He'd called me his daughter...

"Fact three," he continued. "Prasan Aziza was working *with* the graynites"—Nandini made a soft sound of distress—"which means there could be other moles, not only at this academy but higher up."

One of the council members bristled. "What are you suggesting?"

"What we all should be considering," Lionel said. "This incident has taught us that we must look *within* and increase our security protocols."

"I think we're forgetting another important *fact*," Ulrickson said. "Your *daughter* was fated to a sigma and kept it a secret. She broke the law."

"And we have discussed this," Lionel snapped, his eyes bright with anger. "As the only adult Basque, Cameron has been absolved of her crime. It has been agreed. We need her for the elite team."

"At present we have no team," Ulrickson said. "Something that must be addressed."

Finally.

"The council has spoken on the matter," Ulrickson said. "Selas Mason may not be fit for duty for some time and therefore must be replaced. We have agreed that Curi Mason step into her place, and Sharniza Aziza fill the role left by Prasan Aziza. And the Halle spot..." His gaze flicked across the room to where Levi stood, and my pulse stuttered. "The Halle spot will be taken by Levi Halle. My son."

CHAPTER 4

CAMERON

I was the first out of the assembly hall, leaving the others behind in my desperation to get away.

He'd known. Levi had known what his father was going to do. Had he suggested it? To take Serath's place?

My stomach rolled with nausea as I hurried out of the building and down the steps, where I stopped to suck in huge gulps of crisp, cool air.

"Cam! Cameron, wait. Please!" Levi hurried toward me.

"No." I backed away from him. "I don't want to talk to you."

"You can't avoid me forever."

"No, I suppose I can't, not now that you've insinuated yourself onto the team. I told you we were over. I fucking told you there could never be anything between us. Why can't you back off? Why can't you let it go?" My voice rose, clawing at the night.

"Because you could die!" He glared at me, chest heaving. "The trials could kill you, but if I'm there, I can help. Once I'm in the trial with you, I can help. I can tell you what to expect."

I stared at him in dawning comprehension. "Of course...you know what the trial entails..."

"Yes, but the council doesn't know that I know. I had to convince my father how badly I wanted to prove myself. He likes the idea of his son being elite, so he pushed it through." He reached for me, but I backed away. "Cam, I want to help. That's all. Nothing more. I would never presume..." He put his hands on his hips and tucked his chin in, taking a moment to compose himself. "Look, I know you're hurting, and if it makes you feel better to hate me, if it helps with the pain to have a target for your rage, then I'll be that for you, but you need to let me help you pass the trials. Let me help you save Romi and then...then I'll step down and leave. I promise."

My anger evaporated, leaving me drained. What was I doing? I turned away and headed for the elite tower.

"Cameron? Cam?" Levi called after me.

But I didn't stop.

And this time he didn't follow.

THE OBSERVATORY WAS my go-to place when I needed to be alone. No one came up here anymore. Not even Orix. I'd claimed it as my spot, bringing Orix's favorite chair up close to the window and claiming it as mine also.

Taz, however, didn't understand the concept of privacy. If the darn cat wasn't with Orix, then he was trailing me. Jumping up onto my lap and expecting to be petted.

Orix said it was Taz's way of soothing me. That he could sense my sadness, and when I looked into his peridot eyes now, it felt like he was peering into my soul.

"I'll be okay, Taz. I will...eventually."

The pain would fade...eventually.

But until then, it would be a constant ache in my soul. "This was Serath's favorite spot. He loved looking out at the world from here."

Taz yawned and bumped my shoulders with his head before padding to the door, then looking back at me expectantly.

"We need to put a hole in that door, don't we?"

He made a soft chuffing sound but didn't scratch to be let out.

"Is someone there?"

A knock sounded a moment later. "It's Sharniza. Can I come in?"

Guilt pricked at me because this space should be for everyone to enjoy. Was I making them feel that they couldn't come up here? "Of course you can come in."

Shar slipped into the room, and Taz took the opportunity to dash out, probably in search of Orix.

"You mind some company?" Shar asked.

"Not if it's you."

She smiled, but it didn't quite reach her eyes, and unease bloomed in my chest. "What is it? Has something happened?"

"I've moved my stuff into the tower," she said. "Curi is here too."

"That's good though, right?"

"And Levi is joining us later."

My stomach tightened. "Oh."

"I heard your conversation with him outside the main building."

"You did?"

She winced. "I think everyone in the hallway did."

"Shit." I stood and began to pace. "I don't know why I got so mad at him."

"You're hurting, and you need to lash out, and Levi is a safe option. You know he'll take the tongue-lashing. You know he loves you too much to hate you. Too much to walk away."

"That's not true. Derek loves me more. I could take it out on... on..." But Derek was a part of me, my responsibility to love and care for, and there was no way I would ever hurt him, but Levi... Levi was strong enough to take it. Take my shit and still be here. "I hate that you're right."

She pulled me into a hug. "I hate that you've turned me into a hugger."

I laughed into her shoulder. "I love that you're a hugger now." I pulled away slightly. "And I'm sure Derek will appreciate it too."

She blinked sharply, looking away. "What has Derek got to do with anything?"

I tried to catch her eye. "He loves hugs."

Twin spots of color bloomed on her cheeks. "Hugs from you."

"Hugs from the people he cares about and who care about him..."

She met my gaze levelly. "I do care about him."

"I think it's more than care, isn't it?"

She looked away again. Was she hiding her joy because I was grieving? "Shar...you can be happy. I would never begrudge you that. I *want* you to be happy. Being in love is...It's beautiful and wondrous. Please don't hold back on account of me. I'd hate that."

She exhaled. "I know. It isn't that. Well, not entirely..." She gave me a sheepish smile. "The timing is all wrong. Maybe once we have Romi back. Once the graynite threat is dealt with...Maybe then, but not now. Now isn't the time to start anything, and I'm happy with that."

I studied her for a moment, looking for any signs of deception and finding none. "Okay. I believe you. Speaking of Derek, where is he?"

"Training with Yarrow. He's determined to be an asset to the elite."

He'd been training a lot since the attack. Yarrow had even given him a special bracelet to help ground him. The goal was to help Derek become his own person, completely independent from me, so that he didn't need my energy but could use his own. He'd still be my shield but by choice. We'd still have a bond, but he wouldn't be reliant on my existence to live.

I wanted that for him. "He's already an asset. He's saved my life on more than one occasion."

"I know, but after what happened..."

"That wasn't his fault." I'd made Yarrow keep him away from the cadet exams. I'd made him promise to keep Derek in lockdown. "That was all on me."

"He understands that now, but I think he wants to make sure

it never happens again." The corner of her mouth lifted, and her gaze grew soft. "He's pretty amazing."

"Yes, he really is."

There was another knock on the door, and Orix popped his head in. "Food's ready, and I have to say, it smelled delicious."

"Curi?" Shar and I asked in unison.

Orix's eyes crinkled in a smile. "Why don't you come and see?"

Shar and I exchanged glances before following Orix down to the second floor, where delicious aromas danced on the air. My stomach grumbled in appreciation. I'd eaten on autopilot, keeping fueled so that I could function, but the desire for food had died with Serath.

Curi's voice drifted into the hallway. "Plates are in the next one along. No. Not that one. The other one."

Who was he talking to? We were all here.

At the door now, Orix stepped aside to let me go first.

I pushed it open a fraction to peer in.

"We need more onion in the salad," Palia said, her back to me as she arranged stuff on the table.

"No more onions or I'll be farting all night," Ginia replied from the other side of the room.

Palia's back straightened. "Passing wind." I imagined the prim look on her face.

"What?" Ginia said.

"You'll be *passing wind*."

"I know, that's what I said!"

"You said fart," Touron pointed out from a spot behind the door I couldn't see.

"Touron, please!" Palia turned, hands on hips. Her gaze snagged on me standing in the partially open doorway. "Cam's here!"

I stepped into the room. "You guys came for dinner?"

Touron cleared his throat and rounded the kitchen island to stand beside Curi. "It's a little more than that."

"We're moving in," Ginia said with a grin.

"Roomies once more," Palia added.

"We cleared out a couple of rooms on the third floor," Orix said. "They were just filled with furniture and odds and ends."

"I've taken Selas's room on the same floor with you and Shar," Curi said.

"I'm on the fifth with Orix," Touron said.

Prasan's old room.

They were here. They were staying, and I hadn't realized until this moment how much I needed this. Needed them.

I looked to Orix, heart in my mouth. His face blurred, and I blinked to clear it.

"I got authorization off Carter," he said. "I told her they were part of the team, even if they weren't elite."

I pressed my hand to my mouth to staunch a sob as my lips curved into the first real smile in days. "I love you guys. I love you so much."

The area behind the island bloomed with shadow, and Derek materialized, carrying a basket. He froze for a moment, taking us all in, then held up the basket. "I bring eggs."

For a little while, it felt like the old days, like everything was normal. Touron and Curi had cooked up a feast of wild rice, flavorful chicken, salad, and potatoes. There was even dessert in the form of a delicious cheesecake, courtesy of Palia, and the eggs were put aside for breakfast.

For a little while, I convinced myself to forget about the loss, but conversation soon steered itself to business.

"When's Willowman back?" Curi asked Orix.

"I'm picking him up from Outpost Ten tomorrow," Orix said. "He'll have strengthened the wards by then."

Usually, Orix or Serath would have stayed with Willowman, taken him and brought him back, but with a shortage of elite, that wasn't feasible. So, it was a drop off and pick up situation now.

Outpost Ten was the elites' home when they weren't at the academy. It had been Serath's home. "I want to come with you."

Orix's gaze flicked to me. "I'm sorry, I can't take you. You're our only Basque and not fully qualified as an elite yet."

I didn't have the energy to argue. "Fine."

Silence fell, and the pressure of everyone's regard made my scalp itch. My beast shifted, irritated by the attention. The dining room table was suddenly too full, the air too thick.

"I'm going to go check on Varsa." I fixed a smile on my face as I pushed my chair back. "I'll see you guys later. Thank you for the amazing dinner. It was just what I needed."

The looks on their faces told me that my smile wasn't fooling anyone, but no one called me out on it as I crossed the room to the stairwell exit.

I made it to the ground floor before the clatter of boots behind me pulled me up short.

Curi joined me by the door. "Mind if I tag along?"

"That depends. Are you tagging along to keep an eye on me or just because you want to hang out?"

"Will you hurt me if I say it's a little of both, but more the hanging out thing?" He gave me a disarming smile, and I rolled my eyes.

"Fine, tag along."

The night was crisp, cool, and filled with starlight and a moon that was almost full.

We walked in companionable silence, and I took a moment to study the strong, clean lines of his brutally handsome face, softened by blue tendrils of hair that had escaped from their band to brush his cheekbones. His face had become a comfort to me, and I couldn't recall ever disliking it. Disliking him.

I bumped my shoulder against his arm. "I'm glad we're friends."

He glanced down at me, his expression serious. "Yeah, me too, Cam." He reached for my hand, and I allowed him to take it.

The grounds were dotted with goyles going about their evening, and we garnered a few curious looks. Heck, we were famous now. The cadets that survived a graynite attack.

"Are you going to square things with Levi when he moves into the tower later?"

"Yeah, I'll speak to him."

"He's taking Serath's room, by the way, but I can take it instead, if you want."

I ignored the pang of resentment. "No. No, that's fine. He needs a room. It's just a room."

Serath's room. His space. But he was never coming back.

Curi squeezed my hand. "We're going to get through this, Cam. We're going to make those bastards pay."

I stepped closer to him so that our arms touched, and I could rest my head on his shoulder. "Thank you for being here. For being with me."

"Always."

Willowman's cottage came into view a moment later. The windows were dark, and the place looked empty. Willowman had asked me to keep an eye on Varsa, but I'd been too busy to check in today. What if he was hurt?

The door was ajar. Heart pounding, I pushed it open and stepped into the dark, empty living room.

"Varsa?"

His bedroom was somewhere at the back of the house, but I'd never ventured that far. Never needed to, but now...

Curi followed me through the door at the back of the living room and down a short corridor with three more doors coming off it—a bathroom, an empty bedroom that smelled of incense, and finally a closed door.

I knocked. "Varsa?"

A soft thud was my only answer.

"Varsa?" Panic bloomed inside me. "Varsa, answer me, please." The door was locked.

"Out of the way," Curi said.

I stepped aside, and he shoulder-slammed the door. It opened with a splinter of wood.

"Shit," Curi said.

Varsa lay face down on the floor by the bed. Unmoving. "Varsa!" I fell to my knees beside him, immediately checking for a pulse. "He's alive." I rolled him onto his side, and he looked up at me with glassy, vacant eyes. "Hey, it's me. Varsa, can you hear me?"

He blinked slowly.

"Let's get him onto the bed," Curi said.

We hauled him up and got him settled while he continued to stare blankly at us. "He usually talks to me." I wasn't sure why it mattered that Curi know this. "He's so smart. He knows so much stuff." I stroked Varsa's forehead. "Are you there? Can you hear me?"

Varsa coughed, his body going into a spasm.

"I'll get some water." Curi bolted from the room.

Varsa stopped coughing. "Cameron..."

I exhaled shakily. "Hey...You're here."

"I wish I could stay longer, but I can't hold on anymore. I have to go."

"What?"

He reached up to touch my face. "I'll see you soon." His hand dropped to his side, and his body went limp and heavy. I laid him down gently as his eyes fluttered closed.

Curi hurried back into the room with a glass of water. "Here."

A soft crackling sound filled the air as Varsa's skin hardened to stone.

Varsa had no use for water any longer.

He was dead.

CHAPTER 5

CAMERON

Guilt had me in a chokehold as I paced the living room back at the elite tower. If I'd gone to check on Varsa sooner, maybe he'd be alive. Why had I left it all day?

"It isn't your fault," Shar said.

"She's right," Orix said. "Varsa has been sick for a long time. What the graynites did to him...It's a wonder he lasted this long."

"My Cameron couldn't have stopped his death," Derek said. "But Varsa not die alone."

"Derek's right," Shar said. "Even if you had gone to see him earlier, it wouldn't have prevented his death. You were there at the end, and he didn't die alone. That's what matters."

I latched on to that fact like a lifeline. "He said he would see me soon."

"The afterlife is a comfort for many," Palia said. "Even us goyles."

"It didn't feel like he was speaking metaphysically."

"How else could he have meant it?" Curi asked.

I was being ridiculous. "I don't know. What will happen to him...to his body now?"

"They'll take him to Arcadia for proper goyle rites," Orix said.

I had no idea what those were. "I want to be there. I *need* to be there."

Orix put his hand on my shoulder. "Okay. I'll take you."

"I'm coming too," Curi said.

"I'd like to visit Selas," Touron said. "I'm in love with her."

It took a moment for his words to register, and silence yawned for several seconds before Curi broke it.

"I knew it!" Curi said. "I fucking knew it."

Touron loved Selas? He loved her, and she was hurt, but all this time he'd stayed here with me. My throat throbbed. "Touron, why didn't you say something sooner? You should be with her. Not here with us."

He waved off my words. "We never...we never talked about that stuff...Love. I never told her, and I don't know...don't know if she feels the same. I don't even know if she'll want me there or want...want anyone to know." He roughly raked his fingers through his hair. "Dammit, it's been hell the past few days. If Curi hadn't been giving me updates, I don't know how I would have coped. But...I need to see her. I need to tell her how I feel."

"Don't," Orix said. "Don't do it."

"What?" Was he serious? "Why not?"

He sighed. "Because he's not free to love her. Not the way that she needs."

"Orix is right," Shar said to Touron. "What happens when you find an omega?"

Touron's jaw tensed. "I won't."

"You can't say that for sure," Palia said. "If the scent takes you, and an omega chooses you, then your beast *will* take over."

"It won't. I won't let it," Touron said. "I love her too much."

"Then you'll keep your mouth shut," Orix said. "Tell her how you truly feel and you'll lose her. Trust me. I know."

Orix and Selas? "You two were a thing?"

"For a while." His smile was wry, his eyes clouded with memories.

"You're still in love with her," Ginia said.

"Ginia!" Palia admonished.

Ginia winced. "I'm sorry."

"No, it's all right," Orix said. "I love her. I always will, but what we had is over. It had to be, although I resisted at the time. But Selas, ever practical, logical, realist Selas knew that our romance had a shelf life. She ended it before we could get too serious."

Touron pressed the heels of his palms into his eyes with a soft growl. "So, if I tell her I love her..."

"She'll end it with you," Orix said. "I guarantee it."

"You *should* end it," Palia said. "Before you hurt her and yourself."

Touron plopped onto the sofa. "I'm an idiot. I didn't think...I just..."

"Fell in love," Orix said. "It happens."

There was rarely a happily ever after for an alpha female. Born to fight. Warriors, not nurturers, they were made for the battlefield. While the omegas made sure that the gargoyle race continued through procreation, the alpha females protected the nests—at least that was the way it had been. Now they protected humanity. I was sure they found partners, lovers, but there was always the risk that their lover would be enraptured by an omega at some stage. Always the potential of losing them, not because they wanted to be lost but because nature intended the males to pass on their seed, and as far as I was aware, alpha females couldn't reproduce.

Touron pulled himself to his feet and lifted his chin. "I won't tell her how I feel. I'll just be with her for as long as she'll have me and for as long as I can."

Orix dropped him a nod. "Wise move."

"I think we should all go to Arcadia," Shar said. "I didn't know Varsa well, but I respect Willowman, and we should support him."

"Agreed," Palia and Ginia said in unison.

"I'll break the news of Varsa's death to him later," Orix said.

He'd planned on going to pick up Willowman tomorrow, but with Varsa's death...it felt wrong not to tell Willowman right away.

"If I'm not back by midday tomorrow, hit the training room with Levi," Orix continued. "He knows what the trials entail, and even though he can't tell us, he can make sure you're physically prepared."

A queasy sensation unfurled in my stomach at the mention of Levi. I still had to apologize for treating him like shit the last few days. It was a much-needed conversation but not one I was looking forward to.

I WAS IN the observatory when Levi arrived and watched him coming down the path, carrying a rucksack and a duffel bag. Watched like a creep from the shadows as he got closer, his frame highlighted in moonlight, but he stopped a moment before he'd have to go out of view. Stopped and looked up at the tower as if he could see me. As if he knew I was here.

I stepped away from the window, pulse pounding as if I'd been caught doing something illicit, when in fact there was nothing wrong with watching the world go by.

I gave him an hour to settle into Serath's old room—his room now—before gathering my courage and heading down to the fourth floor. How many times had I made this journey? Less than a handful. Each time to see my mate. To be with him. Would his room still smell like fresh linen or had Orix had it stripped and cleaned like they'd done for Romi? Leaving the air tinged with the tang of disinfectant.

The corridor was dark, but a strip of light shone from beneath Serath's...Levi's door.

I took a breath, then knocked.

Levi opened the door a moment later, eyes widening a fraction at the sight of me. "Cameron..."

"Hey, I was hoping we could talk."

"Of course. Come in." He stepped back to admit me, but my feet refused to budge. I looked past him into the room with the neatly made bed. I'd slept on that bed with Serath, held him while poison tore at his body.

Levi groaned. "Shit, this was his room, wasn't it?"

"You didn't know?"

"No, I didn't." He ran a hand down his face. "I'm sorry, I'll move. I'll ask Orix for another room."

There were no other rooms. "No. No, it's fine. I'm fine." I stepped past him into the room that smelled like fresh air and lemon fabric softener. Nothing like Serath. "I wanted to apologize for the past week. I've been awful to you, and I'm sorry."

"You don't have to apologize."

I set my shoulders and looked him in the eye, speaking from the heart and admitting my guilt. "Yes, I do. I had no right to take my anger out on you, to punish you for Serath's death...to make you the villain. I...I'm sorry. Can we...can we start fresh. Friends?"

"Oh, Cam, we never stopped being friends, and there is nothing to forgive."

His words unraveled the knots of awfulness inside me. "You're too good, Levi. Too fucking kind."

"Only to the people that matter," he said. "And you matter, Cam. I promise you that I'll get you and the others through the elite trials, no matter what it takes."

"Orix said you'll be training us tomorrow."

"Yes, he spoke to me before he left. Told me about Varsa. I'm sorry for your loss."

Again. Another loss. I fixed a smile on my face. "He was a good goyle. He didn't deserve what happened to him."

"No, and we'll make the bastards that are responsible pay." His words echoed Curi's, echoed my intentions. "Serath and Varsa and everyone else they took from this world will be avenged once we kill the alpha."

It was the only thought fueling me now.

The two factions of graynites, Ignus's agenda—neither would matter once the alpha who kept them all alive was dead.

And if I could strike the killing blow, then maybe I'd finally find inner peace. Maybe Serath's soul, wherever it was, would find peace also.

CHAPTER 6

CAMERON

I woke in a cold sweat, heart pounding like I'd been sprinting.

The image of the moon filled my mind for a moment, bright, dazzling, and almost full, but the night was long gone. I'd watched it die. Watched the gray haze of dawn before falling into a deep slumber. But only four hours had passed, and I was wide awake, my body buzzing for action.

I'd dreamed of the moon, and that was bad. It had to be bad, right? Because the last sidhe moon had seen me sleepwalk into the forest, pheromones spiking to attract goyle males. It had left me hungry for Serath and only him. The next time the needing had hit me, I'd begged Curi to fuck me. Thank goodness he hadn't taken me up on my demand, realizing that I wasn't myself. But we still weren't sure if that episode was related to the fated mate bond, my fae blood, or to something that Prasan may have done.

Willowman had found herbs in Prasan's room, a tincture that might be able to loosen inhibitions, and since Prasan had cooked that night, then been so against me going out, maybe...maybe he'd wanted Serath and me to consummate. It would, after all, have resulted in my death and driven Serath mad.

Mission accomplished.

But nothing was certain. We'd know for sure in a few days

as the sidhe moon grew closer. Willowman had promised to try to come up with a solution, some concoction to help temper my needing, and since Mirrowind was back in a couple of days, she might be able to help us. The woman was fae and might know what kind of fae I was descended from.

But if neither of them could help, then what?

What would I do to quell the hunger?

I couldn't allow it to ruin my chances of passing the elite trial, which meant there was only one way to soothe it, and that was to give it what it wanted.

Satiation.

Serath had succeeded in calming it without consummation, but he'd been my mate. I wasn't sure that the needing would accept the same methods from a goyle without that kind of connection to me.

Which meant...

No. I wouldn't think about that. Instead, I'd put my energy into hoping that the needing was absent. That it had all been a trick of a tincture. That without Serath to fuel it, my desire would remain dead.

Yes, all I could do was hope.

Hope and ignore the prickling beneath my skin.

GONE WERE THE days of needing more sleep. If anything, I seemed to require less. I'd gotten used to retiring before the others, but now I walked the corridors like a ghost while the academy slept.

Speaking of ghosts, it was time to check on Melanie again.

The specter had been absent since before the cadet exams, but I was certain she was still around.

Maybe the crystals that Derek had gotten off Yarrow were helping. The crystals were supposed to exude energy vibrations that might help Melanie to manifest if she was struggling to do so. I considered waking Derek to come with me, but he was still developing, and his sleep was important.

I grabbed the key to my old dorm room and stepped out the door, smack bang into Curi's solid chest.

He grabbed my arms to steady me. "Hey." His voice was grumbly and gruff from sleep. "I thought I heard you moving about."

His eyes were still puffy, telling me he needed more shuteye. "You don't have to be up just because I am."

He stretched and yawned. "Nope. I'm wide awake now. Where are we headed?"

He was too sweet to me. "You don't need to hang with me all the time, Curi. I'm okay. I'm not going to fall apart."

He gave me a wry smile and slung his arm around my shoulder, drawing me away from my room. "Maybe I *like* hanging with you."

"I've hardly been fun to be around."

"I've heard losing your fated mate can do that to a goyle," he said lightly.

I paused in my step and arched a brow at him. "Did you just make a joke about my loss?"

He winced. "Too soon?"

Maybe it was too soon. Maybe it was highly inappropriate, but the fact he was doing it made me feel...normal. No more kid gloves.

Just teammates preparing for the fight of our lives. "Thank you."

He leaned in and dropped a kiss on my head. "So, where are we headed?"

"To check on Melanie."

He stifled another yawn. "You can buy me coffee on the way."

"You know, caramel lattes aren't half bad." I took another sip. "Yep, I think I'm a convert now."

"I told you, best beverage." He took a long gulp of his and smacked his lips.

Stone Comfort had been empty, so we'd been served quickly, but in a couple of hours, the place would be teeming with goyles eager for breakfast. Although each dorm had a kitchen, cooking wasn't something many of the cadets enjoyed doing. To be honest, if I hadn't met Shar, Tour, and the twins, I probably wouldn't be into it either. Not that I cooked that often. Touron took on most of the culinary roles, and now Curi too.

I was lucky to have them.

We entered our old dorm, and nostalgia washed over me. "I miss this place."

"Elite tower has better mattresses," Curi replied.

"You think?"

"Definitely."

The dorm was quiet, the halls shrouded in gray light. Most of the goyles would still be asleep, so we made our way silently to my old room.

It was strange being back here. In the grand scheme of things, I'd hardly spent much time in this space, but it had been home for a while. There were memories here, even if the bed was stripped bare and every surface lightly gathering dust. Even though it looked like a room fit for a ghost.

Curi closed the door behind us. "Now what?"

"Now we wait. See if she shows. Melanie?"

Several crystals dotted the room, an effort to provide Melanie with an energy source if she was struggling to manifest.

I ventured farther into the room. "Melanie, are you here? If you're here, show me a sign."

Silence was my only answer. I parked my ass on the edge of the mattress. "I usually wait a few minutes. Just in case."

Curi joined me. "This really matters to you. Why?"

"You know she helped me...to get information about Romi from the secure files..." He nodded. "Yeah, well something happened to her. Something that messed her up." I'd been so wrapped up in my grief that I'd put off helping her. "I spoke to Flora a couple of days ago about what happened. She can't remember a thing, except...she said she has this image of golden eyes in her head. But not witch eyes, more...glowing."

"And that's all she recalls?"

"Yes. Not much to go on."

"No. But if we can help Melanie, then maybe she can tell us more. This feels like too much of a loose end to leave dangling, especially after what happened with Prasan. This might be unrelated to everything, but then it may not. Either way, Melanie doesn't deserve to be lost like this." My breath misted in front of my face. "Temperature drop."

"She's here?"

"I think so. Melanie? Melanie, can you hear me? Can you manifest?" Goosebumps rippled up my arm. "That's it. You're doing great. Use the energy from the crystals. Channel from us if you need it."

Curi shivered. "Fuck, it's freezing in here now."

The coldest it had ever been. She'd never had to siphon so much energy from a room before. My skin crawled with the wrongness of it all.

A low moan filled the room, the sound so mournful and unearthly that goosebumps rippled up my arm and cold fingers of foreboding tightened around my nape.

The air by the window rippled, and a form manifested—gray and wraith-like with a long pale face and dark pits for eyes. Its mouth yawned wide, head canting to one side. I got the impression of long dark hair rippling around its head, but it was too spectral and ethereal for me to make out.

"*That's* Melanie?" Curi asked.

"I think so, but it doesn't look like her. Melanie..." I stood slowly and took a step toward her, but Curi grabbed my wrist.

"Don't. This feels wrong."

He was right. The energy she exuded was dark and hungry. The kind of hunger that takes with impunity. But I had to try.

"Melanie, is that you?"

The specter moaned and reached for me. It had to be her, right? I drew the vial containing the tincture from my pocket. This could help her. Could bring back her memories, but would it work if she was this far gone?

What if I wasted it?

A wave of dizziness had me reeling. I staggered against Curi, who grabbed hold of my shoulders to steady me. "Whoa..."

"Cam, I don't feel too good," he said.

It was Melanie. She was drawing from us, too much too fast.

My knees felt watery "Get to the door..." My voice came out slurred. "Curi..."

I buckled, and the specter rushed me, maw yawning wide, but Curi snagged me around the waist and hauled me out of the room and into the corridor. He slammed the door and stood with his back against the wall, my body cradled to his chest.

"What the fuck just happened?" he asked. "It looked like she wanted to eat you."

Yes. That's exactly what she'd looked like. "Ghosts don't eat people, but spirit ghouls do."

"What's a spirit ghoul?"

"A ghost that exists solely to feed on the energy of the living." I slowly lifted my head, and my nose grazed his jaw. "Curi, I'm afraid that Melanie may be too far gone for us to save."

CHAPTER 7

CAMERON

Another caramel latte and two cinnamon buns later, I was beginning to feel almost normal.

"You can't go back to that room," Curi said. "Fuck, if I hadn't come with you today..."

I'd been thinking the same thing. "Something did that to her, Curi. We've got to help her."

"She tried to drain your life force, Cam. I think she's beyond help."

If Curi hadn't been there to drag me from the room, who knows how much damage Melanie could have done? She could have killed me.

"You're still too pale," Curi said. "I don't think you should train today."

"I'll be fine. Missing training is not an option."

"Then eat one more of these." Curi placed another bun on my plate. "I'll get us refills on our drinks."

He headed back to the counter, leaving me at our table for two by the window. I bit into the bun and chewed, trying to pinpoint what was bothering me about my encounter with Melanie, and then it hit me. Derek hadn't materialized. He always materialized if I felt threatened, and Melanie hadn't evoked that fear, that threat, because there'd been something in the depths of her dark eyes—a plea, a desperation—that had nothing to do with hunger or malice.

I wrapped the rest of the bun in a napkin and hurried to join Curi at the counter. "Curi, get those drinks to go. We need to see Yarrow."

THE ACADEMY WAS waking up as we headed to the main building. With the elite trials around the corner, we'd been excused from other classes, our only goal to train for the trials. Any later and we might have risked catching Yarrow in class, but this early, he'd probably still be in the tutor wing.

We passed an alchemist on the stairs, and a prickle of awareness skimmed over my mind like fingers caressing my bare flesh.

"Urgh." Curi shook his head. "I hate that they're allowed to do that. My fucking mind is not free viewing."

I gave him a teasing smile. "Why? What you got in there?"

He arched a brow. "Trust me, Basque, you don't want to know."

For a moment, we were back in the teasing, banter stage, a mode that had existed before the cadet exams, before my world imploded.

I dropped my gaze.

"I'm sorry," Curi said.

I shook my head. "No." I linked arms with him. "It's good. It's...normal. I want us to be normal." Maybe it would make the deadness inside me a little less cold.

I spotted Dayn in the hallway, chatting with a few cadets I didn't recognize.

"We have new recruits," Curi said, his tone low, "and it looks like Dayn is also recruiting for his fuckwad team."

Dayn was a blackmailing son of a bitch. He liked to control

goyles. He didn't have friends; he had puppets, and since he'd lost his current crew, he was obviously recruiting more.

"We can't let him do this, Curi. Not to any more goyles."

"Trust me," Curi said. "He won't be." A wicked smile tugged at his lips, the kind I hadn't seen since my first weeks here.

A shiver rushed up my spine. "You found out something about him?"

"I sure did, and I've been waiting for the perfect time to use it."

Dayn broke off conversation as we approached. His gaze dropped to our linked arms, and a dirty smirk bloomed on his face. "When I found out you were mated to the sigma, I figured you two were faking it, but I guess you weren't." He raked Curi up and down. "Did you enjoy fucking her while she thought of him?"

The new cadets looked uncomfortable, which said a lot about their characters. Dayn was the last person they needed to be hanging around.

"I had a little chat with my sire a few days ago," Curi said. "We haven't been on great terms ever since the accident with Selas." He leaned in. "You know, the one you found out about and were going to blackmail me with?"

A couple of the cadets exchanged glances, and Dayn cleared his throat. "I dunno what you're talking about."

"Anyway," Curi continued, "topic of the Lowthers came up. Turns out my sire has connections at the registration offices all around the fringe. Knows what goes on in records. The coverups. The misinformation...How names can be altered to protect the affluent goyle families from unnecessary claims from halfbloods." He shrugged. "That type of thing."

Dayn's face drained of color. "Right...I suppose that could be interesting."

"Oh, it is. It was a *very* interesting conversation. But someone like you, from a family who prides themselves on having not a single halfblood in their family tree, wouldn't be interested in such things."

I'd never seen someone gulp before. "I should...get going," Dayn said quickly. "Classes to prepare for." He backed away, turned on his heel, and strode off.

"Stay away from him," Curi warned the newer cadets. "He's bad news. Trust me."

"You're Mason, aren't you?" a slender male with a shock of blond hair asked.

"I am."

"And Basque." He smiled shyly at me. "We heard what happened at the cadet exams. We're so sorry."

My mouth was suddenly dry, but I forced it into a smile. "Thank you."

They wandered off, and Curi steered me toward the stairs. "Not a bad bunch."

"No. Not at all."

We climbed side by side. "So, Lowther has halfbloods in his family?"

Curi shrugged. "I don't know."

"What? But you just said...You lied?"

He shot me a mischievous smile. "Not at all. I did speak to my sire, and he does have contacts at the registration offices, and forms are falsified all the time to hide halfbloods' true lineages. I never said Lowther was one of those lineages."

"But he just assumed." I let out a bark of laughter. "Curi, you aren't just a pretty face, are you?"

"Aw, you think I'm pretty?" he teased.

I smiled up into his warm brown eyes. "Gorgeous." And he was. He was gorgeous to me not just because of how he looked, but because of who he was—kind, thoughtful, and funny. He was all those things, and I was so grateful to have him as a friend.

We bumped into Yarrow as he was exiting the tutors wing with his sister, Flora. Her eyes lit up at the sight of us, but his brows came down in concern.

"Is everything all right?" he asked.

Flora nudged him. "Good afternoon would be a better place to start."

Yarrow rolled his eyes. "Good afternoon. Now, is everything all right?"

"Actually, I was hoping you could help me." I filled him in on what happened with Melanie.

"That can't be right," Yarrow said. "It takes years for a ghost to turn into a spirit ghoul. Melanie may have been haunting the campus for decades, but you said that she was coherent and placid up until a few weeks ago, right?"

"Correct." I glanced at Flora. "She was fine until the night that you were attacked. Melanie was attacked then too."

Flora's bright eyes dimmed. "I wish I could recall what happened. I can't even remember what I was doing in that part of the building." She wrung her hands. "Every time I think on it, I get so...anxious."

"Then don't." Yarrow gently took her hands. "Don't think on it." He turned his attention on us, his golden eyes narrow, jaw tight. "It was powerful allure, enough to steal her memories not only of those few moments but those of the several hours prior. We've tried to recover them but to no avail."

Curi frowned down at me. "If Yarrow can't get Flora's memories back, then what makes you think Melanie will remember anything?"

But helping Melanie was about more than that one incident. "It's not about helping her remember what happened in that filing room. I want to help her become...her again. Willowman got me a potion that can help her remember her past and be whole again. It's my fault that she was in that filing room in the first place. She's lost herself because of it."

"Spirits hold memories in a different manner to flesh and blood beings," Yarrow said. "There are no neural pathways to navigate, no synapses to eradicate. In Melanie's case, her memories are held in the ether around her, and the attacker, whoever it may be, has cut off her access to it. Not just the memories of that incident but to all her memories." He nodded as if he were coming to understand something. "It would explain how she might be turning into a spirit ghoul so quickly. Maybe...But I believe she can be restored." His lip curled. "And when she is whole, we will find the culprit responsible."

"We should check the crystals," Flora said. "Just to make sure they're charged and working."

"Give me the key to the room and leave it with us," Yarrow said. "I'm eager to get my hands on the person responsible for tampering with my sister's mind. I want to help."

I handed him the keys. "Be careful, though. She almost knocked me out."

"Oh, don't worry," Yarrow said. "We'll be prepared."

We left the witches to their plotting and headed back down the stairs and out of the main building. Training started in an hour, which meant the rest of the team would be up and about at the elite tower.

"Do you think Touron will make pancakes?" Curi asked wistfully.

"We just ate a plateful of buns."

"Are you telling me you'd say no to pancakes?"

We stepped off the porch and onto the path. "Not if they come with syrup."

He chuckled. "Blueberries."

"Ice cream."

We spent the rest of the walk back to the tower thinking up pancake toppings and hoping that Touron would make our dreams come true.

CHAPTER 8

CAMERON

Touron didn't make our pancake dreams come true, but he promised to make some for dessert later. Instead, we scarfed down eggs, courtesy of Derek, along with crispy bacon and hot buttered toast. Derek passed the teapot so we could refill our mugs.

"Levi should have stayed for food," Touron said. "I'm worried about him." Levi had left before Curi and I returned, gone to set up for training, Touron had said, whatever that entailed. "He looks exhausted. Like he hasn't slept or eaten properly. Cam, did you guys talk?"

I sighed. "Yes. We did, and we're all good."

"Maybe if you invite him to eat with us later," Touron suggested.

My chest tightened. Had I been *that* bad to Levi? Was he avoiding meals because of me? "I'll speak to him. Insist he join us."

"Orix might be back with Willowman by then," Shar said. "We can eat together."

"We'll need more chairs," Palia said.

"There are some in the living room," Ginia reminded her.

"Those aren't proper dining chairs."

"It hardly matters as long as they're somewhere to park an ass."

Palia shot her a reproachful glance, and Ginia pretended not to see it.

We finished up our meal, tidied away, then headed out of the tower.

The twins walked ahead. They had their hair up in high ponytails today so that Ginia's waves cascaded about her shoulders, and Palia's poker-straight locks swayed against her back. I forgot they were twins sometimes, despite their physical similarities, because their personalities were so distinctly different.

"I can't believe that Melanie is a spirit ghoul," Ginia said.

"Do you even know what a spirit ghoul is?" Palia asked.

"Of course I do." Ginia sniffed. "A ghost who's become a ghoul, duh!"

Palia rolled her eyes. "They're not common, you know. Most ghosts who lose their memories become angry spirits, not ghouls. Only the ones who've experienced a terrible loss become ghouls, feeding off the lives of others to replace what they subconsciously know they have lost. They never succeed in being whole again."

This was news to me. "I didn't know that."

We hit the main path to central campus, and the hubbub of goyles hurrying to classes and training surrounded us. No one gave us a second look, though, and even the alchemists that floated about campus were ignored. It was strange how quickly things went back to normal after a tragedy, especially if that tragedy didn't directly affect you. Only a handful of us had been on the battlefield a week ago; the rest of the cadets here were unscathed, untouched by the nightmares that the encounter had paired us with.

"You know, if not for the alchemists hanging around, you'd think nothing had happened," Ginia said, echoing my thoughts. "But everything has changed. We were breached."

We slowed as we rounded the main building and came abreast of the initiate training grounds. I spotted Waxen and Saffe among the other initiates and raised a hand in greeting.

"See you later," Touron said as he and the twins broke off to join them.

Curi, Shar, and I continued down the path toward the training room. A group of cadets strode toward us, Hawke at the helm. He raised his chin in greeting and slowed his pace. The others with him peeled away.

"How are you, Basque?" Hawke asked.

"I'm coping. Headed to training now. You?"

"Still reeling. Look, I'm sorry for your loss. But I know you guys will get the bastards responsible. I just wish I could help."

"You can, by keeping the academy safe when we're gone. I don't for one second believe there aren't more spies here."

"Agreed," Hawke said. "We'll keep our eyes peeled, trust me."

A prickle rushed over my skin, a magnetic force drawing my attention toward the back of the main building where two alchemists stood watching us. "They give me the creeps."

"Me too," Hawke said. "They've been here a week and found nothing, which is odd."

"Or they've found something, but we've not been told," Shar said. "I'm pretty sure anything they find will be passed straight to the council."

"Or not..." Hawke muttered.

"Hawke!" Farnell called from the training ground.

"I've got to go. But we'll catch up soon. Be safe." He jogged off toward Farnell and the initiate camp.

I glanced across at the alchemists before following Curi and Shar to the training room. "What do they do when they're not mind-diving?"

"No idea," Curi said.

"I heard that there are two groups," Sharniza said. "One that works directly with the council and provides protection and interrogation, while another works with the humans in the lab project."

"Lab project?"

"They make the tinctures, potions, and various other healing tonics for the guardians."

"Like Willowman?"

"There aren't many like Willowman, Yarrow, and Flora left," Shar said. "Witches are rare, and we're lucky to have three here on campus. I'm sure the council would have loved to have them on staff at HQ, but you don't strongarm a witch into doing your bidding."

So, they were here because they *wanted* to be. Because they wanted to help. "But what are the alchemists, exactly? Not witches or mageri, so...what?"

"Humans with abilities," Curi said. "That much I know." He pushed open the training room door. "And we can talk about this later."

He was right. We were here to train, so why was the room so dark, and where was Levi?

The smell of incense teased my nose as the door closed behind us. It took a moment for my night vision to kick in and spot the two figures standing on the far side of the room.

Levi and a woman.

They broke from their conversation and crossed the room toward us. I got a closer look at the woman—slender but not athletic, dressed casually in jeans, a sweater, and sneakers. It was hard to determine her age in the gloom, late twenties, early thirties maybe?

"Why the gloom?" Shar asked.

"It's necessary to the training," Levi said.

"You want us to fight in the dark?" Curi asked.

"You won't be fighting," Levi said. "Not in the traditional sense." He looked down at the woman, who nodded in agreement, her sleek bob swaying against her jaw.

There was something familiar about her. About the curve of her brows and the dips at the corner of her mouth. "And who is this?"

The woman smiled, and I suddenly knew exactly who she was.

"I'm Levi's mother, Adaline. It's nice to meet you all."

His mother? He'd brought her here? My gaze whipped up to Levi. "I don't understand. I thought you weren't allowed to help us, but you told your mother?"

"Now that the whole elite team is down, it benefits us all if you three survive the trial. I spoke to my mother a couple of days ago and explained the situation."

"And Ulrickson knows about this?" Sharniza asked.

"He knows that she's visiting me..." He looked uncomfortable, and his mother continued for him.

"Ulrickson hopes we might rekindle our romance. I'm meeting with him later."

She was using her wiles as a diversion. Nice.

Levi cleared his throat. "One dinner, that's all. It was the only way for her to meet you all and deliver the real reason for her visit."

"I thought you couldn't tell us what to expect," Curi said.

"I can't," Levi said.

"And neither can I," Adaline added. "But I can help you prepare." She drew a pouch from her pocket and extracted a locket dangling from a chain. "I have one for each of you. The locket contains a special concoction of herbs to allow you to fall into a deep meditative state. It is there that you must find yourselves."

"You want us to meditate?" Curi asked. "*That's* the training?"

"It's the only training," Levi said. "The better you know yourselves, the more likely you are to pass the trials."

Shar held out her hand. "Fine, let's get on with this."

Adaline handed each of us a locket, which we slipped around our necks.

"They must be touching the skin to work," Adaline said.

I tucked mine beneath my T-shirt, and the others did the same with their lastonflex tops.

"Now what?" Curi asked.

"Now you take a seat, close your eyes, and relax," Adaline said.

"I want you to focus inwards," Levi said. "Just forget the world and focus on your own breath and the beat of your heart.

Sink into those sensations."

I found a spot on a mat and sat down cross-legged. "How long do we do this?"

"We'll start with thirty minutes today," Levi said. "I'll let you know when the time is up. Don't worry, just relax."

I closed my eyes and exhaled, allowing my body to relax with each breath until there was nothing but me and the darkness. Nothing but me and the gentle warmth spreading across my collarbones. Nothing but the even pulse in my throat.

I floated for long moments until the darkness turned gray, then amber, and I was looking down at a large, pink cage sitting on a desk. There was something important inside it. Something that mattered greatly to me.

"It's all right, love. He's gone to a better place," my mother said.

"No, he hasn't. He's right there. Why isn't he moving? Is he broken? Mumma, can you fix him?"

"No, sweetheart."

I could see what was inside the cage now: a small white mouse lying stiff and unmoving on its side.

I knew this mouse. My buddy. My buddy Derek. Mum had named him for me because I'd struggled to come up with a name. I'd played with him every day. He'd been a four-year-old's best friend. How could I have forgotten him? How could I have forgotten the pain of his loss?

Mum gently scooped him out of the cage.

"Where are you taking him?" four-year-old me asked.

"We'll find a nice box and bury him."

"In the ground?"

"Yes, sweetheart."

"No. No, you can't take him. He'll be scared."

Mum's face came into view, her beautiful blue eyes filled with sadness. "He can't be scared anymore, Cameron. Because he's gone. This here"—she held up the dead mouse—"it's just a shell now. The power that made it work and move and be Derek is gone."

I didn't understand. I didn't get it. "Where? Where is he gone?"

"To a better place."

"Then I want to go there too!"

"No!" She looked horrified. "Don't...don't say that."

I blinked back tears. "Why not?"

"Because Derek is dead. He's dead, and he can never come back, and I don't want you to be dead and never come back."

I could feel my panic, the panic of my four-year-old self. "I don't get it."

She exhaled shakily. "It's a special cycle that makes us human. We get to live here, and then, when our time here is over, we go to a special place. But not today and not for a very long time. Today, we get to stay here. Today, we have to say goodbye to Derek."

But I didn't understand, and my heart was breaking. "Why? Why, why, why?"

"Oh, sweetie, everyone has to die sometime."

Everyone has to die...

Everyone has to leave...

I was standing in the doorway, partially hidden by Miss Miller's skirts as the police officer spoke to her in a hushed voice. My stomach formed knots, making me feel sick as the officer continued to speak.

"Terrible incident. Crime. Investigation."

And then Miss Miller saying, "Dead? You're saying she's dead."

Dead and gone.

Never coming back.

I was back at Pizza Delight, standing in the gloomy corridor with Levi, preparing to tell him I didn't love him in order to keep him at arm's length, when my phone buzzed.

No, don't answer it.

Don't answer it.

But I was trapped in a memory with no control, and no way

to change the events. So, I answered and held the phone to my ear.

"Hello, is this Cameron?" the gruff male voice asked.

"Who is this?" I echoed the words from the past.

"Is. This. Cameron?"

"Yes, who—"

"Romi's dead. I thought you should know."

Dead and never coming back.

No, no, no.

Serath reached for me, bloody mouth parted. "Live free..."

And he was gone.

Gone.

All gone.

The darkness surrounded me once more as I curled into a ball, wanting to stay here. Wanting to be alone because my heart was safer this way.

"We've got you, Cam," Touron said.

"We love you," Palia added.

"So much," Ginia said.

"You can do this," Shar added. "And we're here to help you."

"Get up, Basque," Curi said. "We're not quitting. We're a fucking team."

My eyes snapped open on a gasp.

I was back in the training room, but the memories lingered.

"Cam. You okay?" Shar asked from across the room.

I nodded. "Curi?"

"He stepped out for a moment. Levi went with him."

"I won't ask you what you saw," Adaline said from the window. A strip of light slid across the room as she raised the blinds. "What you see is private. It is a part of you, and it is for you to speculate on and learn from."

"What...what does it mean?" Shar asked.

Adaline shrugged. "It's different for everyone. The mind walk herb takes us to memories forgotten or misconstrued. It's a mirror to our psyche, and the rest...the rest is for you to decipher."

"And how will this help us in the trial?"

Adaline smiled. "You'll understand once you're in the trial. Trust me." She clipped past us toward the door. "Now I have a dinner date to get to, but I wish you all the luck in the trial ahead." She paused at the door. "Embrace your true self, and you'll be fine."

She slipped out of the room.

"I won't ask you what you saw," Shar said.

"I won't ask you either..."

"Dammit, now I want to know," she said with a smile.

I exhaled on a laugh. "Mine was...It wasn't so different from what I saw when Yarrow was testing our shields. I saw the police officer deliver the news of my mum's death, the phone call that informed me that Romi was gone...Serath's death." I licked my lips. "Yeah...but there was one memory I'd forgotten. I had a mouse called Derek, and he died. I was so upset. I didn't understand why I couldn't keep him."

"How old were you in that memory?"

"I think...maybe four."

"Death is a difficult concept to grasp for a child."

"Yeah. I think that was my first experience of it. I'm not sure why this mind walk showed me that memory, though."

She stretched out her legs. "They all have death in common, and Derek...the name...I doubt it's a coincidence you chose to call your shield that?"

"Yeah, me too." I canted my head. "You want to share what you saw?"

She waved a dismissive hand. "Nothing forgotten, just suppressed."

It was obvious she wasn't comfortable talking about it, so I let it slide.

Levi returned alone. His cheeks had a little too much color in them. He'd had an argument with Curi.

I pulled myself to my feet. "What happened?"

"Mason is a little upset. But he'll be fine. He understands how important this process is."

"Where did he go?" Shar asked before I could.

"He said he was going to take a walk. We'll pick up again tomorrow." Levi held out his hand. "I'll need the lockets back for now."

I quickly took mine off and handed it to him before beelining for the exit. "I'll see you guys for supper." Supper...Shit. I ground to a halt and turned back to the room. "Levi, I'd love for you to join us tonight."

His brows flicked up slightly as if to say *really?* But then he smiled and nodded. "I'll be there."

I ducked out and hurried into the night. There was only one place that provided a decent walking route, but I had a quick pit stop to make before I headed to the woods.

CHAPTER 9

CAMERON

I'd barely made it onto the trail when I spotted Curi walking toward me, hands in the pockets of his pants.

He looked up, frown melting when he saw me. "Can't stay away from me?"

The shadows in his eyes belied his light tone.

I matched his tone. "You know me too well." I held out the cup as he drew closer. "And I came bearing gifts."

He sniffed the air. "Caramel latte?"

"Your favorite," I sing-songed.

He took it with a wistful smile. "Dammit, Cameron, you make it so hard not to fall in love with you." He laughed softly and took a sip of his drink to defuse the moment.

But although his words were uttered in the same light tone of earlier, they sliced into me, leaving me aching with regret and sadness because it would be so easy to be with Curi. He was like the ray of sunshine that weathered any storm, finding the cracks in the shroud of gloom that surrounded me to touch me with his warmth, asking for nothing in return. No demands. No expectations. Being with Curi was comforting and freeing.

"I'm sorry I left. I needed some air," he said.

I fell into step beside him. "You don't need to apologize for taking a time-out, Curi. I just...I was worried about you."

He bumped me with his arm. "Thanks." He held out the cup. "You wanna sip?"

I took a swig. "Damn, that is good."

"Why didn't you get yourself one too?"

"Why? You don't wanna share?"

He chuckled. "I'll always share with you, Cam."

I bumped my arm against his. "Good, so...you wanna share what upset you earlier?"

"I walked right into that one, didn't I?"

I stifled the pang of guilt and forged on. "You don't have to tell me, just know that you can. I'm here for you."

We trudged in silence for a couple of minutes, handing the cup back and forth before he spoke.

"It was a memory I'd forgotten...or tried to. It was so vivid. I think I must have been eleven or twelve. Living in the omega nest with my mother. We were in the kitchens baking. Ginger snaps, our favorite...at least they used to be. I was rolling out the dough, ready to cut the cookies, when my sire abruptly arrived. We weren't expecting him. If we'd known, Mother would never have allowed me in the kitchens. But...he was there. His face filled with rage at the sight of me in my apron dusted with flour. The way he looked at me...with such disgust and disappointment..." He exhaled. "That was the last time I saw my mother."

"He took you away?"

"That very hour, and when I cried, he struck me. Told me to be a man. That males did not cry."

Heat stung my eyes. "Curi...that's...that's just cruel."

His mouth twisted in a bitter smile. "It's normal. Our sires are tasked with ensuring we're strong enough to do our duty. But no matter what I did, no matter how hard I trained, how fast I ran, how many competitions I won, I was never, ever good enough for him."

I drew him to a halt at the edge of the woods and looked up into his moonlit face. "But you are, Curi. You know that, right?

You know that you're more than good enough. You're the best." I swallowed the lump in my throat. "You're strong, but you know when to be gentle. You're tough, but you know when to be kind. You're strong-willed, but you know when to show compassion, and I...I adore you."

He reached up to stroke my cheek. "I adore you too, Basque, and trust me, I have tried not to." His gaze softened. "Being with you, Sharniza, Touron, and the twins is like finding home." A moment stretched between us, a moment that could become something more if I took the step to make it so. I dropped my gaze, and the moment passed.

Curi dropped a kiss on my head. "Let's get back. You can tell me what you saw in your mind walk along the way."

SHARNIZA

I SHOULD HAVE shared my experience with Cam. Why didn't I? I stir the pasta sauce per Touron's instructions. She's my friend. What is wrong with me?

"You worried about things?" Derek says from over my shoulder.

I resist the urge to lean back against him. "I'm fine."

"No. You are not. I can feel it. What is wrong?"

"Earlier, Cam asked me what I saw in the mind walk, but I didn't tell her. But she told me what she saw in hers."

"And you feel bad for not sharing?"

"Basically."

"But you were not ready to share."

"No, I wasn't...I'm not."

"Then why you worry? You know that Cam not think badly of you for not sharing. Cam loves you."

He makes it so simple. "Thank you, Derek."

"Um...Shar, is the sauce supposed to smell like that?"

I look down at the angrily simmering sauce that I've stopped stirring. "Shit!"

"What's that smell?" Touron comes hurrying across the kitchen. "Is that my sauce?" I step aside for him to examine his creation. "Oh...oh shit. It's burned."

"I'm sorry. Can we save it?"

He takes it off the hob with a huff. "Nope. It's done for. Dead."

My cheeks burn. Such a simple task, and I messed it up. "I'm really so sorry."

His shoulders sag. "It's all right. I've burned this sauce recipe several times myself."

"I'm starving," Ginia whines. "What are we gonna doooo?"

Palia rolls her eyes. "You're acting like there's no more food left in the world."

Levi sniffs the air as he joins us in the kitchen. "Is something burning?"

Touron groans.

"The sauce is ruined," Derek says. "But it is *not* Sharniza's fault."

"Well," Levi says, "Stone Comfort does excellent pizza."

"Oh, yes!" Ginia claps her hands. "So cheesy and delicious."

"I'll go get us some," Levi says.

"I go with you," Derek says. "Help you carry all the pizza." Levi looks a little wary, and Derek's eyes dim slightly. "I not hurt you, Levi. I only hurt those that try to hurt my Cameron."

"Good to know," Levi says.

The door opens behind him, and Orix storms in, looking windswept and angry.

I step away from the hob and round the island. "What's wrong?"

"Where's Willowman?" Palia asks. "What's happened?"

Orix bites on his bottom lip, his chest heaving. "The alchemists have Willowman. They think he has something to do with the attack."

"That's ridiculous," Touron says. "Prasan almost killed him."

"We saw it," Palia adds.

"They're claiming that he used some kind of mind-altering spell to make you believe that he was injured. That he deliberately took longer than necessary to alert the academy about the breach."

"That's fucking bullshit!" Touron snaps as the lift dings

"What's bullshit?" Cameron exits the lift with Curi in tow. "What's going on?"

"The alchemists have Willowman," Derek tells her.

"What? Why?"

Orix reiterates what he's just told us, and Cameron's face takes on the blank look that I've come to associate with an intense wave of rage. "Where did they take him?"

"Carter's office," Orix says. "It's been commandeered by the alchemists while they stay here. They said that they needed to do something called a deep dive."

"But that could kill him!" Palia says, shocked. "I mean...I read about their practices. Deep dives are only to be used in extreme cases where the evidence supporting their use is strong."

Orix's gaze shoots up to meet hers. "You know the law on the methods used?"

She nods quickly. "Our sire has access to certain legal texts. I used to, uh...take scrolls and books to read. The binding laws surrounding alchemists and their interactions with the gargoyles made for interesting reading."

Cam crosses to the stairwell exit, her stride long and determined. "Then we use what you know to our advantage. We are not losing another friend."

CHAPTER 10

CAMERON

A hooded alchemist guarded the door to what had once been Carter's office.

A scream echoed from within, and my pulse jumped.

The guard stepped into my path. "You can't go in there. You can—"

I shoved him aside and slammed the door open. Two alchemists stood by Carter's desk like sentries while another was hunched over Willowman. The witch was tied to a chair with a gag in his mouth and silver cuffs shackling his wrists—muters for his magic.

"What you do to him?" Derek demanded.

Willowman's eyes rolled in our direction, his gaze settling on me. He said my name, muffled and almost incoherent behind the gag, and my blood boiled.

"Get the fuck away from him!" I rushed forward and shoved the alchemist so hard he went flying into the desk.

Derek blocked him from bouncing back at me while I focused on Willowman. "Willowman, shit, are you okay?" I tugged the gag out of his mouth.

"Head...hurts..." Willowman's eyes slipped closed.

"Where are the keys to the cuffs?" Shar demanded, her voice

a menacing growl.

"Answer her!" Derek shook the alchemist like a rag doll.

"The desk. On the desk," he cried.

Orix went for the keys while Touron dropped to his knees to untie Willowman's legs from the chair.

"You can't do this," one of the other alchemists said. "We have the authority—"

"Shut up!" My voice was a gravelly boom because my beast was desperate to maim and hurt someone, and these alchemists were the perfect target. "One more word and I won't be responsible for what my beast does to you."

Derek gave the alchemist he was holding a final shake and then shoved him toward the others.

They shrank away from us, and I turned back to Willowman, gently cupping his head while Shar undid the cuffs on his wrists. He groaned softly, his eyes drifting open for a moment.

"Cameron...he's gone...Varsa is gone." There was a deep sadness in his eyes and a thickness to his tone. He was grieving, and these bastards had done this to him.

I scooped him up into my arms. "It's okay. I've got you. We'll go to Arcadia together and put him to rest."

I turned to the door to find it blocked by Ulrickson's large frame.

"What is the meaning of this?" he demanded.

"I could ask you the same thing." Why the fuck was he still here?

"You cannot interrupt an alchemist interrogation," he said.

"We can if it's unlawful," Palia said. "Section A one thirty-nine point five A of the Gargoyle Codex highlights the binding law, which states that a deep dive can only be performed on a gargoyle in the presence of strong physical evidence of his or her involvement in a crime and—"

"Willowman is not a gargoyle." Ulrickson's lips curved into a smug smile.

Palia's eyes narrowed, and she strode forward. "If you'd allow me to finish," she said coldly. "Section A one thirty-nine point five A *also* goes on to state that the deep dive *cannot* in *any* circumstance be used upon a creature with human genes as it would invariably result in that creature's death."

Ulrickson's smile dropped, and his gaze flicked to the shadows in the corner of the room. Someone was standing there. Had been there all along.

The figure stepped forward now. Hooded and robed like the alchemists, it was one of them, and yet there was something still and ominous about this one. It pushed its hood back to reveal an austere face with deep lines bracketing a mouth I couldn't ever imagine smiling.

"Patrick?" Ulrickson frowned. "Is this true?"

Patrick's dark gaze settled on Palia. "The Gargoyle Codex is not a free text. Which means your reading of it was unauthorized."

"That hardly fucking matters," Curi snapped. "Your investigation is illegal. You were going to kill him."

"Is that what you want, Ulrickson?" Shar demanded.

"No," Levi said. "He wouldn't. He didn't know, did you, Father?"

Ulrickson's brows came together. "Of course I didn't," he said quickly, then fixed a glower in Patrick's direction. "You will be answering to the council for your negligence."

Patrick smiled coolly. "I don't answer to the council, Ulrickson. I answer to the collective, and their only goal is to stamp out this rising incursion, no matter the means. But I'm sure the council will be happy to explain to the Arcadian committee how Stonehaven was breached on so many occasions."

"Prasan did that," Orix said. "We know that."

Patrick raised a brow. "On his own? Unlikely."

"So you break the law?" Levi asked.

"Laws written by your kind, not mine." He lifted his chin and despite being half a head shorter than Levi, managed to look down his nose at him. "Keep your witch if you must. But when he shows himself to be the traitor he is, do not come to us for aid."

He strode toward the exit, minions in tow, and Ulrickson stepped back to let them pass.

Willowman groaned in my arms.

"We should get him to the infirmary," Levi said.

"No..." Willowman whispered. "I need...Calista..."

"Calista?"

"His outer rim contact," Orix said.

"Do you know where she lives?"

"I know the town. I can find out the rest."

"Wait a second. You're not intending to take him off academy grounds," Ulrickson said.

I fixed him with a steely gaze. "Why not? Is he a prisoner?"

"No but—"

"Are we?"

"No but you—"

"Then we're going. This witch is essential to the elite team, and if you want to stop us, then you'll need to use force."

"There's no need for that," Levi said. "Is there, Father?"

Ulrickson had the look of a cornered animal.

"They'll be with me," Orix said. "We have a funeral to attend in Arcadia, so as soon as Willowman is healed, we'll head there. I'll make sure to send a magigram to the academy to keep you updated."

"You're supposed to be training," Ulrickson reminded us.

"We will," Levi said. "I'll make sure of it."

"It isn't safe out there."

"It isn't safe here, either," Curi said. "But we're safer if we stick together."

Ulrickson ran a hand down his face. "Very well. But you'll take precautions. Travel by secure warps that have been checked thoroughly by..." His gaze dropped to Willowman. Because he was our warp guy.

"Yarrow will help," Orix said. "Please let me do what I do best."

"What in the world is going on here?" Carter pushed past

Ulrickson. "Willowman!" She rushed toward him. "What happened?"

Travani was close behind, her usually sleek hairstyle slightly disheveled. The lamplight caught her eyes, and for a moment they seemed to glow like amber, but then Carter was blocking her, the human's face a mask of genuine concern.

"Oh goodness, what is this? Did the alchemists do this? They said they merely wanted to talk to him. Simply talk..."

I didn't have the time or energy to find soothing words to assuage her guilt. "I'm sure our councilman will fill you in." I hoisted Willowman up in my arms securely and headed for the exit.

There would be no sleep for any of us this dawn.

CHAPTER 11

CAMERON

I'd never been this far into the rims, into the gray where my lungs felt too tight and my skin itched. Orix had commandeered a minibus from Outpost Two, large enough to transport us all. If not for Willowman's dire condition, this might have been a fun field trip into an area filled with pockets of mundane land.

Before leaving, Orix had agonized over whether to bring Taz or not, but in the end, he'd opted to leave the feline in Yarrow's care. It seemed that Taz was officially becoming the academy mascot.

The vehicle we'd commandeered might have been spacious for humans, but it was a crush for goyles.

The goyles' larger size made it impossible for them to share a bench, let alone drive this thing. Levi and I took turns at the wheel.

He was in the driver's seat now while I sat at the back, close to Willowman stretched out on the long back bench. We'd strapped him down as best we could to prevent him from rolling off. Derek had taken the spot on the floor below the seat, the only space large enough to accommodate his frame. Shar sat opposite me, her legs stretched out across her double seat, and I was hit by déjà vu from our first meeting.

She met my gaze and smiled. Yeah, she remembered too.

"I can't believe how far we've come from that first bus ride," Touron said from the seat beside mine. "I knew as soon as we met that we'd be friends."

Shar snorted. "Of course you did."

"I did, even with you giving us the cold shoulder."

Shar sighed. "I was a little harsh, wasn't I?"

"But you softened up to my charm." Touron made a kissy face, and Shar rolled her eyes.

"It looks so bleak," Ginia said from her window seat.

The sun was rising, its fragile rays casting fingers across a barren landscape either side of the winding road.

"Our eyes see color differently," Palia said from the spot behind her. "But they don't work as well when there is no magic. We're basically seeing what a human would see."

"That sucks," Touron said. "For them."

The minibus went over a bump, and Willowman moaned softly. I slipped off my seat, and Derek tucked in his legs to allow me to crouch beside the witch. He'd been unconscious for hours but cracked an eyelid now, looking up at me blearily. "Cameron?"

"Yes, it's me. How are you—"

"There are so many stars." He looked through me. "It's so beautiful." His eyes slipped closed.

"He's still not fully with us," Curi said.

"What if we were too late? What if they broke him?" Ginia said.

"We can't think like that," Shar replied. "This Calista person will help. She has to."

I needed to believe that. I stroked Willowman's dark hair back off his clammy forehead. "You're gonna be fine. I know it." I moved to the front of the van, squeezing past Curi's and Orix's legs to get to Levi. "How much farther to this Mistlegate place?"

"Not long. Another ten miles," Levi said. "We'll see it soon."

"And it's half mundane, half magical?" Palia asked.

"That's what Willowman told me," Orix said.

"Well, we need to get into the magical region soon," Curi said. "My skin hurts."

"Mine too," Touron said.

"I feel tingling," Derek said. "But no pain."

Levi hadn't been very communicative since leaving the academy. I climbed into the passenger seat.

"You okay?"

"Not really."

"What's wrong?"

His jaw tightened in that way I recognized when he was deliberating his words. "I'm not sure my father was telling the truth. I think he knew about the deep dive."

"Why didn't you confront him?"

"If he *is* lying to me, if he's...hiding things, then I don't want him to know that I'm on to him. I need to play the trusting son."

"But you don't trust him now?"

"I haven't spent much time with him. Not face-to-face. Not until recently, and now that I have...Cameron, I have warning bells going off inside me."

Finally. He was seeing his sire for what he was: the person who'd orchestrated his brother's and sister-in-law's deaths and abandoned his nephew. It was time that Levi knew the truth. "He didn't look for Serath, you know? He sent him away. Put him in an orphanage and made sure that his records went missing. Farnell found Serath by accident. He took him in."

A muscle in Levi's jaw jumped. "A few days ago, I wouldn't have believed you, but now..."

"There's more. Serath believed that your father had something to do with his parents' deaths."

He threw a sharp glance my way before focusing on the road again. "I may not trust what my father said back in Carter's office, but I can't allow myself to believe he could be a murderer. Not his own brother."

But the tension around his eyes told me differently, which was good because I hadn't believed a word that came out of Ulrickson's mouth.

"We're here," Levi said. "That must be it."

Curi hung over the back of my seat, his cheek close to my head. "Mistlegate population five-fifty, forward slash, four-fifty. Clever."

"Step on the gas, Levi," Orix said. "I need to breathe."

We accelerated over the town line and into Mistlegate proper.

CROSSING THE HALFWAY point of the town was surreal. Going from a winter scape to summer in a roll of a tire was enough to make my head spin. But the itch under my skin abated, and the band around my chest eased, allowing me to take a full, satisfying breath.

"Fuck, that's better," Curi growled.

"No more tingles," Derek said.

"I don't think I like being mundane," Palia said.

"Me either," Ginia replied.

"Which way?" Levi asked Orix.

"I'm not sure. Park and I'll go get directions."

Levi brought the van to a halt against the curb, and Orix climbed out and stretched. The others followed, eager to be out of the tin can. Derek looked torn, glancing from Willowman to the freedom of the street.

I smiled down at him. "Go stretch your legs. I'll keep an eye on him."

"You sure, my Cameron?"

"Positive."

Derek carefully unfolded his body and ducked out of the bus, stretching and expanding to his full height. He'd somehow made himself smaller to fit in the bus. That couldn't have been comfortable. Maybe I should have asked him to stay behind, but... but Derek was his own person, and I needed to allow him to make his own decisions.

I crouched beside Willowman again. "We're here, Willowman.

We're going to get you to Calista. Just hang in there."

If he heard me, he gave no sign of it.

Across the street, Orix was in conversation with a small man. The others stood on the pavement on this side of the road. Orix broke away from the man and jogged back to the van.

"There's a port across the road," he called out. "We take that, and it will drop us opposite her store."

I scooped up Willowman, Levi locked up the van, and we headed across the street to an ornate lamppost that had a peacock statue on top of it.

"What do we do?" Ginia asked.

"Just touch it," Orix said. He reached out and did just that and vanished.

"Cool," Ginia went next, and Palia followed.

"Go on," Levi said. "You go next."

I pressed my back to the lamppost, Willowman held tightly in my arms, and the world tipped, righting itself quickly to leave me standing on a pavement opposite a row of pretty storefronts.

"I think it's that one," Orix said, hands on hips.

Shar and Derek appeared, then Levi, Curi, and Touron followed a moment later.

"Couldn't we all have ported together?" Ginia asked.

"Best not to," Palia said. "Small numbers mean less chance of a mix-up."

"What do you mean?" Levi asked.

"Body parts being switched, for one," Palia said.

All the males looked down at their crotches.

Ginia stifled a giggle.

"Thank fuck I went through solo," Shar said as we crossed the street toward what seemed to be a bookstore.

The bell above the door tinkled as Orix pushed it open for me.

I carried Willowman to the counter. "Hello? Calista?"

A man stepped out of the back room, ducking slightly to get through the door. The gray hair at his temple spoke of age, but I'd have put him in his mid to late thirties at a guess; however, if he was supernatural, that number could be way off.

"Can I help—" His eyes widened at the sight of Willowman in my arms, then narrowed when they fell on Derek standing a step behind me. "What happened?"

"We need Calista," Orix said. "Where is she?"

"She popped out to get milk. She'll be back in a moment." His gaze went back to Derek, and I could almost see the questions forming in his mind.

I hoisted Willowman up. "You have a back room? A bed? Somewhere we can lay him down?"

The man looked thrown but recovered quickly. "Are you friends of Calista?"

"No," Orix said. "But he is." He pointed to Willowman. "Now please, do you have somewhere we can put him down?"

The man pressed his lips together for a beat, and I thought he might argue, but then he nodded. "Yes, there is, but it's not a large space. You won't all be able to fit." He looked to Derek once again.

"I'll stay here," Derek said.

"We all will," Orix said. "Levi can go with Cameron."

Levi stepped forward. "I can take him, Cam."

"No, it's fine. I got him."

The man's gaze settled on me again before flicking across to Levi. "Follow me." He led us across the shop floor to another door that opened onto a narrow staircase, which he struggled to squeeze up himself. It opened onto a cozy lounge filled with color and soft patchwork designs.

"You can put him on the sofa," the man said.

I carefully laid Willowman down.

"Now, I'm assuming she knows you, because if not...Well, Calista doesn't like her private space being invaded."

"Honestly, I don't care about upsetting anyone right now. My friend is hurt, and the last person he asked for before losing consciousness was her."

The man nodded. "Very well, please make yourselves

comfortable. I'll send Calista up as soon as she's back."

He hurried back downstairs.

"What is he, do you think?" Levi asked me.

"No clue. But he's a big guy."

"I didn't get a supernatural vibe off him."

"A large human, then?"

"Likely. Maybe he and Calista are a thing."

"Could be." And we were making small talk. "I don't want things to be awkward between us, Levi."

He sighed, gaze softening. "It won't be...It isn't. We're good."

But something had changed. The connection we'd always fostered was tainted. My fault for pushing him away, but...it was for the best. Maybe now we could build a fresh friendship, one that wasn't overshadowed by attraction.

The door opened, and a woman came flying into the room, wild-eyed and urgent. "Fuck, Willowman." She shoved past me and fell to her knees beside the couch. "Hey, you..." She stroked his cheek. "What have they done to you, eh?"

"The alchemists attempted a deep dive," Levi said. "We're not sure how much damage—"

"I heard. I've got this. You can go."

"What?"

She looked up at me, fire in her eyes. "I said, you can go."

My neck heated. "I am not leaving him."

She stood slowly, her small frame vibrating with indignation. "And you're not staying either, so I guess we're at an impasse."

"Whoa, whoa," Levi said. "Look, Calista, Willowman means a lot to Cameron. He's her friend, our friend. We just want to make sure he's okay."

Her eyes narrowed in my direction, nostrils flaring slightly. "Was it your blood he brought to me?"

"Yes."

Her stance relaxed a little. "He obviously cares about you. Wouldn't have made the journey otherwise." She sighed. "Look, this isn't something that can be fixed in a few hours. It could take days, and I work best when I'm left alone."

"You want us to leave him here?"

"Yes." She stared at me levelly. "I want you to leave him, and I want you to tell your council that he's dead."

"What?" Levi asked.

"You heard me. You tell them that he died along the way. Tell them that you buried him on the road, tell them whatever the fuck you want because there is no way I'm allowing my friend back into servitude for those motherfuckers."

"Servitude? What are you talking about?"

She gave a small, incredulous exhale. "You think he works at the academy for free by choice? Because he loves being an errand boy to your kind? No. He did it to be with the man he loved. He took an oath so that he could stay with him, and when that man lost his mind, they made them both stay. They refused to dissolve the contract. But he's done. I won't allow him to throw his life away any longer."

Wait...Varsa? "Varsa was his lover?"

"Yes, and from what I've heard, the goyle is lost in his own head now."

"Varsa is dead."

She stared blankly at me. "What?"

"He died last night. Willowman only just found out before they...they did this."

She looked down at Willowman. "And it all makes sense. Varsa's death dissolves the contract. They knew he was free. That he could leave and take all their secrets with him. Those bastards." She lifted her chin, eyes glittering with anger.

"No," Levi said. "If that was true, they'd never have let us leave with him."

"Unless..." I looked up at Levi. "Unless they believed he wouldn't recover?"

Calista's mouth twisted in a bitter smile. "But they don't know me. They don't know what I'm capable of. Leave now. They have no claim on him any longer, but if they ask, tell them he died.

Trust me, it's for the best."

The last thing I wanted to do was leave Willowman, but if what she was saying was true, and there was no reason for me to believe she was lying, then he was safest here with her. Varsa's funeral was tomorrow, and there was no way he'd be recovered enough to attend anyway. This was for the best, but my heart ached anyway.

"Please tell him...Tell him I'm sorry. Tell him I'll miss him and that...just, thank you for being there." I blinked back tears, and Calista's expression softened.

"I'll tell him. Now please, you should all leave."

The man with the graying temples popped his head around the door. "Is everything all right?"

"It's fine, Ivor. They were just leaving."

Ivor's brows went up. "So soon?"

"Yes," Calista bit out.

Ivor smiled, and his kind eyes warmed. "Well, safe journey. Maybe we'll meet again soon."

I followed Levi down the stairs, my heart heavy with the knowledge that Willowman had effectively been a prisoner for such a long time. And now that he was free to leave, they'd decided to use him as a scapegoat. To placate the Arcadian committee that all the moles had been found and dealt with.

Calista was right. It was best if they believed him to be dead, even if that meant we would probably never see him again.

CHAPTER 12

CAMERON

"I didn't know," Orix said, breaking the silence in the van.

I sighed, my eyes on the road ahead. "I believe you."

Arcadia was several hours away, outside of the pockets of magic and in the rim that we knew and tolerated. There were no ports into the stronghold, not that regular goyles knew of, anyway, but I doubted that the Arcadian committee would have left themselves without a quick escape route. I'd always believed that the headquarters was also housed in Arcadia, but apparently it had a separate location, which, now that I thought about it, made sense because humans also worked there.

We'd fueled up in the mundane half of Mistlegate before leaving, so we were good to go.

"Are you sure you don't need to rest?" Shar asked me. "You and Levi have done a lot of driving."

"She's right," Curi said, stifling a yawn. "We should all get some sleep."

"We can park and get some shut-eye."

"We probably should have stayed in town for a few hours," Ginia said. "Gotten some rooms."

"And paid for a whole day?" Palia looked affronted. "No way."

"I'm fine." I stifled a yawn of my own. "Okay, maybe I'm not."

The road was bordered by woodland, an empty stretch where our van was the only vehicle.

"There's a track coming up on the left," Levi said. "Pull in there, and we can take a nap."

I swung us onto the track, wheels bumping along uneven ground as I took us a little way along the trail and deeper into the cover of trees before killing the engine.

"Is it safe here?" Palia asked, peering out of the windows.

"A van filled with gargoyles?" Ginia said. "I think we're safe."

"I will keep watch," Derek said.

"You need to rest too," Shar reminded him. "Yarrow said sleep is essential for your development."

"I can sleep later," Derek said. He lowered himself onto the floor closest to the door, legs crossed.

I climbed out of the driver's seat, careful not to step on Derek, to find that all the seats were taken.

"There's room here," Curi called from the longer back seat. It was a deeper seat than the others.

"Or if you want a seat to yourself, *I'll* snuggle with Mason," Touron said with a cheeky grin.

"Cameron can sleep in my lap," Derek offered.

"I can take the front passenger seat," Levi said. "You can have my spot here." He made to get up.

I held up my hands. "It's fine. I'm good." I shooed Levi back down. "It's too cramped in the front. My thighs ache from driving, and you're much taller than me. I'll share with Curi."

Curi moved over to make room, lying on his side so I could lie down next to him. He put his arm around me to anchor me to him, and I snuggled close. I was used to hugs from him. Used to being close, but this was my first time sleeping with him. There was no discomfort, though. No sense of awkwardness.

"You good?" he asked, his voice low.

"Mmmm...You?"

"I'm good."

My eyelids drifted closed, warm lethargy infusing my limbs.

BLADES OF LUSH grass tickle my bare feet as I walk toward a circle of light. The world around me is dark and empty, and I know, instinctively, not to stray from this grassy trail. The light ahead holds warm golden hues that invite me to safety, but the darkness watches me, waiting for me to slip up so it can take a bite. The closer I get to the light, the more the dark presses in until there's nothing but a narrow strip of grass to guide me. I pick up my pace, falling into a jog, then a full sprint that takes me into the light, leaving the hungry dark behind.

Sunlight stings my eyes, and the world is fuzzy at the edges, giving the impression of greenery and flora, but my attention is drawn to the one spot of clarity in this strange vista: a lake with three benches lined along it, two brown with a bright red one in the center that houses a figure with his back to me. That back... That form...

My heart leaps. "Serath?"

The figure tenses and turns his head, offering me his profile.

"Serath!" I rush forward, and he stands abruptly to face me.

His mouth parts in shock. He reaches for me. I'm so close I can almost touch him, but the world rocks, and I'm thrown backward, snatched away from him and tugged into the claws of darkness once more.

"—UP. YOU NEED to wake up."

I surged into consciousness with Curi's hands on my shoulders, his face a mask of concern.

The van shook, and someone howled.

"What the—" There were figures outside the van, circling and banging against the metal. Something smashed against the glass.

"Leave!" Orix yelled through the window.

"Why dontcha come out and say that, big guy?" one of the males outside goaded. He was small, maybe five seven, with a scraggly goatee beard and a beanie hat that made him look like he had a peanut head. His coat was all leather and dirty gray fake fur, and the bat clutched in his hand was encrusted with reddish brown stains.

Blood.

There were five others with him, all men. Humans.

"They'll go away," Shar said. "They'll get bored and leave."

"And if they don't?" Levi asked. "That one has a blade." He indicated a weaselly looking guy.

The man hopped from foot to foot in his battered boots and skinny jeans, his jacket a little too tight across his belly area.

"I can't believe we have to sit this out," Ginia groaned.

"What would you rather do?" Orix demanded. "Go outside and risk an altercation?"

"If you hadn't noticed, we're already in an altercation," Curi said dryly. "The only difference is they're doing all the altercating."

"I'm confused," Derek said. "Why can't we *make* them leave?"

I'd only learned about the rule a few months before joining the academy. "Gargoyles are prohibited from attacking a pure human. They're bound to protect them, and there are some humans who know this and, from time to time, take advantage." Romi had told me a few stories about such groups. About a gargoyle who'd been attacked, beaten, and tortured by a small group of humans who took pleasure in inflicting pain on what they called Otherworlders.

A bottle smashed against the side of the van, and laughter rose.

I glanced at Levi in the driver's seat. "Why are we still here?"

"They've blocked off the road behind us and in front," Levi said. "I can't reverse or go forward."

"So...gargoyles can't attack them," Derek pondered. "What about me? What about you, my Cameron? You are not full gargoyle."

He had a point. "Orix, is it just pure goyles who are prohibited from hurting a human?"

Palia sat up straighter in her seat. "Yes, yes, it's purebloods. There's no mention of halfbloods in the edict."

"Good." I made to squeeze past Orix, who was blocking the door, but he grabbed my arm.

"Don't. What if you hurt them?"

"They'll have had it coming."

He released me with a sigh, and I pulled the lever to open the door.

The group backed up as I exited.

"Bit small for a stone bastard, aintcha?" the ringleader said. He sucked on his teeth. "You a runt?"

I gave him a closed-lipped smile. "Nope. I'm a halfblood. Do you know what that means?"

His eyes narrowed. "You one of them abominations."

I shrugged a shoulder. "I've been called worse, but what's relevant to this situation is that I have no qualms about kicking your ass." I strode forward, and he backed up a step before catching himself and standing his ground.

"We can take you."

The air shifted as Derek materialized beside me. "You're not taking my Cameron anywhere."

Their eyes rounded as they took him in.

The driver's door opened, and Levi climbed out, stretching to his full six-two height. "They won't touch her, Derek," he said. "Or they'll have three of us to contend with."

The human raised his bat and smacked it against his free hand. "I reckon we still might be able ta take ya."

His companions didn't look too sure, though. Time to drive home my point. I lifted my hand and willed my talons to extend. My hand morphed, fingers elongating as thick, vicious talons pushed out the tips.

Beside me, Derek expanded into his larger form, his arms elongating, shadow talons protruding from his fingers.

Blade guy's eyes bulged. "Um, Gaz, I think we should go."

The three of us took a unified step forward, and this time the whole group backed away.

"I suggest you listen to your friend, Gaz. I've had a shitty day, and there's nothing better than a little evisceration to lift the mood." I fixed a manic smile on my face and looked from my talon-tipped hand to his abdomen.

He lowered his bat and backed up into the underbrush. "Let's go. These fuckers ain't worth it."

I moved forward, and he let out a yelp and ran into the woods.

"Nothing like a little evisceration to lift the mood?" Levi asked.

I tucked away my talons and offered him a sweet smile. "The way I feel recently, it's exactly what I need." I strode to the back of the van. "Get in and start this tin can. I'll move the tree trunk, and we can get the fuck out of here."

No more naps. No more almost-dreams about Serath. The ache of loss it left inside me was too painful. I'd been denied the closure of a funeral for Serath, but maybe saying goodbye to Varsa would allow me to say goodbye to Serath too.

CHAPTER 13

CAMERON

Levi was at the wheel when Arcadia finally came into view. After three stops to stretch our legs and one stop to grab a bite, we were finally approaching the impressive gates to the gargoyle stronghold as the sun was preparing to set.

Romi had lived here growing up. This place had been his home, and he'd painted a picture of tall sturdy walls and thick wooden gates reinforced with steel and iron. He'd told me of the wide winding streets that led to gated properties housing the elite bloodlines, and the elaborate streets lined with huge mansions made of sandstone to weather all elements, and now...Now I was about to see it all for myself.

"Fucking hell," Touron said. "It's massive."

"Have you never been here?" Ginia asked him.

"Nah, my bloodline never made the cut."

"Ours either," Ginia said. "But our sire has friends here, so we visited often."

I was confused. "I thought all the omega nests were in Arcadia." There were omegas at the academy, but once they found their mates, they'd move back to Arcadia to birth and raise their young. At least that's what I'd been led to believe.

"Not all of them," Orix said. "There are many approved and

some unsanctioned nests out on the rim."

The gates loomed higher as we approached.

"What if they don't let us all in?" Touron asked.

"It's Derek I'm worried about." I glanced across at him, curled up on the floor at the back of the van, recharging in slumber. "If they try to hurt him..."

"They won't," Orix said. "I'm familiar with the guard here."

Levi brought the bus to a halt, and Orix jumped out and jogged to the gates. He pressed a button on the intercom fixed to the door and waited.

"I wish we weren't here for such a sad reason," Ginia said. "Arcadia is beautiful."

"Oooh, we should go to the bakery on Maple," Palia said.

"I'm going to go home and shower," Curi said with a sigh.

Orix opened the bus door. "We're good to go."

"We'll need somewhere to stay," Touron said.

"You can stay with me," Orix said to Touron. "We have a guest house on grounds."

But my attention was on Shar, who sat silently across the aisle from me. The tightness in her jaw spoke volumes. She wasn't happy to be back here.

"Hey, Shar, is it okay if I stay at yours?"

Shar sat up straighter. "What?"

"Can Derek and I stay at your place while we're here?"

She looked momentarily thrown, then her expression warmed. "Sure you can."

I woke Derek, and we all clambered out of the bus and followed Orix to Arcadia's gates. My stomach trembled with excitement and apprehension as a smaller door in the mammoth gates trundled open.

"Home sweet home," Shar said, her tone laced with bitterness.

Orix ran his hand through his golden hair, teasing the darker highlights into disarray. "Let's just get this over with. Funeral is tomorrow afternoon. We can leave straight after and be back at the academy in time for a late supper." He led the way into the stronghold.

This had been Romi's home, but it had also been Serath's, and now...Now I would be a part of it, even if only for a little while.

THERE WERE NO vehicles emitting gasses into the air in Arcadia; instead, sturdy trams designed to carry goyles ran all over the city. There were trees and bushes wherever I looked. They bordered every street and dappled the many gardens that could be found here. The buildings were huge squat affairs with balconies built for landing and taking off. Everything was larger—more space, more air, more everything.

My eyes struggled to take it all in as we rode the tram across the city to the elite quarter. Even the night couldn't hide the beauty of this place.

"The air smells clean," Derek said from his seat beside me.

"All the trees," Palia explained. "Arcadia is committed to a greener world."

The guards had given Derek a wide berth as he'd entered the city, but Orix assured me that there would be no issues. They understood that he was a shield and only a threat to anyone who tried to harm me—Lionel Basque's daughter.

Was he here? My sire, my...father? Should I go and visit? No. Not without an invitation. That would be awkward.

The street widened out, and an arch came into view up ahead.

"Elite quarters," Ginia said excitedly, sitting forward in her seat.

We passed through and onto a woodland-lined road. There were gaps in the trees at regular intervals—roads leading into deep woodland.

"All the properties are farther back," Palia explained to me. "They overlook the lake."

"This is my stop," Curi said as the tram came to a halt. He hopped out. "I'll see you tomorrow." His gaze snagged on mine for a beat. "If you need me before then, just call." He began to walk away.

Call? How? "Hey! Curi, I don't have your number."

"Just ask the operator to connect you." He threw the words over his shoulder. "Everything here is connected."

The tram set off again without him, and there was no denying the empty feeling his absence evoked. I was getting too attached to the blue-haired goyle.

"This is us," Shar said a moment later as the tram slowed again.

"I'll pick you up for the funeral tomorrow," Orix said. Derek and I joined Shar at the edge of the woods and waved goodbye to the others as they set off again.

"I'm starving," Shar said. "I'm going to ask Berta to fry us up some steaks."

We followed her down the moonlit road.

"You sure you have space for us?" Derek asked.

Shar smiled up at him. "I'm sure."

The trees grew sparser, then fell away, but the road continued, bordered by neatly clipped lawn snaking toward a huge three-story building that reminded me of a castle.

I let out a low whistle. "*That's* your house?"

Shar glared at it. "Yep. *That's* my house."

"You will definitely have space," Derek said.

"Too much of it." She picked up the pace toward the moonlit monolith. "Come on. Maybe we'll get lucky and Father won't be home."

"You don't like your father?" Derek asked.

"I like him just fine, in small doses."

We went from the road to a gravel drive that seemed redundant since they didn't have cars here.

Three steps led to a porch and an unlocked door. It was dark inside with only one lamp burning low in the entranceway, but there was enough light to make out the impressive staircase curving upward to the first-floor balcony.

"You best take off your shoes," Shar said. "Berta will have a fit if you get her floor dirty."

She kicked her boots off and carried them to a door to our left. "You can put them in here." She tugged it open to reveal a walk-in cloak room with hooks for coats and scarfs and shelves for boots and shoes on the opposite side.

Boots stored, we followed Shar down a corridor lined with closed doors, down a short flight of steps, and into a spacious kitchen where a female goyle sat at the table reading a book.

She looked startled as we entered, but her face soon broke into a warm smile.

"Niza!" She dropped her book and hurried over to pull Shar into a hug. "Look at you. Just look at you." She reached up to touch Shar's curls. "Your hair's grown. It suits you." She cupped her cheek. "Oh, my child. You look well, but what are you doing here? I wasn't told to expect you. And you brought company." She smiled at me, but her eyes widened in shock at the sight of Derek.

"This is Cameron Basque and her shield, Derek," Shar said. "They'll be staying the night here."

"A shield..." She peered up at Derek, all curiosity now. "Can it...Can it talk?"

"I can talk," Derek said. "And I'm a *he*."

"He's a person," Shar said with pride. "His own person, but also Cameron's shield."

"Well..." Berta beamed up at Derek. "It is very nice to meet you."

Derek inclined his head. "You too."

"And Miss Basque, you have been the talk of Arcadia ever since your sire revealed your existence. Our hope for the future." She clasped her hands to her chest. "I was devastated to hear about your brother. He was such a sweet boy."

"You knew Romi?" Shar asked.

"We met several times on social occasions. He was always polite and helpful. He never looked down on anyone of a lesser station." She bustled over to the stove. "Tea?" She didn't wait for a reply before putting the kettle on. "How long will you be staying?"

"Just the night," Shar said. "We came for a funeral."

Her face fell. "Ah, yes, I heard. Such a terrible loss." She sighed and shook her head. "Your father won't be back till dawn, but I'm sure he'll be delighted to see you. Are you hungry?"

"Actually, we are," Shar said. "Would you mind—"

"*Pfft*, of course not. Sit, sit, tell me all about your training... well, the parts that you're permitted to reveal, and Derek..." She smiled kindly at him. "Tell me about you. I've never seen a sentient shield before."

WE'D TRAVELED FOR hours, and I'd driven for miles, so by the time midnight drew up, I was ready to retire. Shar showed me to the guest room next to hers and left me to pass out while she took Derek to the cinema room to watch a movie.

I didn't have the energy to scope out the room, didn't even bother to turn on the lights, content to strip and climb into bed with just the moonlight for company.

My head hit the pillow, and I sank. Deep.

I'm back on the grassy path with the darkness pressing in on me, but this time, a figure is framed in the circle of light up ahead.

"Hurry!" Serath reaches for me. "Run!"

I break into a sprint a moment before the darkness clamps its jaws shut.

Arms encircle me, crushing me to a taut chest and cutting off my scream of horror. "I've got you," Serath says. "I'm here."

I pull away just enough to be able to peer up at him. My gaze grazes his hard jaw and then sweeps across his full mouth and up to his pale blue eyes filled with triumph.

"You found me," he says.

This is a dream, and yet it feels so real. I don't want it to end. I don't want to wake up. "Yes, I found you."

He cups my nape and brings his mouth down on mine in a crushing kiss that steals my breath.

"Cameron..." He breaks the kiss and presses his forehead to mine. "I thought I'd never see you again."

My heart breaks. I want to pretend, want this to be real, but it isn't, and that hurts. "I can't do this." I pull away. "I won't. I watched you die, and this...this is too painful." I squeeze my eyes shut. "I need it to stop. I need you to go away."

He grabs my arms. "Open your eyes, dammit. Look at me. I'm here. I'm here. I'm real and I—"

A rumbling growl cuts over his words, and the hackles on my nape quiver.

"You have to go." Serath cups my face. "Go, but don't forget this. Remember. You need to—" Another growl. "Dammit." Serath presses a kiss to my lips, and then he shoves me away. Out of the light and into the gray.

The mattress bows beneath my body as Serath presses me into it, his mouth on my neck as he trails kisses up toward my jaw.

There's something...something I need to—

He claims my lips, and our tongues meet. I'm lost, all train of thought abandoned to sensation as heat pools low in my belly, a glowing coal that gets warmer and warmer. Until my pussy is throbbing so hard it's almost painful.

I need him.

I need him inside me badly.

But this is wrong. We can't. We shouldn't. I shove at his shoulders, and he breaks the kiss, and all I see are his eyes, dark with desire. Hungry, so hungry...

I woke sweat-soaked, the apex of my thighs pulsing with need. I needed...Fuck, I needed...I shoved my hand into my pants, into my slick heat, and finished what the dream had started, coming hard, mouth clamped shut to stifle my cry. I rode the orgasm, pulse pounding in my head, chest aching with trapped breath.

The fever ebbed slowly, and my muscles relaxed. I turned my head to look at the window, at the almost full moon hanging in the starless night like a warning.

It was happening again, and I wasn't sure how I'd cope.

CHAPTER 14

TOURON

The goyle who opens the door to the Mason mansion is old and hunched over. "Can I help you?" His attention flies from me to Orix, and his eyes light up. "Master Albion, how wonderful to see you."

"Benny, it's good to see you too."

Benny steps aside to let us in. "Mr. Mason is out at present, but you may wait in the parlor if you wish."

"Actually," Orix says, "we were hoping to see Selas before we head to the funeral."

His face falls. "Ah, yes. Such a terrible thing."

"It is," Orix says. "But I hoped to make the journey less gloomy with a visit with Selas."

"I'm afraid Mistress isn't accepting visitors at present."

My heart sinks. "Please. Can you speak to her and ask?"

His brow furrows. "And you would be?"

"One of my most promising initiates," Orix says. "Selas had a strong hand in training him. I'm sure it would do her good to have the company, even if for a few minutes."

Benny gives a curt nod. "I'll see what I can do. Please take a seat in the parlor while I speak to her."

He shuffles off up the steps, and Orix leads me across the

polished wooden floors into a room with high vaulted ceilings and a large, airy feel. A hearth crackles with a generous fire, and there are enough seats here to host several goyles. A large gilded frame containing a family portrait hangs above the hearth, and I spot Selas right away. She can't be more than fifteen or sixteen in the painting, and her eyes aren't milky but a rich shade of brown, but it's the slight dips on the corner of her mouth that give her away—that almost smile that I love.

"I'm afraid Mistress has declined a visit," Benny says from the doorway.

The pit in my belly yawns wide. She doesn't want to see me...

Orix sighs. "Ah, a shame, Benny. Such a shame." He pauses, index finger going to his lips. "But, since we've come all this way, maybe you can make us some of your famous tea?"

Benny's eyes light up. "Of course. Right away." He makes to leave.

"I'll come with you," Orix says quickly. "The kitchens are so much more hospitable."

Benny presses his lips together in a suppressed smile. "You always did love the window seat."

Orix leans in as he passes and whispers in my ear, "Take a right at the top of the stairs, fourth door on the left." Then louder, "Touron, you said you needed the washroom? It's the first door on the left when you get to the top of the stairs."

He drops me a wink and places an arm about Benny's shoulder to steer him away.

Heart in my mouth, I take the stairs to the top floor two at a time, then take a right. It's plush and carpeted up here and smells of furniture polish. There isn't much light, though; all the doors are closed, and so are the drapes at the end of this hallway.

I hurry to the fourth door on the left, go back to make sure I've counted correctly, screw my courage into a ball that vibrates in the middle of my chest with a thump, thump, thump, then knock.

Three raps.

"What is it now?" Selas calls.

I take that as a cue to enter and crack open the door. It's dark inside, but a sword of light lances across the room from a gap in the thick drapes, slicing across the expensive-looking bedding on the large ornate bed.

Selas sits, propped up against a tumble of pillows, her dark hair loose and wild about her shoulders. One leg is stretched out and covered in a thick cast, resting on more cushions. There's a book propped open on another pillow on her lap, and her fingers graze the pages, sliding over them as she reads. They pause now, and she slowly lifts her head.

"I told Benny to tell you I wasn't taking visitors."

I swallow past the fist in my throat. "He did."

"You snuck up?" The corner of her mouth lifts. "You must want to see me badly."

"I do."

"Okay." She turns her head and sits forward so that her face is bathed in light, and I suck in a breath. The skin is puckered and swollen where the graynite sliced open her cheek.

"They're not sure it will ever heal fully," she says bitterly. "I'll be scarred for life."

"I'm sorry."

"Yeah, so am I."

She almost died because of toxin in the graynites talons. Her leg, which had been broken in two places, was still in a cast. Goyles heal fast, but leg bones aren't meant to snap this way. Insides aren't meant to spill out of torsos, but hers almost had. The graynite tried to rip her open. So much blood...so fucking much and Curi holding her together.

She sighs and sits back, casting her face in shadow once more. "You shouldn't have come." She turns away from me, as if she can't bear for me to see her like this, and my stomach wrenches, twisting in pain because she's hurting.

"I would have come sooner, but I didn't want to push boundaries."

"I'm glad you stayed away."

I have to play it cool. I can't let her know how much she means to me. I can't let her know how much this...being here, seeing her, breathing the same air as her, matters to me. I can't let her know I'm in love with her or I'll lose her.

"I stayed away, yes, but..."

"But what?" she asks.

"It didn't mean I wasn't thinking about you every day." I know as soon as I say the words that they reveal too much. "I mean, everyone was...thinking...about you. We've been worried. Nothing is the same without you." *Fucking shut up, Touron.*

Shit, she's looking at me now. Right at me with beautiful eyes that gleam like pearls in a face so filled with light and beauty that her scars are barely visible to me.

"Oh, Touron..." She closes her eyes. "Sweet, sweet Touron."

Oh no...She knows...She sees it. Of course, she sees it. "I'm not in love with you."

Her smile is sad and bitter all at the same time. "You're a terrible liar. You carry your heart on your sleeve, and it leaches into your aura so beautifully...All the colors, all the wonderful colors that any female would be honored to see. But not me. Still, you knew that, right? I bet Orix had words with you. Prepared you for what is to come."

"It doesn't have to be this way. We can still be together." I sound desperately weak, and I hate it.

"Maybe..." she says. "Maybe if you were in love with me, but I wasn't falling in love with you, then...maybe..."

My heart slams against my ribcage, once, twice, a third time as if it can't believe what it's hearing. "You...you're falling for me?"

That smile again, filled with the aching longing of all the things she can't have. "I am. But I don't want to. Do you understand that? I don't want any more pain, and if you love me, truly love me, then you'll walk out of this room, and you'll forget about me."

"I can't do that. I'm staying at the elite tower. Helping Cameron and—"

"I'm not coming back," she says. "I've filed for an honorable discharge. I'm done, Touron. So, leave, and please, don't ever come back."

I want to argue, to make all the promises to never leave her, to love her forever. I want to insist that it will be different this time, with us, with me. But there is no escaping the truth of our natures. If an omega binds me with her scent, then I will be lost, and Selas...Selas will be broken again.

I won't do that to her.

I can't.

I love her too much to be the cause of her pain. "Thank you... Thank you for being my first. First love, first...Thank you." I turn to the door and stop, my chest so tight I can hardly breathe. "I need you to know that if there was a way to turn off my nature, to be free of it completely, then I'd take it in a heartbeat just to be with you."

"Goodbye, Touron."

Her tone is thick with emotion, and it takes every ounce of will for me to walk out of the room. And as I close the door softly behind me, I hear her sobs, quiet and muffled, and for the first time in my life, I truly hate myself.

CHAPTER 15

ORIX

With Touron and the twins ensconced in the guest house of my estate, I'm free to spend the afternoon how I wish, and there's one special place that I've been itching to visit.

The cat sanctuary sits behind my estate—acres of woodland belonging to my father, to me—home to every stray cat I've ever come across, which are many. There are no bars, no walls to hold them in, just freedom, nature, and the hunt.

A long time ago, these creatures were kept as pets, domesticated so that some weren't even allowed outside, but now they've been allowed to return to their true nature as predators, and each of them has a story.

But only one of them ever speaks to me.

I walk deep into the forest, toward the river that runs through it and across the rickety bridge into a clearing dappled in sunlight and littered with the leaves shed by the towering trees. I settle on the downy ground and wait.

He knows I'm here, and if he wants to speak, then he'll find me.

Long minutes pass with the sun on my face and a cool breeze running its fingers through my hair before I sense his arrival.

And he's not alone. Other felines trail after him, their

inquisitive eyes fixed on me. New additions, born here in the sanctuary. But the one who leads them is an old friend. Maybe even ancient, although he's never confirmed it. His large, inky form pads closer, eyes like emeralds glittering in welcome.

Murnoch is the largest cat I've ever seen. His head sits three feet off the ground, his paws are the size of dinner plates, and when he yawns, the action exposes a serration of teeth designed to tear and shred. He's fearsome and agile, lethal when he wants to be. My friend and my savior.

"Well, hello there," he says. "It's been a while." He pads closer, circles me, and sniffs the air. "You have the scent of a new feline? A new addition to our sanctuary?"

Of course he would smell Taz on me. "No, not this one. This one belongs with me."

"He's chosen you, then. Good. You could do with a feline eye on you."

"So you've been saying. How are you, old friend?"

"Would you believe me if I told you there was an ache in my bones?"

"Not at all."

"In that case, I'm well. Busy with all the new additions to our numbers. We'll need more space soon." He looks over my head, up into the canopy. "Soon it will be time to return to the rest of the world."

This is a safe place. A home where the cats can breed and claim territory. Where they can live side by side but still alone if they so wish, but there is only so much land to go around. "Is it time, then?"

"Soon. I still have much to teach them about survival in the true wilds, about living alongside other much larger predators, about the cycle and circle of life." He settled beside me and laid his head on his paws. "You may stroke my fur if you wish."

An honor indeed. I lightly stroke between his ears and down his neck, and I'm rewarded with a soft rumbling purr. "Are you ever going to tell me?"

His purr becomes a deeper rumble. "One day. When the time is right. Then I will tell you. But you remember your vow, don't you?"

"Yes, I remember." Never ask. Never demand. Never expect.

He'd saved my life all those years ago. Without him, I wouldn't have lived long enough to make guardian. He'd lost his own kin in the process, and I'd given him a new family, an ever-growing one, along with my word that I would never ask him who or what he truly was.

But one day he will tell me. One day he will confide in me, maybe even show me what is hidden behind his feline façade.

Until then... "You want to race?"

He chuckles softly. "You'll lose. Again."

"Are you scared, old boy?"

He chuffs and pulls himself to his feet. "I'll give you a head start. One. Two—"

But I'm already loose, leaping across the bridge and into the woods, the rustle of pursuit close behind me, and the thrill of the chase buzzing through my veins.

The race has begun, and even if I lose, simply being here is a win.

CHAPTER 16

SELAS

I wake from my nap to late afternoon sunshine and my father silhouetted on my balcony.

I sit up and push my hair back off my face. "When did you get back?"

He turns to me with a smile. "An hour ago. Benny said you had visitors."

Touron... "Yeah, but I wasn't up to seeing anyone." I don't want to get Benny in trouble by letting Father know that Touron made it to my room. Knowing him, he'd up security and fire our long-time butler. My father can be a little overprotective. I am, after all, his only child. Mother told me he'd been less than pleased when he discovered I was an alpha, that I'd have to be on the frontlines. Most sires were eager to throw their spawn into the arena, but I'm certain mine would have kept me wrapped in cotton wool if he'd had the choice.

"You need to see people," he says. "You can't stay locked away forever."

"I'm still healing."

His mouth tightens. "Yes, but that doesn't mean you have to isolate yourself." He rounds the bed and sits on the chair beside it. "I've spoken to your mother, and she's agreed to host you for a few months. I think it would be good for you to have a change of scenery and—"

"No. I don't want to go."

"Why not?"

He knows why. He must. "Seriously?"

He sighs. "Procreation isn't everything, sweetheart."

As much as he tries, he will never fully understand what it's like to have your choices taken by nature. To watch other females find their mates, fall in love, and have younglings. He'll never know the deep ache in my soul that can only be assuaged in combat, and now... "It's procreation or guardian, Father. I can't procreate, and now, with this injury, I can't even be a guardian."

My leg throbs as if to remind me of the shattered bone, so damaged that I will never be able to fight again. I'll be left with a limp and pain. Always pain. I should have told Touron the truth, but I'm not ready to face it. Not yet.

Another sigh. "There are positions at headquarters," he says. "Or you could continue to train cadets at the academy. Mentor or—"

"No." I can't go back there. Not like this. Not ever. "Please. I just...I just want to wallow for a while. Is that all right?"

He leans in to kiss my temple, and I breathe in his familiar soothing aroma, gripped by guilt because he's doing his best. He's always done his best.

"I'm sorry, Father."

"You have no reason to be sorry, my child. You are and always will be my pride and joy. We will find a purpose that makes you happy. I swear it."

I want to believe that. I really do, but as the sun dips and shadows fill my room, it's hard to imagine there ever being sunshine in my life.

CHAPTER 17

CAMERON

Berta put on a spread of pastries and bacon for our midday breakfast. The dream was a faded memory in the back of my mind, but the fever wasn't. I needed to do something before it got out of hand.

With Willowman gone, I'd need to turn to Yarrow for magical assistance and Mirrowind for information on the kind of fae blood I might have. I needed to make the connection and fast.

"My Cameron, you think hard today," Derek said from across the table.

"Just tired."

"You didn't sleep well?" Shar asked. "I'm so sorry. Was it the bed? The room?"

"No." I glanced at the door. Berta had just left the room, so it was safe to speak. "I had one of my fevers last night."

Shar looked confused for a moment before her face softened in comprehension. "Shit. You think it's going to get worse?"

"Yeah."

"What can we do?"

"I don't know. Serath usually...He was here for me."

"I can be here for you," Derek said.

"No!" Shar and I said at the same time.

He looked between us, his diamond eyes clouded. "My Cameron, I want to help you."

"I know, but not with this. You can't help with this.'"

"Why not?"

My cheeks warmed. "Because...because I don't want you to, okay?"

He flinched and looked down at his plate. I shot Shar a *help me* look.

She gently placed her hand on his arm. "Derek, it's a sex thing. The kind of thing that lovers do, not best friends."

He looked up slowly. "I see. My Cameron, you can explain these things to me. I will understand." Then to Sharniza. "Thank you. And I do have a solution. You can do the sex thing with Levi."

"No, I can't. Because...because we used to be lovers, and now we're not, and it would confuse things."

"For who?" Derek asked.

Damn, he was too astute for his own good sometimes.

"Derek has a point," Shar said. "What other options do you have? Curi? He'd do it for sure, but he's already half in love with you, and Touron would probably be sick at the thought. He sees you as a sister."

"Then some random goyle." I shuddered.

"Levi," Sharniza said. "Better than a random guy who might turn into a stalker."

Derek nodded his agreement. "He is the safest choice if need be."

Urgh. "I don't want to. I don't want anyone but Serath."

Sharniza looked me dead in the eyes. "Serath is gone."

I reminded myself of this fact regularly, but hearing it said was a fresh kind of torment. "I know, but...it feels like he's still here." My dream surged to the forefront of my mind. "Last night, I—"

A gargoyle male strode into the room. "Sharniza, when did you arrive?"

Sharniza sat up straighter, her expression smoothing out like glass. "Father. We arrived last night and will be leaving after the funeral."

This was her father? This tall, wiry goyle with a heavy brow and frown lines that made me think he never smiled? I couldn't see the resemblance between them at all.

"And who are your guests..." His brows shot up at the sight of Derek. "Miss Basque and her shield, I presume?"

"News travels fast." I forced a smile. "Nice to meet you." Although it didn't feel nice. It felt cold and uncomfortable being in his presence, as if he sucked the heat right out of the room.

He barely looked my way before turning his assessment on his daughter. "You've let your hair grow out." His nose twitched as if he smelled something bad. "You'll fix that."

"I'm sorry," Shar said smoothly. "Things have been busy. I'll get it cut back at the academy."

"No need. Berta can do it before you leave."

A little light bled out of my friend's eyes. Her throat bobbed. "Of course."

"Do you want to cut your hair?" Derek asked Shar.

Her father looked at Derek as if he couldn't believe he'd dared to speak. "Excuse me?"

Derek took his time tearing his attention from Shar and fixing it on her father. Then he simply said, "You're excused" before dropping his attention back to Shar. "Do you *want* to cut your hair?"

Shar stared at him for long seconds, as if she couldn't believe someone was asking her that question. Asking her what she wanted.

"Shar..." He gently touched one of her curls. "Do you want to cut your hair?"

"No," Shar said softly.

"Then you shouldn't." A gentle smile bloomed on his lips, showcasing the tips of his canines. "I'm glad. I think it suits you, this length."

"Sharniza? What is the meaning of this?" her father

demanded.

Shar held Derek's gaze when addressing her father. "It means I'm not cutting my hair." She smiled, and it lit up her eyes. "In fact, I plan to grow it out. I might even put a pink bow in it." And there was the twinkle that had been absent since coming to Arcadia.

Her father's eyes bugged. "Don't be ridiculous. I won't allow it. You are a warrior. A guardian, an alpha female who—"

"Likes pink." Shar pushed back her chair and stood, eye to eye with her sire. "I *like* pink, *and* heels, *and* dresses. I like makeup and bows and pretty, shiny things, and I am *done* denying myself. It's enough that my nature stripped me of the chance to bear children and put me onto the frontlines of a war that I didn't choose to fight. It's enough that I can never be mated to my own kind. I've *given* enough, and I'm done."

Her father's eyes narrowed, his lips thinning. "You would bring ridicule and shame on this family?"

"If my being happy makes you ashamed, then so be it." She jerked her chin my way. "We should get going. Orix will be here to pick us up soon."

She strode from the room, but I took my time pushing back my chair and standing. "I'd say it was a pleasure meeting you, but that would make me a liar. But I will give you a piece of advice. Rethink your priorities before you lose your daughter. Trust me, don't leave it too late."

I followed Derek out of the room, suddenly eager to be out from under this oppressive roof and go to a funeral.

CHAPTER 18

CAMERON

Gargoyles didn't originate from this world. Our kind came from the stars. From distant planets that were now cut off to us. The oldest of our kind remembered their home and recalled the pilgrimage away from it when it died. Back then, they called the death of a goyle the long sleep, and the funeral was a farewell into dreaming. We'd adopted many of the earthly customs now, though, but the oldest of our kind remembered. At least that was what Romi had told me.

My brother had taught me so much over the years, things I'd probably forgotten that would come back to me when the timing was right. Like now.

We stood in a circle surrounding a large platform that housed a plinth—its tip pointing at the sky and the base decorated with the effigies of grotesques.

Varsa's stone body lay on the platform, looking up at the sky.

They called it a farewell, not a funeral, and the whole process would take place out in the open, in the Meandering Garden—several beautifully kept gardens that were intersected by twin rivers that fed the lakes of Arcadia. This part of the garden was called the Central Garden, and according to Shar, this was where all social events and important gatherings happened. Under sky and air.

Everyone wore dark colors, but every outfit had some silver in it, be it a cuff, a collar, or a scarf. Shar had loaned me a silver belt, and Palia and Ginia had silver scarves in their hair.

Palia had explained that silver was the color of mercury, which was considered a mutable yet connecting force, durable and transformative just like the gargoyle race.

A robed goyle slipped through the crowd and climbed onto the platform with Varsa.

I leaned closer to Palia. “Who’s that?”

“That’s the sleepsinger,” she whispered. “He has the power to release a goyle to eternal rest. There aren’t many of them in existence. Legend says that they are born as and when needed to maintain the cycle of life and death.”

A large gargoyle male I didn’t recognize broke away from the crowd and came to stand before the dais, hands clasped in front of him. Like several others, he was dressed in dark blue and silver, his shirt and pants loose enough to hang off his solid frame.

“Who is he?” Touron asked, his voice low.

“That’s Terinin Storm,” Orix replied. “The head of the Arcadian committee. Here in Arcadia, he is the law.”

“But he answers to the council,” Palia added.

“Why a Storm and not one of the five bloodlines?”

“Balance,” Palia replied. “The five have enough power. They weren’t even on the council until over a decade ago.”

“Ulrickson?”

“Yes,” Palia said. “My sire told me it was a shock to everyone, and there was some debate and friction with the other families when he was appointed.”

“Welcome, brothers and sisters,” Terinin said. “Today we gather to say farewell to Varsa Orbrin, our brother of over a century. A male of great purpose and great resilience. He did not bow to the graynites when they bent his mind. He did not allow them to steal our secrets despite the cost to himself. Varsa was a true guardian. A true warrior, and today we gather to send him into the arms of the spirit, where he will sleep until it is once more his time to awaken."

Terinin gave the sleepsinger a nod before stepping back into the circle.

The sleepsinger pressed his lips together, and a low, resonant hum filled the air. He tipped his head up, mouth parting to let loose a melody—an echoing light sound that made something inside me tug, drawing me to the precipice of a larger comprehension only to pull me away again.

As his voice rose, the timbre changed, becoming higher and higher until it was a whisper on the edge of my consciousness, slipping into a range that my ears couldn't register.

On the dais, gray matter rose from Varsa's body and dissipated into the air. He was disintegrating, his stone form breaking and rising until he was gone.

The sleepsinger dropped his chin and closed his eyes. "And so, he shall rest. And so, he shall find his way home. And so, he shall return to us once more when the spirit permits." He stepped down, and everyone began to move away.

"That's it?" I looked across at Palia, who nodded sagely.

"That was...beautiful," Derek said softly. "He will return one day? Reborn?"

"That's the theory," Sharniza said.

"I like that theory. It means...it means that nothing ever dies."

My mind flashed back to my dream of Serath. It had felt so real. The way he'd looked at me, the things he'd said...I could almost believe he'd been reaching out to me from beyond, but the fact that we'd suddenly ended up in bed proved it was all a dream.

"You okay?" Curi asked me.

"Yeah, I'm good."

"Ready to get out of here?"

The look on his face said he was more than ready to leave. "Yeah, let's go."

The gardens had emptied out, and the expanse of water that had been blocked off to me was now visible. I zeroed in on a bench, the wood painted red while the other two benches on either side of it remained brown. My blood went cold.

"Cameron?" Curi said.

I tore my gaze from the bench. "I dreamed of this place. That bench...It was in my dream."

"What? When?"

"Last night, I dreamed it and...Serath was there."

"Is everything all right?" Orix joined us. "What are you looking at?"

"Cameron says she dreamed of this place last night," Curi said. "That bench and Serath."

"Maybe he told you about this place?" Orix suggested. "It was his favorite spot. His mother used to bring him here as a child."

"There are no ducks..."

"What?"

"He said he used to feed the ducks, but there are no ducks here."

"There haven't been for some years," Orix said. "Cameron... It was just a dream..."

"I'd believe that, but the bench is red. He never told me that the bench was red, so how come it was red in my dream?"

CHAPTER 19

CAMERON

The bench held me transfixed. It was the same bench. Exactly the same, down to the shade and the distance it sat from the other two. Down to the scratch on its leg where the paint had worn away.

"Cam, you're freaking me out," Ginia said.

"You can't believe your dream was real?" Levi said.

I forced myself to look at him, tearing my gaze from the lake scene. "I'm not sure what to believe. I mean, how do you explain what I saw...what I felt..."

"Dreams are strange things," Palia said. "You might be filling in the blanks now."

That was a possibility, but, "It felt so real. He was trying to warn me, to ask me for something. He wanted my help and then..."

"Then what?" Curi asked.

My cheeks heated. "The dream changed."

"To what?" Ginia pressed.

Shar caught my eye, and she made an *O* with her mouth, connecting the dots to our earlier conversation about my fever state returning.

But I didn't want to discuss that right now. Not here. Not with everyone. "It doesn't matter. We should get back to the academy. To training. I need to speak to Yarrow about Melanie."

“The van’s all packed and ready to go,” Orix said. “Touron and I grabbed some snacks for the road.”

“We can get some training in on route,” Levi said. “I brought the lockets my mother made.”

“What about the incense?” Shar asked. “Don’t we need that too?”

“You’ve all mind walked once, so we shouldn’t need the scent this time and—”

“Cameron?” My sire stood just outside our group. “May I have a word?”

When had he arrived? Or had he been here all along? “Sure.” I slipped away from my friends and followed him toward the lake.

“I heard what happened at the academy with Willowman,” he said, his expression solemn. “Carter called me. I’m so sorry I wasn’t there. I was at headquarters, but I made my way here as soon as Carter said you’d be attending Varsa’s funeral. Did you manage to get Willowman to the special healer you were taking him to?”

I dropped my gaze. “We did, but he...he passed away once we got there. His friend asked us to leave him so she could bury him.”

“Oh...” He put his hand on my shoulder. “I’m so sorry. I understand that you two were close.”

I hated lying to him, ironic considering the fact he’d lied to me all my life, but it still felt wrong, especially after how he’d gone to bat for me the last week or so. “Willowman was a decent guy. He taught me a lot about herbology and tinctures, and Varsa...Varsa was my friend.” My voice cracked. “I’ll miss them both.”

That part was true.

He gave my shoulder a reassuring squeeze. “I’ll let Carter and the council know about Willowman. You focus on your training and the trials, and if you have any other issues with anyone, you can contact me through Carter. You’re a Basque, Cameron, and no one messes with a Basque.”

I met his steely gaze, except this time there wasn’t a sheet of glass between us, and I felt the warmth of his regard. “Thank you.”

The words came out on a whisper.

His smile held sadness, and the echo of moments lost. "I wish I could have brought you home sooner. I wish there was time for me to take you to the estate but...time is something we seem to be running out of. But once this is over, once Romi is back, we'll celebrate in true Basque style."

"I have no idea what that is."

His eyes dimmed. "I suppose you don't. But you'll see. I promise." He looked over my head. "You have a strong support system, despite everything. I'm so very proud of you, Cameron."

And why did that give me the warm fuzzies? "I should...I should go. We have a long drive ahead of us."

"Yes. I suppose you do. I'll see you after the trials. We'll have a lot to plan."

His confidence that I'd pass meant the world, and I walked back to my friends, feeling lighter than I had in days.

I was ready to focus. Ready to mind walk until my spectral feet ached.

I may have lost Serath, but I'd be damned if I lost anyone else.

CHAPTER 20

CAMERON

The mind walk in the van was a bust because my mind was too busy going over everything that had happened on the trip. My dream of Serath, the fever, the coincidence with the park bench and my father's hopes for me.

Curi and Shar seemed to manage it fine, but both were silent and reflective for the rest of the journey, so it was a quiet bunch who returned to the academy.

It was almost eight in the evening by the time we strolled into the elite tower, and we were all too wiped to cook, so Derek and Touron headed to Stone Comfort to grab pizza.

I showered and changed into a baggy T-shirt and leggings and slipped on my lastonflex shoes before heading down to join the others for supper. I had a lot to do before I could wind down for the evening, but my stomach grumbled incessantly, reminding me that food had to come first.

Five large pizza boxes were laid out on the kitchen island, open to showcase the variety of piping hot, cheesy goodness. Derek handed me a plate, which I loaded up before joining everyone at the table.

Curi patted the spot beside him, and I slipped into the seat, mouth already filled with deliciousness.

We ate in silence for several minutes, and I noted that even Derek had a slice. Shar watched him, hiding the hearts in her eyes. She had it bad. But I understood why she was holding back, although I doubted they'd be able to keep from professing their feelings for much longer. The way Derek had stood up for her in Arcadia...the look they'd shared...A weight settled on my heart—a reminder of what I'd lost. The fact that I'd never again feel the flutter low in my belly or the heat spread across my chest and up my neck. I'd never experience the agony of longing to touch someone. Having Serath here but not being able to *be* with him had been painful, but...but there'd been comfort in that pain. A rightness that was now absent.

I was alone.

I'd always be alone.

"Cam?" Curi was looking at me, brows drawn. "Hey..." He reached up to gently wipe a finger across my cheek.

I blinked, dislodging more tears. "Shit. I'm sorry." I wiped at my face. "Just tired."

"Yeah, it's been a long day."

The look on his face told me he didn't buy it, and my stupid eyes heated.

"I think we should watch a movie later," Ginia said quickly. "To unwind. Popcorn and snacks. Ice cream!" She clapped her hands.

"Excellent idea," Palia replied, her gaze stoically on Ginia.

And suddenly everyone was looking at Ginia and discussing movie options, taking the attention off me completely and giving me the moment I needed to pull myself together.

The only person that didn't engage was Touron. He watched me solemnly from across the table.

"What do you think, Touron?" Ginia asked him.

He smiled, but it didn't reach his eyes. "Sure, whatever."

Wait...Touron had gone to see Selas? He must have, and now he was all subdued, which meant it hadn't gone well. Orix must have taken him over...

Once again, I'd been so caught up in my own emotions... No. I wouldn't be that person. I wouldn't allow grief to make me selfish. "I need to pop in and see Yarrow. You wanna come with me, Touron?"

His forehead wrinkled, and he dropped his gaze, and for a moment I thought he was going to refuse, but then he nodded. "Sure."

"Can you pick up Taz for me?" Orix asked.

"You mean, can I ask him to come back with me?"

Orix rolled his eyes. "Yeah, that one. And tell him I missed his furry face."

It was my turn to roll my eyes. "Sure."

The rest of the meal passed quickly, but my attention kept going to Touron, to his plate where one pizza crust sat.

My goyle friend who loved his food had barely eaten.

I had no doubt how the meeting with Selas had gone now. It was time for me to be there for him, just like he was always there for me.

It was good to be walking and not cramped into a metal can on wheels. My legs thanked me for the exercise as we made our way down the winding path toward the main building.

It was prime time on campus with goyles milling about and enjoying the moonlight, many in their gargoyle beast forms, wings out to take to the air. I couldn't help but wonder what it would feel like to have wings. To fly on my own steam.

Beside me, Touron seemed lost in his own thoughts, but a muscle in his jaw jumped the longer I studied his profile.

He exhaled softly. "Go on, then, ask me."

He sounded resigned, and that hurt my heart. "You don't have to talk about it if you don't want to. We can just walk. I just...I'm here, Tor, and I'm sorry that I didn't check on you sooner."

He glanced my way with a frown. "What? Don't...don't do

that. You have enough on your plate."

"Never too much to care about my friends. I love you, Touron, and I hate seeing you in pain."

He swallowed hard. "You're in pain too."

"It doesn't mean I can't be here for you. I want to be here for you. Please."

He dropped his gaze to the gravel, boots crunching with each step. "She broke up with me."

"You told her you loved her, didn't you?"

"No." He looked across at me, indignant. "I did not say that. But...I didn't have to. She read it in my aura."

"Oh, fuck."

"Yeah, I forgot she could do that. I guess I'm walking around with hearts floating around my head or something." He gave a weak smile. "She told me she isn't coming back to the academy either."

"I'm sorry, Tor. I wish there was something I could do to help."

"I don't think I'll ever feel this way about anyone, ever. I love her, Cam. It fucking hurts."

"I know." I reached out and took his hand. "I know."

"I'm such a dick. It's worse for you."

"Not worse, just...different. Serath is gone, but Selas is still here. Two kinds of pain, each as awful as the other."

"Your dream...Do you really think he was reaching out to you?"

My pulse quickened. "It seems silly now."

"I know, but...we never saw a body. They took him."

"There was no way he could survive the wound that thing inflicted on him."

"Maybe...but what do we know about the graynite abilities? About their technology or their medical facilities."

My stupid heart beat faster with each word. "You really think he might be alive?"

"I think you have the right to hope."

Hope, that fickle yet insidious bitch, flared to life in my chest. There was no body, and the dream...the dream had felt so real, not to mention the red bench. How could I have known about it even subconsciously without ever having seen it?

"Next time you dream of him, don't fight it," Touron said, eyes bright. "Ask him where he is. Ask him...ask him if he's alive."

My heart leaped, and Serath's voice filled my mind, a memory from the dream, forgotten up until now. *Look at me, I'm here—*

Oh God. Could it be true? Was Serath alive?

CHAPTER 21

SERATH

A soft beep and click breaks the silence of my prison, then light spills into the room. I close my eyes. They can't know that I'm conscious. Not yet.

I need time.

Time to reach her. Time to convince her.

"How is he doing?" a cultured male voice asks.

"Wounds were bad, but he's healed nicely," another male voice, this one sounding younger, says.

"Strong enough to begin the procedure?"

"I believe so. We can start tomorrow."

"Good. The sooner we complete the conversion, the better. The powers that be are beginning to get antsy."

"Do they want another incident like the Basque boy?" There's a bite to the young male's voice.

Romi? They're talking about Romi...

"I raised this precise point. The only reason they've been agreeable to taking it slow with this one. How is Basque doing?"

"He's viable...if contained. We're working on compliance."

"Good, good," the older male says. "Give this one another day, then start the procedure. Take it slow and increase the pain. We need to ensure that—"

"I know how to do my job."

"So, you've extracted the female's pheromones from the items provided?"

"Of course I have."

"Good, that should make the process smoother."

The door clangs shut, and my heart squeezes painfully in my chest because I'm running out of time.

CHAPTER 22

CAMERON

I hadn't intended to lead with my new conviction that Serath was alive, but as soon as Yarrow let me into the tutor's quarters, that's exactly what I did. I relayed my dream and what Serath had said and explained the whole red bench theory because that bench was the most grounding factor.

Yarrow listened without interruption, his face giving nothing away.

I finished and waited for his verdict. When it didn't come immediately, I couldn't help but prompt, "So, he could be alive, right?"

His eyes twitched. "Cameron..."

I didn't like his tone, soft and almost pitying. "No, but wait. How do you explain the dream and the bench?"

Yarrow pressed his lips together. "Grief plays tricks on the mind, Cameron. Now if you two had consummated your mating, then maybe Serath would be able to reach out this way to you, *if* he was alive somewhere."

"But she's a halfblood," Touron pointed out. "Willowman always said it was a gray area with them because of that. They couldn't be sure how a fated mating worked for them."

"True," Yarrow said. "But it's a long shot. I don't want you to get your hopes up just for them to be dashed."

But if my father could hope and believe that Romi was alive after all this time, then why couldn't I hope that Serath was too?

"Didn't a graynite rip through his chest?" Yarrow continued.

I sucked in a sharp breath as the image filled my mind once more.

"That was cruel," Touron said.

"I wasn't trying to be cruel. I'm merely stating a fact. An injury like that, from a graynite, with the toxin it would have put into Serath's system, isn't something he'd recover from. It would kill him."

But now that Touron had helped ignite this fire, I wasn't letting it burn out. "We can't be sure of that. Serath could be alive. They might have healed him so they can then feed on his soul."

The room echoed with silence as the meaning of this fact settled in my bones. Lionel had told me the truth of how graynites were made. That they were just gargoyles without a soul, but did Yarrow know this?

We eyed each other warily for a moment or two.

"You know, don't you?" Yarrow said finally. "You know what that would mean."

I shook my head. "He'd fight them. He'd resist. He's strong."

But even as I said it, doubt crept in. Romi was a Basque, and the graynites could use him as a bargaining chip, but Serath... Ulrickson had made him an orphan, and whatever information he had, Romi had it too...

"Look, Cam, I'm not trying to hurt you, but it's obvious they intended to kill Serath in order to undo you. They wanted to eliminate your mind, your ability to take Romi's place on the team."

I closed my eyes and exhaled. "Forget it. Please. I don't want to talk about it anymore."

"Cameron..." Touron lightly touched my arm. "Nothing is certain. Don't lose hope."

I wasn't. I couldn't.

Yarrow's jaw tensed, his gaze hardening as it settled on Touron. "As her friend, you should be helping her come to terms with her loss, not feeding her delusions."

"As her friend, I'm being honest about what I believe," Touron said.

"Even if Serath is alive, there is no way to get to him. No way through the wards around graynite territory."

His words were a fist to the gut because of course there was no way in. How had I not considered this? But then why did Lionel say he wanted me to save Romi?

"The alpha will emerge, and when we take him down, the wards will fall too," Touron said with confidence.

"You don't know that for sure," Yarrow pointed out. "No one knows for sure, and false hope is toxic. We must work with the facts. The elite team is vital in the event of the alpha emerging. That is all we can say. Whether the wards will fall or whether Serath is alive is all speculation."

"Enough. I didn't come here to talk about Serath. I came to check in about Melanie."

Yarrow was kind enough not to remind me that I'd been the one to bring up the topic in the first place. He released Touron from his golden gaze and fixed his attention on me.

"Flora and I found something in your room. Something that explains why your ghostly friend is unraveling."

THE BLACK CRYSTAL was smaller than the others Yarrow had given us to place in Melanie's room.

Yarrow held it up to the light, and the sheen on its surface flattened out and went matte, almost as if it were absorbing the light. "We found this beneath your bed. This particular crystal absorbs energy and vibrations. I believe it was negating the effects of the crystals we gave you and hastening Melanie's unraveling."

"You think someone planted it, don't you?" Touron said.

But who? "Who has access to my room and to this kind of crystal?"

"I could speculate," Yarrow said crisply, "but I would rather prove my theory. And we will do so, once Mirrowind returns tomorrow."

"She can help," Flora continued. "She has an artifact that can transport certain types of energy. If she can move Melanie here, then we can put her in the room that we housed Derek in. It's a revitalizing and healing space, and it should help her to recover."

I looked from Flora to Yarrow. "So, it's not too late?"

"No," Yarrow said. "Not too late. But you need to keep this plan between us. Someone found out what we were doing with Melanie and tried to thwart our plan, and that same someone is likely responsible for the attack on Flora and Melanie. If we want to discover their identity, then we need to keep this plan a secret. The less people that know, the better."

Whoever it was could have been working with Prasan and the graynites, and we were one step closer to catching them.

CHAPTER 23

CAMERON

The moon was partially hidden behind a cloud when we left the main building with Taz in tow. The feline hadn't been too eager to leave the cozy confines of Yarrow's quarters and had waited until we were out the door to shoot after us.

He trailed behind us now, vanishing into the underbrush only to pop out ahead of us, then wait for us to catch up before trailing us once more...or stalking...Maybe he was stalking. Either way, it seemed to be a game to him, and it was kind of sweet.

"I don't like keeping this Melanie thing from the others," Touron said as we approached the elite tower.

"I know, it feels as if we don't trust them. But it's better this way. The more people that know, the more likely that the information will spread, even inadvertently. We can tell them once Melanie's recovered enough to speak to us."

He unlocked the door and held it open for me, but Taz dashed in first and vanished up the stairs. "You need to make sure you speak to Mirrowind about your sidhe moon problem too."

Wait, had I told him about that? No...I'd told Shar and Derek. "You see, this is what I mean about information being spread."

He shrugged. "It's hardly the same. We all care about you and want to help you. I just can't..." He looked down at my crotch. "Do that for you."

I hid my smile behind a frown. "Do *that*?"

Twin spots of color bloomed high on his cheeks. "You know what I mean."

I leaned closer and stage-whispered, "Sex?"

"Urgh." He shuddered. "Stop."

A giggle climbed up my throat. "I love you, Tor."

He slung an arm around my shoulder. "I love you too, Cam. In a totally platonic, brotherly, non-sexy way."

THE TWINS, SHAR, and Derek were deep into a movie where a couple danced on screen, twirling, bodies indecently close. There was no sign of Levi, Curi, or Orix.

Shar spotted us and grabbed the remote to pause the movie, leaving the characters mid hip grind.

"How'd it go with Yarrow?" Shar asked.

"He wasn't there," Touron lied for us both.

"But you managed to pick up Taz?" Shar asked, glancing at the door behind us where the feline now sat watching us with his intelligent peridot eyes.

"Oh, yeah, Flora let us in," Tor said quickly with a light chuckle that sounded fake.

Shar frowned. "You're lying. Why are you lying?"

Touron's eyes flew wide. "How dare you suggest such a thing. I'll have you know I am no liar."

"Um...why are you talking like a character from a historical novel?" Ginia asked.

"I knew you'd been raiding my stash!" Palia said to her sister.

"So what? I love a good bodice ripper."

"Touron?" Shar said, her tone stern. "Cameron?"

Touron looked to me, sheepishly. "I probably should have mentioned I'm a shit liar."

He really was, but, "You managed to keep your romance with

Selas a secret."

"Only because no one confronted me about it."

"Hello?" Shar waved a hand. "What happened with Yarrow?"

I trusted each person in this room with my life. "Okay, so this is what Yarrow thinks..."

I filled them in on the black crystal, Yarrow's theory, and how he felt Mirrowind could help.

"And he counseled you to keep it a secret?" Shar asked.

"Even from me?" Derek looked hurt.

I ran a hand down my face. "I don't even know what I was thinking. I trust you guys with my life." I smiled at Derek. "Especially you."

"But I get it," Palia said. "The more people that know, the more chance that they might speak about it to each other, and someone else might overhear."

"So we agree not to speak of it," Derek said. "We don't speak of anything important or vital unless we here, in this tower."

"Agreed," Shar said.

"Now come watch the movie," Palia said. "It's only just started."

"I'm in." Touron climbed over the back of the sofa and settled beside her, but I begged off, hands in the air.

"I think I'm gonna curl up with a book."

"I didn't know you read," Palia said, eyes brightening.

"It's been a while, but I fancy it tonight." I wandered over to the bookshelf across the room and ran my finger across the spines. "I'm sure I'll find something." The titles meant nothing, so I grabbed three at random. "These'll do. I'll see you for breakfast." I ducked out of the room before anyone could stop me.

A few weeks ago, I'd have wanted nothing more than to hang out with them, but now there was a strange comfort in solitude. Solitude, my thoughts, and dreams.

I wanted to sleep. To dream. I wanted to find Serath again and ask him if he was real. If he was alive.

I needed to know if my suspicions were correct. I needed to

know that I wasn't going crazy.

THIS TIME THERE is no grassy path. This time I find myself standing by the red bench opposite the lake, and there is no sign of Serath.

The world is fuzzy at the edges, as if it's been erased by invisible forces, and I'm gripped with a sense of urgency. "Serath! Serath, where are you?"

A finger of awareness slides up my spine to rest at my nape.

"Here," Serath says from behind me.

I turn to face him, and ice pricks at my senses. He looks gaunt, his eyes dark smudges in his face, his skin pale and drawn.

"Serath? What's happening? What's—"

He gathers me to him, solid and real. His scent fills my head, chasing away any doubts. He cups my face, and the calluses on his palms tease my skin. His eyes are all pupil. Unfocused and dazed. "Serath, what's happening to you?"

"They have me, Cameron. They have me, and I'm not sure how long I can hide this part of me before they find it and tear it away."

This place... "You've created this place as an anchor?"

He scans my face with dark eyes. "I did. But I have no idea how you're able to find it. Find me. But you're here, and I am so grateful to have seen you once more." His tone holds defeat.

"Don't you dare give up. I'm going to find you. I'm going to save you. You've got to hold on a little longer."

He tucks his chin in, wincing as if in pain. "I'm trying, but... Cameron. I'm afraid I'm failing."

"You're stronger than them. You can fight this. I'm going to find you. Just...hold on."

He drops his forehead to mine, his breath warm on my lips. "I'm trying. I'm just...I'm so tired."

A little more color leaches from his skin, and the world around us dims. His hold on this place, on this sanctuary is slipping. "No.

I won't let you go." But his skin is so cold against my warm hands. A bad sign.

I press my lips to his and breathe my life into him.

He's mine, and I'm his, and we are one. I won't let him go. I won't let them have him.

I break the kiss, lips moving against his as I speak. "Stay with me, Serath. You can stay with me. Fight until I can find you because I *will* find you. I swear it."

He wraps his arm around me and crushes me to him, claiming my mouth, hungry and desperate. His fingers weave through my hair and clutch at my scalp as he deepens the kiss to a bruising intensity that leaves me reeling.

A wave of prickly heat rushes up my body, and a phantom hand squeezes my nape. Serath gasps and breaks the kiss, his gaze stunned as it moves off my face and up to the sky.

The world is dark, the sky a vista of twinkling stars, and set in the center is the moon—too large, too round, and outlined in crimson. My pulse beats hard in my throat and between my thighs, and my gums throb strangely. When I speak, my voice is lower, a deep, sultry timbre. It belongs to my beast, but it's different, laced with something else. Something new. Something ancient. And suddenly I know what must be done to protect what belongs to me.

To us.

"Cameron?" Serath stares at me in awe. "Your eyes..."

But all I see is the color in his cheeks and the life in his veins. Life that belongs to me. I won't let them take it. I won't.

"Mine." My head whips forward, and I bury my fangs into his neck.

I woke with the tang of iron in my mouth, heart thundering in my chest, and peeled off the covers stuck to my body. I was burning up, my lungs so tight I was afraid they'd fracture on my next breath. I tried to swing my legs off the bed, and my lower abdomen tightened with need.

Oh no. Not again. I pressed my thighs together against the swollen throbbing between them that ached for release, but that just made it worse. Dammit. I shoved my hand into my pants, thighs falling open as I touched myself. It didn't take much to tip me over the edge, and I bit back a cry, my whole body shuddering with pleasure. But the relief was momentary. The twisted need never ebbed, rising instead, tightening, and growing stronger. I worked it, finding release once more, but the need grew greater until it was bordering on pain.

Hunger.

This was hunger. Strange, awful, and empty. A yearning that couldn't be filled by the thrusting of my slick fingers.

"Cameron?" A knock on my door. "Cameron, are you all right?"

I clamped my mouth shut to cut off the needy sounds spilling from my lips.

"Cameron, answer me!" Curi demanded.

Yes. Need him. Want him. Thoughts filled my mind. Thoughts of his body on top of mine, of his cock pushing into me. No!

Pain ripped through me, sweet and sharp.

I flung myself off the bed, yanked open the door, and threw myself against Curi. His scent filled my head as I grabbed at his biceps, digging my nails into the lastonflex.

He wrapped an arm around me. "Fuck, Cameron...fuck, you smell so good." His tone was thick, just like his cock would be.

My pussy throbbed eagerly, hungrily. I needed him. I needed him to make the need stop.

CHAPTER 24

CURI

"Curi, it hurts. Please..." She rubs her body against me.

I grab her arms to hold her still. "Fuck."

"Yes!" She twists her fingers in my shirt. "Fuck me. Please." A sob breaks from her lips. "Curi, please. Help me..."

This is déjà vu, and I know exactly what's happening here. "Cameron, you're not yourself."

She grabs my nape and crushes her mouth to mine, and oh gods, she tastes like nectar and caramel lattes, and I want nothing more than to push my tongue into her mouth and taste every fucking inch of her. It takes everything I have in me not to act on my desires. Instead, I gently cup her jaw and force her away from me.

"Look at me. Cameron, look at me."

Her eyes are unfocused, the color all wrong. The stormy gray is now laced with streaks of crimson. "Cameron!"

She blinks, and her gaze sharpens, nostrils flaring. "Curi, I can't make it stop. I need you...to...to..."

"What do you need, Cameron?" I need her to say it. I need her to be clear.

She squeezes her eyes closed, leaking tears. "I need you to touch me. I need you to...to make me come."

My heart is a fist in my chest because although I offered myself to her for this very purpose all those weeks ago, now that the time is here, I'm not sure I want to cross that line. I don't want to lose her. I don't want to lose our friendship.

"There has to be another way."

She grips my shoulders, fingers digging in as she cries out in pain. "Maybe, but not right now. No time right now. Please. I need you to do this for me."

My blood is on fire as I scoop her up into my arms and carry her into the room, kicking the door closed behind me.

I try to lay her on the bed, but she clings to me, sobbing softly, her need an aroma that my beast can't resist, but I tamp down on it as I climb onto the mattress with her. I won't let him out. I can't risk it.

Whatever happens between us now will be clinical and necessary. No emotion. There can be no fucking emotion.

She grabs my wrist and guides me to the apex of her thighs, her face buried against my shoulder in shame.

My throat is tight, eyes burning as I touch her over her slick panties. She's so fucking wet and hot. Her lips swollen with need. Dripping beneath the fabric. I want to touch her bare pussy, to taste her with my tongue.

My chest vibrates, and she moans, parting her thighs for me.

No.

I can't. I have to focus.

I can do this for her without crossing that line. I stroke her through the fabric, running my fingers over her clit, then circling it. She bucks hard against me, her strangled cry music to my ears as she comes. But it's not over. Her body is on fire, pressing against mine, hips rolling against my hand begging for more.

"Inside," she whispers, her voice as tight as the string of a bow. "Please."

Fuck, she's testing me now. I squeeze my eyes shut, holding on to the reins of my beast as I slip my hand into her panties and touch her bare skin. My cock is so hard I'm afraid it will explode as

I slide first one, then two digits into her. She's so tight, so fucking tight.

She sobs. "Yes, yes, yes." Her walls hug me as I thrust, squeezing me tightly as she comes, over and over, leaving me wet, hard, and hungry. A strange prickle washes over my skin, a haze fills my mind, and the air is suddenly thick with a sweet, cloying scent.

I stay inside her until her body relaxes and she slumps against me, and then I slowly withdraw my fingers.

She curls her body into a ball against me and lies there breathing, just breathing for long seconds. Silent fractures make their way across my heart because she's so small, so vulnerable, and all I want to do in this moment is erase what just happened between us and take us back to the easy comradery of before.

Finally, she raises her head and looks up at me through misty eyes, her wobbly mouth turned down in shame. The crimson is gone from her irises, which are now clear and bright, and her cheeks are flushed like she's been for a run.

"I'm sorry," she whispers. "I didn't want to have to do that. I'm so fucking sorry, Curi." Tears track down the side of her face, and I brush them away with the same fingers that were inside her a moment ago. I can smell her on me—honeyed and tempting. I breathe through my mouth, past the need that presses against the base of my spine.

She has no idea the lengths that I would go for her. "Don't you dare be sorry." I gently pull the sheet up over her body—she's shivering now that the episode has passed. "We'll find a way to fix this, and if we can't do that, then we'll find a way to manage it. You don't ever have to be sorry with me. Do you understand?"

She nods, dislodging more tears, then presses her cheek to my chest. I should leave now, but instead I hold her tighter. Just hold her.

Fuck, I could just hold her forever, and that...that could be a problem.

CHAPTER 25

CAMERON

Curi was gone when I woke up. I was glad for that because I needed time to compose myself before seeing him again. The fever was gone, too, but only because he'd given me what I needed last night. He'd given me what I needed, knowing that I could never give him what he needed in return.

My heart.

Guilt was a live thing burrowing inside my chest because I'd used him. I'd used him to relieve my need, knowing how he felt. Knowing that he'd been falling for me.

As far as he was aware, Serath was gone, there was no barrier for him to lean on, to stop his feelings from resurfacing, but I'd forced him to test that barrier last night. I'd pushed him, begged him, pleaded for him to capitulate.

Shame burned a path up my neck and settled in my cheeks. I covered my face and squeezed my eyes shut at the memory of his hand on me. Of the pleasure that had rocked my body.

I'd let him touch me. Begged him to help me find release, and Serath...I'd betrayed him. I'd allowed another male's hands on me and...and I'd liked it. I felt...revitalized. Energized.

No. That person hadn't been me. It was the fever. This inexplicable thing linked to the fae blood in my veins or...or maybe not. If Serath was alive, then the mate bond was still alive and... No, Willowman had explained that distance would mute the bond, which was why Serath had planned to leave.

Urgh, I was going round in circles.

Focus, Cam.

I needed to tell the others that Serath was alive, but first things first, I needed to speak to Curi and apologize. I needed to tell him about Serath and fix us because I needed him in my life, I needed our friendship.

CURI WASN'T IN his room, and his bed looked unslept in because... because he'd slept with me.

I'd slept with Curi.

Together.

My stomach churned.

He was probably at breakfast already. I hurried down to the third floor and into a room filled with the sound of voices, the clink of metal on ceramic, and the smell of bacon. Derek stood at the cooker, apron tied around his waist as he expertly flipped pancakes, and Shar leaned against the island watching him with a look that was a cross between pride and lovesick.

She caught my eye and quickly composed her features into something that was more light interest than anything else.

I arched a brow, and she rolled her eyes with a smile.

Yeah, she was so gone for him.

"Cameron, just in time!" Touron passed me a plate loaded with bacon, eggs, and toast. "Unless you want pancakes. I mean, you can have pancakes too." He headed to the table with a second plate piled higher than mine for himself and parked his ass opposite the twins, who were already stuffing their faces.

"You should eat," Levi said as he slipped past me, holding the coffee pot. "We have physical and mental training today."

"Where's Curi?"

"Here." He came up behind me, and my body tensed. I forced myself to relax and look at him as he came abreast of me.

His easy smile didn't reach his eyes, and my heart hurt. "You okay?" I kept my voice low.

He dipped his chin. "Are *you* okay?"

I nodded, my mouth dry.

"That's all that matters, Cam."

But that wasn't true. "You matter too, Curi."

His smile slipped, but he fixed it back into place quickly. "Course I do. And I can take care of me just fine. But we need to tell the others your fever is back."

"Shar, Touron, and Derek know, but there's more I need to tell everyone. Curi, I believe that—"

"What are you two whispering about?" Ginia called out.

I took a deep breath and finished my sentence for all to hear. "Serath is alive."

Silent faces stared back at me, and Shar was the first to speak. "I know you dreamed about him the other night, but—"

"I did. And I dreamed about him again last night. He's alive. He told me. The graynites have him. He says he's running out of time and—"

"He's alive?" Curi said softly. "You knew last night?"

I looked up at him, stomach in knots. "I woke up from the dream with the fever and—"

"Your fever is back?" Palia asked.

"What fever?" Levi asked.

"What were you doing with Cam last night?" Derek demanded of Curi.

And suddenly everyone was speaking at once.

"Enough!" Orix stood by the stairwell, Taz at his feet. The room fell into pin-drop silence as he raked us all over with a stern glare. "Now one person, tell me what the fuck is going on."

All eyes turned to me, and my stomach sank. I fixed my gaze on Orix. "Serath is alive, and we need to save him."

❧

NO ONE SPOKE while I filled them in on my dream about Serath and how I was certain he was alive, that it was more than a dream. "He said he made a place to hide. An anchor. The lake and the bench...I think he's fighting them by hiding a part of himself there."

"If he *is* alive, then I believe it," Orix said. "I believe he could do it. Serath is the most mentally strong of us all."

"This is insane," Levi said. "A wound like the one you described isn't something he could have survived."

"They must have healed him," Touron said. "I believe Cam. I think he's alive, and she's somehow able to connect to him."

"But you never consummated," Ginia said.

"She's a halfblood," Palia retorted. "The rules don't apply. In fact, we don't know the rules."

"He's alive..." Curi said softly. "What you felt last night...the fever...that was you yearning for him..."

"You had another episode?" Shar asked.

"What is this fever?" Levi asked again.

Shar filled him in quickly about the fever, the needing, the sidhe moon, and my fae blood.

His gaze whipped my way. "You have fae blood?"

"Supposedly, yes."

"And you were there last night when she had an episode?" he asked Curi.

Curi met his gaze levelly. "I helped."

Silence fell, thick and heavy, and my cheeks burned. "It was bad, and Curi...Curi was there." I knew how bad it sounded as soon as the words were out, as if he'd been convenient. As if the fact it was him didn't matter. "I mean...I mean he was close. No. I mean that—"

"I know what you mean," Curi said stiffly. "It's fine. Serath being alive would explain her episode."

"Not really," Palia said. "Distance mutes the needing."

I agreed. "I think this fever is related to my fae blood."

"Your eyes changed," Curi said. "During..." He swallowed hard. "They were darker and laced with crimson, and the air...it felt...different."

"These episodes need you to..." Levi licked his lips. "You have to orgasm?"

"Yes, but not solo. I...uh...It doesn't help if I do it."

"Well, this is awkward," Ginia said.

"But necessary," Orix added. "If these episodes are linked to the sidhe moon and your fae blood, then we have a huge problem. The elite trials are on a sidhe moon. You can't enter if you're..."

"Horny?" I finished for him.

Ginia snort-laughed and then clamped a hand over her mouth.

"Why him?" Levi asked. "Why not me?"

"Because I was there," Curi said. I didn't miss the edge of bitterness in his tone.

"Not true," Derek said. "My Cam spoke to Shar and me about this, and she said she would come to you if need be."

Curi looked across at me in surprise.

"It's true."

"Great," Levi said. "You'd rather go to someone you met a few months ago than come to me, the guy you dated for a year."

How the fuck was he making this about him? "Yes. Yes, I would, and I can tell you exactly why. I care about you both. But if I have to go to anyone for help with this, it won't be to the ex who I know is in love with me. It would be much too easy to get lost in the fever, fall into a familiar rhythm, and cross the line. It'll be with the gargoyle who has the fortitude *not* to cross the line." I turned to Curi. "It's true that you just happened to be there last night, but if you hadn't, then I would have chosen to come to you because of the deal we made all those weeks ago. Because I trust the boundaries you've set. You helped me last night, but I promise I won't put you in that position again. I value our friendship too much. I won't risk losing you."

Curi's expression softened, real light bleeding into his eyes. "I believe you."

I looked to Levi, who had his head bowed. "Levi? Do you understand what I'm saying?"

"I understand," he said. "But I don't agree. Even the strongest boundaries can get blurred when you're falling for someone, can't they, Curi?"

Curi pressed his lips together, refusing to respond.

"This arrangement is not sustainable unless you wish to take Curi as your lover," Orix said.

I couldn't...wouldn't do that. "I won't play with someone's heart if I'm not free to give mine in return."

"Then we speak to Mirrowind," Shar said. "And we find another way to deal with this fae blood fever, get you through the elite exams, and get Serath and Romi back."

All we could do was hope that they both survived long enough for us to get to them.

CHAPTER 26

CAMERON

I was on my knees, surrounded by my friends and their jeering laughter. The world beyond them was a dark expanse of nothingness. I wanted to dart between them, to run away, but they circled like vultures, blocking my escape again and again as they rained down insults like heavy hailstones.

"Pathetic," Shar said. "I can't believe I was friends with you."

"I should have known better," Touron added. "You're weak."

"More like selfish," Curi said. "Taking what you need at the expense of others."

"It's your fault that Serath was taken," Palia said. "He was so focused on protecting you that he failed to watch his back."

They continued to chip away. To make digs at me. Their words more painful than any blade or barb.

No. Not true. Derek's voice filled my head. *My Cameron, you can't believe this.*

But I did; there was a part of me that felt all these things, that held on to them every fucking day. These were my wounds come to haunt me, and as much as I wanted to fight back, to tell them to fuck off, the words refused to come because everything they said felt too real, too true, teasing the doubts and fears inside me.

Their voices grew louder, and I felt smaller and smaller until the buzz of Levi's alarm jolted me back to the training room.

I stared at the mat, tracing the nicks and cracks in the fabric as I waited for my pulse to stop racing and the awfulness that had bloomed in my chest to dissipate. I couldn't look at the others right now. I needed a moment to remind myself that none of what had just happened was real.

Derek put his hand on my shoulder. "It's not true. None of it is true."

I exhaled and nodded, because of course I knew this. But... but it *felt* true. Deep inside me, it fucking felt true.

Derek put his arm around me and pulled me into a sideways hug, resting his cheek on my head. "It's all right now, my Cameron. It's all right."

I glanced at Shar staring at the exit as if she wanted nothing more than to bolt.

I nudged Derek and whispered, "I think Shar could do with a hug too."

He kissed the top of my head, then misted away only to materialize next to Shar and pull her into a hug.

She let out a soft squeak before relaxing against him and closing her eyes.

Curi watched them with an expression I couldn't read. His gaze shifted to me then bounced quickly to Levi.

"How come you're not training?" he asked Levi.

"I defeated my demons a long time ago," Levi said.

"Is that what we're doing?" Sharniza asked. "Defeating our demons?"

"In a manner of speaking."

Curi pulled himself to his feet and rolled his shoulders. "Then we best go again, *after* I get a latte."

"I'll come with you." I made to stand, but he waved me off. "I'll bring you one back."

He didn't look at me when he spoke, and my heart sank as he left without another word.

I caught Levi watching me. I didn't want to see the pity on

his face.

"Take thirty," Levi said. "Get some air."

I followed Derek and Shar to the door.

"Cam?" Levi called. "Can I have a minute?"

Great. I wasn't in the mood for a pep talk or a lecture, or maybe both, but I had too much respect for what he was trying to do with us to tell him that. Besides, right now, I was sucking hard at this mind walk stuff, and if I didn't master my demons soon, then I wouldn't make it out of the elite trial. So, I hung back while Shar and Derek left and waited for whatever pearls of wisdom Levi wanted to hurl at me.

"I wanted to apologize for earlier, at the tower," Levi said. "I was an ass. Pushy and jealous. I had no right to be. I was selfish, focusing on my insecurities instead of supporting you."

Well. I hadn't expected that. "It's okay. I understand. If roles had been reversed, I probably would have reacted the same."

"No, Cam, you wouldn't have. Because that isn't who you are. You don't have a selfish bone in your body."

"I beg to differ. Recently, everything I do feels selfish, and my mind walk confirms it."

His brow crinkled. "Your fears and doubts aren't always real, Cameron. They aren't always valid. It's up to you to weed out what is true and what is false and find the balance that will allow you to be the best version of yourself. Our past experiences don't have to define us." He smiled wryly. "We can take away from them what serves to make us better people and leave the chaff behind."

I wanted so desperately to believe that, but... "And what if we can't? What if *I* can't?"

His smile fell. "Then you'll fail. It's as simple as that."

ANOTHER ROUND OF mind walking, another failure, and two hours of physical training later, we were free to get on with the rest of our day. My limbs had that satisfying ache that came from a good workout, and my head felt a little fuzzy, the kind of sensation that said I'd done a ton of mental acrobatics too. All in all, I'd have been happy to head back to the tower, climb into bed, and dream my way to Serath. But if I was going to save him, then dreams would have to wait. There was work to be done.

Shar dabbed at her brow. "Are you going to see Mirrowind?"

"Yeah. I'm going to shower and change first." I lifted my armpit and sniffed. "Definitely."

"We'll come with you," Derek said.

I slid a glance Curi's way, waiting, hoping that he'd offer to come with, but he wasn't on his mat; he was already at the door, then gone.

"You should talk to him," Shar said softly.

"Why should she?" Levi said from the bench press across the room. "He's acting like a child."

"You don't know what he feels," Derek said.

He was right. We didn't. Everyone had said their piece. Everyone except Curi. "I'll meet you guys at the tower."

I hurried outside and spotted Curi walking toward the tower. "Curi! Wait!" I jogged to catch up, and he slowed his pace to let me. "Can we talk?"

"We don't have to do this, Cam. We're good. Everything is good."

"If everything was good, you wouldn't be avoiding me."

"I'm not. I...Look, I just, I need a little space, okay?"

The yawning pit inside me grew wider. "Oh...Of course. I...I'm sorry. Of course you do. After what I asked you to do—" I was an idiot. Of course, he was upset.

"This isn't about that." He came to halt and turned to face me. "The mind walk today was...difficult, and it centered on you. I just need...I need a little space today. Okay?"

I'd been in his mind walk? "Did I hurt you? Did I hurt you in the mind walk?"

"No, Cameron. I hurt myself."

Because of me...He hurt because of me. "I'm sorry."

"It's not your fault. It isn't real."

"But it feels real."

"Yeah." He reached out to touch my cheek but thought better of it and pulled back his hand. "Caramel lattes tomorrow morning and you can fill me in on whatever Mirrowind says today."

I nodded, unable to speak past the stupid lump in my throat.

He broke away and jogged toward the tower, beautiful blue hair gleaming in the red rays of the setting sun, and even though I was headed there, too, I waited for a couple of minutes before following.

I WAS FILLING a takeaway mug with coffee to take to the main building with me when Orix entered the kitchen.

"How did training go?" he asked.

Ah, so many ways to answer that one, but I didn't have the energy for a long conversation. "Good."

"And everything else?"

"It's fine. We're fine. I'm actually about to go look for Mirrowind now, so hopefully I'll have answers and solutions too."

"Don't get twisted up if she can't help," Orix said. "We'll figure something out regardless."

I needed the vote of confidence right now. "I know, I just...I can't risk failing the elite trial. Romi and Serath are depending on me. On us."

"Not just them," Orix said. "Everyone. We're tasked with bringing down the graynite alpha, Cam. Bringing back Romi and Serath are bonus actions, not the main mission. You do realize that, don't you?"

Ice filled my veins because, no, I hadn't been thinking in that way. For me, Serath and Romi *were* the mission, and my face must have communicated that, because Orix pressed his lips together, breathing raggedly through his nose in a way that told me he was about to deliver some serious home truths that I probably wouldn't want to hear.

"You're not a fool, Cameron. You've hunted. You know how priorities in the field work. The main objective must *always* come first. The secondary objectives can be completed afterward. The lives of the many over the lives of the few."

A bitter tang stained the back of my throat. "You're saying Romi and Serath are dispensable."

He shook his head. "Not to me. Never to me, but for the purpose of this mission, yes. If we must choose between taking down the alpha and extraction, then we choose taking down the alpha."

Choose? How could I choose? "I'm not going to leave them there. I won't do it."

His lips thinned. "Then you'll end up getting us all killed. If we're not on the same page, then we will fail. All of us."

"The others...you spoke to them already, didn't you?"

He nodded. "I did."

"But what do they care? Romi is my brother, and Serath is my mate. *I'm* the one with everything to lose here."

"Listen to yourself, Cameron. Would you really put their lives above the lives of every supernatural and human in our world?"

A vise tightened around my lungs because for a moment only one word echoed in my mind. *Yes*. Yes, in the moment I might just do that. I grabbed hold of the counter, exhaling in shock at the revelation.

"Cameron..." Orix moved closer. "Both Romi and Serath knew the risks when becoming an elite. We are the front line. We are a weapon. Without us there is no hope. They knew what the elite team's sole objective was—to eliminate the alpha. That is what we were chosen to do; everything else is filler. You need to understand this too." He pressed his lips together for a beat as if choosing his words before continuing. "I was going to wait until after the trial to tell you and the team this, but I think you need to hear it now."

My scalp pricked. "What? What is it?"

"All this time we've been prevented from attacking the graynites on their own turf because of a ward they have over their city, but that's changed. It turns out the prototype that Prasan was working on was a dud, probably deliberate on his part, but the science and theory behind it was sound enough for another tech to run with, and we now have a mini disrupter. According to your sire, this other device has been in production for some time, even before Romi was taken."

"Prasan's prototype helped them fix their version?"

"Yes."

So, my father had been confident that we might have a way past the wards when he asked me to run for elite.

"It won't take down the whole ward," Orix said. "But we can punch a hole into it. We can get into their territory without them knowing. We can find the alpha and take him down. And everything must be focused on that objective because we only get one shot. One use of the machine and then it's over. Do you understand?"

He wanted me to agree to put Romi and Serath second, leave them behind or let them die if it came to a choice between saving them or killing the alpha. I wasn't sure I could do that.

"I...I should get going." I hurried toward the exit.

Orix gently gripped my arm. "You can't run from this, Cameron. If you do, you could end up getting us all killed."

I looked up into his eyes filled with doubts and concerns, and my gut twisted. "I know. I just...I need a little time."

"There isn't much of that left. Make sure you've reconciled with the idea before stepping into the trial." He released me, and I ducked out of the room, eager to get away from him and his pointed words.

There would be no elite team if I failed the trial, and that's exactly what would happen if I couldn't get the fever under control.

That would have to be my first concern. The rest would have to wait.

CHAPTER 27

CAMERON

Shar and Derek had asked to come with me to see Mirrowind, and we somehow picked up Levi in the main building. Okay, so he might have been loitering outside, waiting for us to go by, but I wasn't about to call him on it. There was no reason for him not to come, and having a druid with us couldn't hurt. He might even be able to help Mirrowind come up with a solution to my fever problem. I mean, herbs and tinctures and fae magic had to mix well, right?

We headed to Yarrow first, who informed us that Mirrowind had indeed returned at dawn that day and had already moved Melanie to Yarrow's quarters, where my spectral friend was hopefully recharging. But the room was sealed and would stay that way for several more hours before it would be safe to check on her.

Mirrowind's chambers were in the tutors' wing but on a different floor from everyone else, up a flight of stairs and inside what I could only describe as a penthouse suite.

It was a huge, cavernous chamber dotted with comfy fabric seating that fought for space with the wondrous plant life sprouting from large, earthen pots set around the room. Glass cases filled with strange, colorful insects hid among the foliage, and the windows were flung wide, letting in a steady circulation of cold air along with shimmering moonlight that competed with the dazzling lamplight illuminating the room. The air smelled like syrup and freshly baked bread, a combination that made my stomach growl.

Mirrowind stood before us, all five feet four of her, draped in a loose-fitting shirt and pants. Her tiny feet were bare, toes adorned with silver rings, and her slender fingers were wrapped around a goblet. Twin spots of color sat high on her alabaster cheeks, and her sky-blue eyes were bright with curiosity as she took us in.

"It isn't often I get so many visitors at once," she said in her melodious voice.

It was strange seeing her again after all these weeks. I'd forgotten how petite she was. I remembered her as brighter... more alluring...more...everything. And although she was still a captivating creature, she didn't turn my head like she had the last time we'd met.

That didn't seem to be the case for the others, though.

Beside me, Levi let out a soft moan, as if it pained him to be this close to her and not touch her. Shar sighed heavily in agreement, her gaze softening.

Derek frowned down at Shar, unaffected by Mirrowind's presence and probably confused as to why Sharniza was.

But Mirrowind was fae, and this allure must be her power.

Yarrow confirmed it a moment later.

"Dial it down, Gwen," he said, biting back a smile. "They won't be able to think straight to absorb anything you tell them otherwise." He sounded lighter, almost teasing, his golden eyes soft as they settled on the fae.

Mirrowind made a soft *O* with her luscious lips. "Yes, of course. I forget sometimes the effect I have on non-fae."

Levi cleared his throat and dropped his gaze, and I couldn't help but notice that his hands were clasped in front of his crotch. Bloody hell.

Shar shook her head and blinked several times before speaking. "Were you using fae mojo?"

"Not intentionally," Mirrowind said. "This is who I am, but my essence can be...intoxicating. I try to remember to mute it wherever I can, but it can get tiring to do so, and sometimes I slip."

"What are you?" The question popped out before I could think to phrase it more politely.

She turned her attention to me. "I think I should be asking you the same question. You've changed. I sense...kindred..." She canted her head, a slow smile taking control of her mouth. "You have Baobhan sidhe in you."

So, Willowman had been right. "You can tell that from looking at me?"

"Yes, dear, I can, but I should not be able to. Fae blood in humans should be too diluted to have any effect, but then...you're not human. You're a gargoyle halfblood, so the rules do not apply."

"You said kindred," Levi pointed out. "Kindred as in another fae, or as in another Baobhan sidhe?"

"Both." She looked me over. "You have the blood of my people, and I assume it is causing you some discomfort. I assume that is why you're here. Unless this is about the ghost?" She looked to Yarrow who shook his head.

"No, I'm here about this fever." I filled her in on the needing and how it was almost painful now.

"How often are you overcome?"

"Around the sidhe moon. The week leading up to it mainly."

She nodded. "Yes, that makes sense. It doesn't help that there are two sidhe moons so close together this year. But the next won't be for a few months, so you should get a reprieve. Blood or sex, or is it both?"

"Blood?"

"Yes, child. The Baobhan must feed on blood and sex to survive, but you are not pureblood, and therefore you may not need both." She waited for me to answer, tapping a slender finger against the brassy goblet.

I'd bitten Serath in my dream; did that count? "I...I don't feel like I need blood but...I did bite my mate in a dream. It was...

strange..." I recounted my dream, leaving out the romantic details and focusing on the sudden appearance of the moon and my urge to bite Serath. She listened intently.

"You marked him," she said. "Bound him to you. It's a primal impulse with our kind and reserved for the mates we take." Her eyes narrowed. "Not something a fae blood would be practicing..."

"You have more than one mate?" Shar asked.

Her laugh was a short melody. "Of course. One male is not enough to satisfy a pureblood Baobhan sidhe." Her expression sobered. "Our hunger is potent, and we require much satisfaction." Her attention slid back to me. "You may have a fated mate, but your fae blood could still draw others to you and you to them. Not as strongly but undeniably. It is up to you to reconcile your natures as you wish. Serath is a sigma, and even if he lives and you save him, you cannot be together, so he cannot give you what your body needs."

I knew that. I understood it perfectly, but I didn't want to be controlled by sexual urges. "I don't want to *need* sex. Blood, I guess I could handle, although, yuk." I sighed. "I just want the fever gone."

"I'm afraid that's not possible. If you deny it, then it will worsen until it consumes your thoughts, your every breath, and eventually kills you. I'm sorry, child, but the hunger is a part of you. Sex is fuel to our kind. The energy it creates makes us stronger. Faster. Immortal." She took a swig from her goblet, and her lips were stained crimson for a moment before the color sank into her skin.

Was this why she'd been away? To feed? To fuel up? Was this the creature I would have to become to survive? No. I refused to accept that. "There has to be a way to control this hunger."

Her expression smoothed out to something cold and almost alien, and a shiver raced down my spine. "Would you deny your belly food? Your lungs air? Hmmm?"

"No, but—"

"There are no buts in this equation. You will accommodate

your needs or die. And not just you." She looked up at Derek. "Your shield too. He is a part of you, after all, a manifestation viable only because of the fae blood you seem to despise so much." She raised her chin, her eyes narrow slits.

Fuck, I'd pissed her off. "I don't despise anything. I just—"

"Wish it gone. Yes. I understand what you want, child. You want to ignore your nature. Put it inside a box and forget about it. But it is your very nature that gave you this gift." She smiled up at Derek. "A creature created in the image of a strong shadow sylph."

"Shadow sylph?" Derek tested the words.

"That is correct."

"He will be independent soon enough," Yarrow said confidently.

"Not soon enough, if Cameron refuses to feed," Mirrowind countered.

I couldn't put Derek's life at risk.

Panic colored Shar's features. "Cam, you've got to do it. You can't let him die."

The thought of being with anyone else but Serath made my stomach hurt, but last night in the grip of a fever, with the needing strong, I'd allowed, no begged, Curi to help me. I could do it. I could sate the fever, but I didn't want to. It felt wrong. It felt like a betrayal to my mate. "There has to be some other way to get the sexual energy I need."

Mirrowind rolled her eyes with a sigh. "It's sex. For our kind it's like having a meal, or in your case, a feast before weeks of hibernation. It doesn't have to *mean* anything."

Her flippant tone grated. "Well, it does to me."

"What if she has sex with Serath in her dream?" Sharniza asked. "Her mind will make her body feel the sensations."

"That can work," Mirrowind said. "*If* she can hold the connection for long enough."

My dream visits with Serath were short and unpredictable. "I can try."

"Try isn't enough," Levi said. "The elite trial is in a few days and on a sidhe moon. You need to be fueled up by then so you can focus."

"He's right," Shar said.

This was too much. Too much pressure. Too much everything.

Derek had been silent all this time, but he spoke now, his voice a low, soothing rumble. "You don't have to do anything that makes you uncomfortable, my Cameron."

The fresh flash of panic on Shar's face echoed the turmoil inside me.

I looked up into Derek's glittering diamond eyes, my heart too full, my throat tight. "I love you, Derek, and I'm not losing you. If there's no other way, then I'll do whatever needs to be done."

"We could mute it," Yarrow said suddenly. "There are herbs to mute desire, correct?"

"There are." Mirrowind's tone was weary now; it was obvious she was fed up with this whole thing. "But muting won't help her long-term. Her body needs the sexual energy to thrive."

"I understand that," Yarrow said. "It would be a short-term solution to get her through the trial and this moon cycle."

Mirrowind drained her goblet. "Fine. I know of a tincture, but it *is* a short-term solution." Then to me, "It will cease to be effective the longer you deny yourself. It would be selfish to ignore your needs for some twisted version of honor you hold in your mind."

"Whoa," Shar said. "Cameron is the least selfish person I know. She might put herself at risk, but she'd never risk harming the people she loves. Denying herself to preserve someone else's feelings is not selfish; it's entirely the opposite."

My chest warmed.

"It will buy us time to complete the mission," Levi said. "End the alpha, get Romi and Serath back so you can say goodbye properly, and move on."

Because even if I got Serath back, he would have to leave. But at least he'd be safe. He'd have a life, even if not with me, and in time...in time I might be able to move on with mine.

I looked to Yarrow. "Please. Do it."

CHAPTER 28

CAMERON

The lake is a mirror reflecting the starlit sky and heavy full moon. Serath stands silhouetted against the backdrop, a powerful figure inked in silver and shadow. He turns his head as I approach.

"I'm not sure how you did it," he says. "I'm not sure how I'm still here."

I'm not one hundred percent sure either. "I think this has something to do with my fae blood."

There's so much I want to tell him, about the elite training, about Melanie, about my nature, and about the fever and what happened with Curi. Yes, especially the last part, because I need him to absolve me, to tell me it's all right, that I'm forgiven for giving in to the needing. Me. That will be for me. Not for him. No. Knowing won't serve him. It won't help him at all. It will leave him trapped here, torn up, conflicted, and helpless.

I won't do that to him.

The confession, the truth of what I'll have to do going forward, will wait until he's free of the graynites and back with us. It will wait until he can stand before me in the flesh and tell me how he really feels.

But I can tell him about my ability to bind him to me. "Mirrowind says my fae blood allowed me to bind you to me. I think that connection might be helping you anchor yourself here."

"Yes..." He looks up at the moon, then back down at me. "I think you may be right. If this works, then it will buy me time." He winces, his brow furrowing in discomfort.

I cup his jaw, reveling in the real sensation of stubble against my fingers. "What is it?"

"I can feel them chipping away at me, feel...something else. Cold and alien pushing against my senses."

"You can't let it in." I push up on my tiptoes and press my lips to his, wanting to inject my power, my fortitude into him. "We won't let it in."

He sighs against my mouth, a ragged, weary sound. "I'm so tired, Cameron. So fucking tired."

My eyes heat. "I know, but just a little while longer. The elite trial is in a few days, and Orix says they have a way to punch a hole in the graynite wards. I'm coming for you. I promise I'll find you and Romi, and I will bring you home."

A little hope bleeds into his eyes. "All this time we've been waiting for the alpha to emerge so we can take him down, but now... now we can finally take the fight to him." He grips my shoulders. "Cameron, the focus must be on the alpha. Eliminating him must come first. Before Romi...before me." My conflict must have shown on my face because his grip on me tightened. "Promise me. Swear it."

Dammit. "Fine. Alpha first."

His grip relaxes, and he reaches up to caress my face, but darkness creeps over his features, stealing him from me and pulling me away. Away from our shared haven and into the tumult of regular mundane dreams.

For the next four days, I lived for dreaming. Woke, ate, trained, and then hurried to bed, wanting nothing more than to be with Serath once more. Our shared anchor became my world, and the real world felt like a dream.

Yarrow and Mirrowind made good on their word and provided me with a tincture to stave off the worst of the needing, but the nights were still fevered and yearning. Luckily, the tincture made it so that I was able to satisfy myself and calm the waves of intense desire, which I attempted to do as silently as possible.

The elite trial was tomorrow, and I still hadn't managed to resolve my mind walk issues, finding myself trapped by doubt and insecurities over and over again as my darkest fears won.

"Penny for your thoughts?" Palia asked from across the dining table. She was an early riser for a goyle, up by eleven and usually on her second cup of coffee before we all joined her, but the last two days, I'd been up early enough to join her for breakfast.

I dropped the crumpet I was holding, cold now that I'd been staring blankly at it for the past five minutes. "I was thinking about the trial."

"You'll do great. You've worked hard."

"I'm not so sure. Levi said I need to believe in myself, and I think I do, but when I'm in the mind walk, I feel so weak and useless. I feel...vulnerable."

"Don't we all? Deep down, I mean? Isn't that normal? I mean, if we felt invincible, truly invincible all the time, then the world would be filled with egomaniacs with superiority complexes and no fear. Doubts keep us on our toes, they make us think and question before making decisions. They keep us safe...surely?"

She made sense, but...but what Levi had said contradicted her words. I was so confused.

The stairwell opened, and Orix entered, trailed by Taz. The elite was dressed in a sleep tee and baggy joggers, his go-to bedtime attire and the only time he wasn't in lastonflex. "Message came for you just before dawn," he said to me. "Yarrow said Melanie was ready."

I sat up straighter. "What? Why didn't you tell me right away?"

"And interrupt your dream time?" He arched a brow, and my cheeks colored.

"Have I been that bad?"

"It's understandable," Orix said. "He's your mate, you want to be with him, and if sleep is the only time that you can do that, then..." He shrugged and poured coffee into his favorite mug, one that was large enough to be a bowl, then added three heaped spoons of sugar before taking a sip.

"I'm just glad you believe me, that he's alive..."

He turned to face us, leaning back against the counter. "I won't believe it for certain until I see him, same with Romi, but I can concede that what you're telling us is possible. That what you're experiencing is more than regular dreams. And I can promise you we will do everything in our power to get him and Romi out once we've taken down the alpha." His gaze was probing as he waited for my assent.

I'd had time to think about this. To talk to Serath about it in the snatches of time we'd had in our anchor place. As much as I hated it, Orix was right. If we only got one shot at punching through the wards, then the alpha had to be our focus. The needs of the many had to take priority, and Serath had made it clear that's what he expected of me, and Romi...I knew he'd want the same.

"Don't worry. Serath already made me give him my word. Alpha first."

Orix relaxed. "More reason to believe he's alive."

Shar, Ginia, and Curi entered the kitchen, bleary-eyed and all aiming for the coffee machine, which Orix quickly vacated with a chuckle.

Curi raked his hair back and threw me a glance and a smile. Things were easier between us now, but not the same as before. We didn't hang out as much, and maybe that was for the best. If what Mirrowind said about my fae blood was true, and it did attract males, then it was best to keep my distance from him. But it did leave me with the question of whether his interest had been due to the allure of my hidden nature or because of me. Just me. Had muting the needing muted my nature too? Was that why he wasn't spending time with me anymore?

And why did it bother me?

Derek materialized at the table, and Levi entered via the lift a moment later, dressed in lastonflex, looking fresh and as if he'd been up for a while.

"I want you all to take some time off tomorrow," Levi said. "Rest your bodies and your minds before the trial tomorrow. We leave campus at dawn to avoid the pheromone flare."

Pheromone...Oh shit, the omega moon coincided with the sidhe moon, which meant that the air would be thick with their heat tomorrow. Goyle males would be driven crazy with the primal need to rut, and the forest would be a playground of sexual activity.

Once again, I'd been so focused on my own needing that I'd neglected to think about the others, Levi, Curi, and Touron.

"I'm locking the doors and staying inside," Touron said stiffly.

"You can't deny your nature," Orix said.

He raised his chin, defiant. "I can, and I will. I'm not...I don't want to be with anyone else."

"The pheromones don't affect me," Levi said. "Perks of being a halfblood."

But they'd affect Curi...they'd affect him, and he was being forced to miss out and last time...Last time he'd missed out because he'd wasted his time protecting me from all the pheromone-crazed males in the forest.

I tried to catch his eye, but he kept his gaze on the contents of his coffee mug, even though I was sure he could feel me watching him.

He obviously didn't want to engage.

"Make sure you're up with the sun," Levi said. "The council has prepared a port for us, but it's time sensitive."

"The port will take us to a secure location," Orix said. "There you'll activate an orb to take you into the trials."

"And this orb is safe?" Palia asked. "Willowman is gone, so who prepared it?"

"It's a standard orb used by the council for the elite trials," Orix said. "It leads to one location and is set so it cannot be tampered with."

"What about switched?" Touron asked. "Like the last orb?"

"He's right," Palia said. "We can't ignore the fact that every time Cam has left campus, she's been attacked. Someone wants her out of the equation, and the best time to do it is outside the campus wards."

Orix nodded. "That's true, and it's also why Lionel took charge of the port and the transport of the orb. He refuses to take any risks where Cameron is concerned."

"There is another possibility," Shar said. "Maybe they think we're no longer a threat. Newbies with no experience against graynites. Or they could be too caught up in their own war, graynite against graynite."

"Either way, we're not taking any risks," Orix said.

My gut tightened. I'd done my best not to dwell on what was to come the last few days, and sleep had been my salvation, but now there was no avoiding it. Tomorrow would decide Serath's and Romi's fate, because if I failed, there would be no elite team.

If I failed, there would be no way to take down the alpha, no mission to punch through the wards. Nothing.

If I died.

They died.

CHAPTER 29

CAMERON

The twins and Touron had initiate training with Orix, and Levi had a meeting, although he didn't elaborate with who or about what, and I didn't feel it was my place to ask. But Shar, Curi, and Derek were free to accompany me to Yarrow's to see Melanie.

By the time we headed out, the campus was quiet, as most goyles were in class or on the training field. My gaze went to the dome of the omega den, off-limits to everyone but the omegas that lived there. These females' purpose was to find mates among the strongest, most promising goyles—those who'd made it into the academy. Their goal was to procreate. Their omega moon coincided with the sidhe moon, and as my luck would have it, I'd entered the academy at a time when there were two sidhe moons in a row.

Two omega runs, two chances that Curi would miss finding his mate. The first my fault and the second fate's.

Up ahead, Shar and Derek chatted easily, walking side by side, the backs of their hands brushing now and then but neither making the move to take the other's hand.

"How long do you think before they take the next step?" Curi asked.

"I don't think it'll be too long."

"I envy them. They get to choose." He was silent for several seconds, then, "Do you think...Do you think you could have ever chosen me, if you'd had the freedom to do so?"

My heart climbed into my throat. "Curi..."

He exhaled raggedly. "I need to know, Cameron. I need to know that I'm not fucking crazy."

Our pace slowed, and Derek and Shar pulled ahead.

"I can't answer that, Curi."

"Can't or won't?"

"It wouldn't be fair to—"

He gripped my shoulders and propelled me off the path and up against a tree, his large body dwarfing mine. My heart lurched, throat pinching at the wretched conflict on his face.

"Tell me, Cameron. If there was no fate bond. If there were no pheromones or needing, would you want me? Could there ever have been a chance for us in a world like that?"

The answer should be no. No was the right answer, the safe answer, but the knots in my stomach and the hummingbird in my heart wouldn't allow me to lie.

"Yes." The word was an explosion, a release of a truth that I'd been denying for some time. "If there was no fated bond, if my heart didn't already belong to Serath, if we were free of it all, then yes, I think I could have loved you. But Curi...the fact is that Serath does exist, and he...He has my heart. He will always be my first choice, even if I can't be with him. And you...You deserve to be someone's first choice too."

His exhale mingled with mine as he dropped his forehead to my temple. "Thank you. Thank you, Cameron."

I blinked back tears and fisted my hands against the urge to hold him. "I'm sorry..."

"Don't be. This...this helps." He pressed a rough kiss to my head and released me, backing up. "We'd best catch up to the others." He smiled, but it barely reached his eyes. "Wouldn't want them getting the wrong idea."

I took a shuddering breath to free myself of his intoxicating scent, then followed him back onto the path and toward the main building, my stomach still in knots because what we'd failed to touch upon was my fae nature and my needing. It was in control now that I had a tincture, but what would happen when it stopped working? What would happen if I didn't find a permanent solution to my need for sex?

"NOW SHE MAY be a little confused," Flora said as she led us to the crystal room. "So, give her some time to gather her thoughts."

I fingered the vial in my pocket, the one that Willowman had gotten for me all those weeks ago to help Melanie with her memories of the past. Once I administered it, Melanie would not only be able to tell us what happened that night in the filing room, but she'd also have the memories from her life back.

Yarrow joined us, coming from the direction of the kitchen. He was still in his PJs, gown thrown over the top and mug of coffee in his hand.

"We don't want to overwhelm her," he said. "Best if only Cam goes in."

"No," Derek and Curi said together.

Yarrow's brows shot up. "I appreciate your desire to protect, but if you want information, then you need to tread carefully."

He was right. I didn't want to spook Melanie, which was ironic, considering she was a ghost. "I'll be fine alone."

"After what happened the last time?" Curi looked skeptical.

"She was going ghoul, but she's fine now. Just...skittish. She won't hurt me."

"No, she won't," Derek said. "Because I'm coming with you, my Cameron. I am your shield, a part of you, and I lived in the same room as Melanie for several days."

"He has a point," Sharniza said. "I think we'd all feel better if you took him with you."

"Okay." I smiled up at Derek. "Let's do this, buddy."

Flora produced a key and unlocked the door. "Good luck." She looked nervous, understandable because the answers I came out with would affect her too.

We were about to find out who'd messed with both their heads.

CHAPTER 30

CAMERON

Melanie stood with her back to us, facing the wall. Her spectral form had more substance than I'd ever seen it have, which was encouraging, even if she was staring at wallpaper.

"Melanie?" I took a couple more steps into the room. "Melanie, it's me, Cameron."

She turned slowly to face me. "There are butterflies hidden in the walls?"

I glanced at the wallpaper that covered one side of the room—a floral pattern, which, on close inspection, might truly have butterflies hidden in it.

"How are you feeling?" Derek asked her. "Do you remember Cameron?"

Melanie's mouth parted in a warm smile. "Of course I do. We're roommates, except..." She frowned. "This room is different." Her eyes rounded. "Did we move? Can I stay?"

She was here, but she was confused. I needed to get her back on track. "Melanie, what's the last thing you remember?"

Her frown returned, and she dropped her chin, chewing on her cheeks in thought. "Oh...I was in the filing room." She looked up, eyes bright with the memory. "I found your brother's folder and then...then..." She winced. "I was here...What happened?" She wrung her hands. "Cameron, what's happened to me?"

I withdrew the vial from my pocket. "We're going to find out. Trust me. Just relax." I held up the vial. "The solution in this will help you to remember...everything. Not just what happened in the filing room but all the things that happened before. Before you died."

She stared at me wide-eyed. "My past?"

"Yes, Melanie. Do I have your permission to use it? I'll need to break the bottle near you."

Her gaze bounced between the vial and me. "I'll remember everything...good and bad. Everything..."

I'd come in here for answers, but it felt wrong to take them from her without her consent. This was her mind. Her thoughts. Her afterlife. "Do I have your permission?"

Her delicate jaw hardened, arms coming down to her sides and ending in fists of determination. "Do it."

I threw the vial at the ground by her feet hard enough for it to smash. Purple smoke appeared, obscuring her from view for several seconds, and when it cleared, Melanie stood hunched over, her hands in her hair hugging her scalp while a low, keening sound spilled from her lips.

My heart sank. "Melanie?" I made to take a step, but Derek gently gripped my elbow.

"Wait," he said. "Give her a moment."

Several more seconds passed before Melanie finally straightened. She looked the same, except where her eyes had been a wishy-washy gray, they were now as dark as an impending storm.

"It's coming back...the past...I'm remembering. I...I remember home. A small town filled with magic but beyond it...nothing. The pockets of magic were all around us. I remember applying for a job here. Carter interviewed me, and I got the position."

I resisted the urge to ask her about that night in the filing room because it seemed as if she were reliving her past, as if the memories were coming back in layers, and I didn't want to confuse her. She was silent for several beats, nodding to herself, her gaze slightly unfocused, and then her mouth parted.

"Oh...Oh my...How could I have forgotten?" Her eyes welled. "Oh...They took me from him, and they took her from me. They took her. Took her...and I...I waited..." She began to hyperventilate.

"Melanie, calm down. What are you saying? What happened?"

"I was in love. I was happy. I left here because I was happy. But they came for me in the night. They brought me here to the academy and locked me up, and then..." She looked down at her stomach and then placed her hands on it. "They took her. They took my baby."

"WHERE IS SHE?" Melanie demanded. "I need to know what they did to her. I need to know what..." She clutched her head. "They made me forget her. They made me forget." She began to cry with body-racking sobs, and my eyes burned with empathy. "They took me away from him. I loved him. Oh...does he even know I'm gone? Does he know he has a daughter?"

"Who? Melanie, who are you talking about?"

She squeezed her eyes shut. "I can see him in my head, but I can't remember his name. I can see them taking my baby, but their faces are blurred."

"What about the night in the filing room?" Derek asked. "What happened then?"

She looked up at him with a tear-stained face. "What?"

"You went to search for Romi's file, and something happened to you. Someone did something to you to mess with your mind. It could be the same person who took your baby. Can you remember?"

She closed her eyes. "I remember the clip of boots on wood and the smell of jasmine and eyes...eyes burning like lanterns in the dark. Amber, so warm, yet so cold, and a face...so pale. Hair like a raven's wing and—" Her eyes snapped open. "Oh...Remi... Remi found me that night. She did this to me."

Remi? Mistress Travani?

Melanie's eyes rolled, and she swayed. "No, please let me hold her. Regina? Remi, bring her back, please." The voice changed in timbre, an echo of the past. "I'm sorry, Melanie, truly sorry for what I'm about to do." Another voice. "Remi, I don't like this. I don't—" Remi's voice spilled from Melanie's mouth like a spooky recording. "Then leave. Take the baby and I'll finish here." Melanie moaned. "Don't hurt her. Don't...What...what is that? I don't want it. I don't..." She fell silent, her chest heaving with breaths that got fewer and farther between before stopping because ghosts didn't need to breathe.

She opened her eyes and looked right at me. "I remember what happened to me. They took my baby, and then they killed me, and now...Now they're going to pay."

Her face contorted, chin elongating, eyes darkening and sinking into their sockets, her body hunched, and she dashed at the wall.

Bright blue light shimmered across the surface of the wallpaper, throwing Melanie on her ass. She screeched and ran for the door, meeting the same resistance, except this time the light latched on to her.

Her horrific form melted away, and she was simply Melanie again—a frightened specter with blue fire eating away at her body.

"Please," she pleaded with me. "Let me go. I deserve justice. I deserve to know what happened to my baby. I need to—"

And she was gone.

"Melanie!" I hammered on the door and fell through when Yarrow yanked it open. "Where is she? What happened to her?"

"You tell me," Yarrow said. "I wasn't in the room with you."

"She was eaten by blue flame when she tried to leave the room," Derek said.

"Then she's fine," Yarrow said. "It's simply a precautionary measure to neutralize any threat. She'll materialize in due course, but what I want to know is what prompted her to turn into a threat."

"She remembered what happened to her," Derek said.

Yarrow's eyes lit up. "She remembered who attacked her in the filing room?"

I swallowed past the bitter tang at the back of my throat. "Yes, she did. She also remembered how she died and who killed her. They're both one and the same."

Flora gasped, hand flying to her mouth.

"Who?" Curi asked.

"Travani and Carter. They killed her and they took her baby and now I'm going to find out why and make them pay."

CHAPTER 31

CAMERON

"Cam, stop and think about this," Shar said as I stormed down the corridor toward the tutors' quarters exit. "These are administrators of the academy. You can't just accuse them of murder."

"Why not? You think Melanie is lying?"

"Of course not, but we need to think about this. About what it could mean."

"She's right," Curi said. "We can't show our hand so quickly. For all we know, this could somehow be connected to Prasan. What if they're working with whoever Prasan was working for?"

"Then we interrogate them and find out who." Yarrow joined us, dressed now in dark denim and a dark turtleneck that brought out the gold flecks in his eyes.

Flora was close behind, her mouth turned down in disgust. "They can't be allowed to get away with this. We can make them talk."

"How?" Sharniza asked.

Yarrow and Flora exchanged a secretive smile, but it was Yarrow who answered. "We're witches."

❧

CARTER LOOKED UP from her paperwork as we entered her office. Her gaze flicked between us and then settled in a frown. "Is everything okay for the trial?"

"This isn't about the trial," Yarrow said.

Behind us, Flora closed the door, muttering something under her breath, and a shiver of energy washed over my skin, pricking and plucking, almost uncomfortable.

Behind the desk, Carter sucked in a sharp breath. "What was that? What are you doing?"

The side door to the office, a small washroom, opened, and Travani stepped out. Her eyes narrowed, and a low hiss slithered from between her lips. "Magic." Her voice was a rasp. "What is the meaning of this?"

"We just restored Melanie's memories." I studied their faces, noting every tick, every jump of muscle. "She told us who killed her and who messed with her head in the filing room."

Carter's breath quickened, and her face drained of color, but Travani reacted the opposite, her features rearranging themselves, smoothing out like glass.

"Oh?" Travani said. "Her death has been a mystery to us all for some time. I'm interested to know who she *thinks* is responsible."

I allowed the corner of my mouth to tip up slightly. "You. Both of you."

Carter made a soft sound of distress, but Travani covered it with a bark of laughter, recovering quickly to stare at me with a frown. "Wait, you're serious?"

"Don't play games," Yarrow said. "You killed Melanie, took her baby, and attacked my sister in the filing room a few weeks ago. You messed with her mind."

"Listen to yourself, Blake. How could I have messed with a witch's mind? I'm not a mageri."

"No, you're a child of the ancients," Yarrow said.

Travani sucked in a sharp breath. "How...how can you know that?"

"You hide your mark well, but not well enough. Last summer when it was sweltering, a little of the makeup you use to mask it rubbed off."

Markings? "What are you talking about?"

"Nothing you need to worry about," Travani said quickly before she turned her attention back to Yarrow. "You have no idea what you're talking about, and if you expect the word of a specter to hold up against mine when it comes to the council, then you're delusional."

I stepped forward. "Oh, we have no intention of getting the council involved. For all we know, they're in on it. No. If you refuse to tell us the truth, then we'll let Melanie have her way with you. She's on the verge of going malevolent, and I'm sure you both know what a malevolent can do to a person, supernatural or human. So, what do you say now?"

A little of Travani's bravado slipped, but it was Carter who replied.

"I say it's time we told the truth, Remi."

Travani balked. "Regina, what are you—"

"Enough!" Carter said. "I've had enough. What we did has been eating away at me for two decades, and I can't...I won't let it claim another minute of my life." She pushed back her chair and stood. "Sit and I'll tell you everything, and then you can judge us as you wish."

"No," Travani said. "I should do it. This is, after all, my fault."

"Remi, no it—"

"Hush, love." Travani smiled softly at Carter, leaving us in no doubt as to the truth of their relationship. "Let me."

Carter slipped back into her seat with a nod. "Okay."

"THERE ARE RULES for my kind. Many rules where I come

from," Travani said. "But the only one that matters in this case is the one that I broke. I fell in love with a human, and I shared my life force with her, rendering her as ageless as me without the need to consume blood."

My gaze flew to Carter. "Wait...how is that possible?"

"My people have special...abilities. Ones that we are forbidden to exercise and yet...yet I did so."

"To save my life," Carter said.

"The reason doesn't matter, not to the conclave. We were hunted," Travani said. "Mercilessly for decades. For us, the graynites were a blessing. They allowed us to vanish, to become different people. They allowed us to find a home here at the academy. To be safe. Things were good—until they weren't."

"We received a letter," Carter said. "Unmarked, unsigned. Inside was an address and instructions." She rolled her lips into her mouth for a beat. "Instructions to kidnap and bring Melanie Thornton to the academy and hold her here until further instructions."

"The person who sent the letter knew about us," Travani said. "Who I was, what I'd done, and they threatened to reveal our location to the conclave if we didn't comply."

"We should have run," Carter said. "Run that night."

"And have them track us?" Travani shook her head. "No. There was nowhere to run. We had to preserve what we'd built here."

"So, you kidnapped Melanie?" Sharniza prompted.

"Yes. She let us into her home when we arrived. She knew us. We'd worked together. She even came back to the academy with us willingly. We told her there was a function to open a new wing and that it wouldn't be the same without her."

"She was our friend," Carter said, biting back a sob.

Travani continued, her tone unwavering and without emotion. "Once we had her here, we gave her a room in the new dorm that was still under construction and locked her there. We kept her there for three months. I was forced to make her forget most of it to keep her calm. I may have...have broken her a little."

"But the letters came, every week. Reminders," Carter said. "Threats. To keep her there and wait for the baby to be born. And then..."

"Then to drop it off at a specific location," Travani said. "We were told that once we left the baby at the church, we'd be free of our obligation. That all we had to do was administer a tincture to Melanie, which would heal her body and wipe her memory of the last few months."

"You'd already wiped her memory, though," Curi said. "Over and over."

"No, I'd altered them to calm her, made her believe she was on a retreat and that we were taking care of her, that it was all willing."

"But then you killed her," Derek said flatly.

Carter let out a sob. "It was supposed to make her forget. I didn't like the idea, but...but we agreed to do it. To end the threats."

"But it was a lie," Travani said. "The tincture killed her."

The room fell into silence as we all absorbed this. I could empathize with their fear. Their desire to protect each other, to be safe, but I couldn't justify the cost. "Melanie paid the price for your safety with her life, and what if this blackmailer had come back and asked you to do more nefarious stuff?"

"He didn't," Travani said. "He or she kept their word."

"But they could have," Carter said. "We always knew it was a possibility, but we took the risk anyway. Remi, we were selfish."

"Maybe," Travani said. "But I would do it all again to save you. To keep this. Us. I regret Melanie's death, but I do not regret saving our lives."

"And the baby?" Yarrow asked. "Did you not want to know what happened to her? Why this nameless, faceless, blackmailer wanted it?"

"No." Travani lifted her chin. "I did what was needed to keep the woman I love safe, and if you want to punish me for that, then so be it. I don't care, just leave Regina be. Please."

"And the filing room? Why did you attack Flora?"

Travani sighed. "When I stumbled upon Melanie in the filing room, I panicked. She was going through Romi's file, and the information in there was classified, so I wiped her mind, but to do that, I needed to show my true face." She looked to Flora. "You happened along at that moment and saw it, and if I hadn't wiped it from your mind, it would have driven you insane. My kind can manipulate memories, but wiping them is much harder, and we don't do it often because it can render the subject insane, but with a specter..."

"You broke her." How could she think that was okay? "You messed with her memories, you killed her, then you broke what was left of her mind over a fucking file. You make me sick." My lip curled. "How do you sleep at night?"

"I don't...not well," Travani said. "I went back to the church that same night to look for the baby, but it was gone, and not a day has passed when I haven't wondered what happened to her."

"What are you going to do now?" Carter asked. "Now that you know what we did."

Yarrow met my gaze with bright golden eyes and gave me a nod, leaving the decision to me. "We're not going to do anything. You are. You're going to make amends with Melanie. You're going to tell her the truth, and then you're going to do everything in your power to find that baby."

"Don't you think we've tried?" Travani said. "It's been decades; the baby could be anywhere."

"Do you have the blackmail letters?" Flora asked.

"Yes, why?"

Once again, she and Yarrow exchanged glances.

"Give them to us. We might be able to use them to locate this blackmailer."

"There are no postmarks, no blood, nothing. Not even fingerprints," Carter said. "We checked."

"We don't need any of those things," Flora said. "Just the whiff of an essence."

"Give us the letters," Yarrow said. "And if there's anything to find, we will find it."

We'd solved one mystery only to be saddled with another, but my gut told me that the identity of the baby and its father were vital, and I had faith that Yarrow and Flora would succeed in finding her and reuniting her with her mother.

I had an elite trial to mentally prepare for, and that required some serious decompression time and maybe a caramel latte or two with my buddies.

CHAPTER 32

CAMERON

After we'd filled the others in on the revelations from Carter's office, we decided the best way to spend the rest of our day would be to order pizza and watch movies. Curi and Levi went to get the pizza, while Ginia and Palia argued over which movie to start with. Derek and Touron prepared snacks, and Taz claimed a spot in the cushy armchair, but Orix remained slightly apart, merely watching us. It hit me that his team, his friends were gone, about to be replaced by a bunch of newbies with their own strong dynamic. Was he wondering how he'd fit in? He was probably grieving the loss of his team, but he'd been here for us. Mentoring, supporting. He'd been our rock, and we wouldn't be able to do this without him. He needed to know that.

I sidled up to him and leaned back against the counter. "You all right?"

He threw me a quick smile. "I'm good."

"You don't have to be, you know. It's okay to be sad. To grieve. Trust me, I know."

He tucked in his chin. "I know, but it's better to hope. To plan and take action. This team is my plan, my action, and my hope. The hope that I can maybe bring back my friends, and if I can't, hope that I can avenge them." He turned his body toward me. "That's all I can think about."

All that was keeping him going. "We need you, Orix. We can't do this without you."

"You won't have to." He smiled with his eyes. "I'm so proud of you all. You've worked so hard, and once you clear the elite trial tomorrow, the real work can begin."

I smiled up at him. "So, are you glad you didn't kill me now?"

He let out a surprised laugh. "Will you ever let that go?" I pushed up on my toes and kissed his cheek.

"Consider it forgotten."

He sighed and hugged me to him. "When you see him next... tell him...tell him I fucking miss him."

I hugged him back. "He already knows."

"Pizza is here!" Curi entered, holding several boxes, and Levi followed with several more.

Orix and I broke the hug, and standing here, surrounded by all the people I loved, it was impossible to stave off the warm fuzzies. I accepted the feeling, let it wash over me, then stamped it out. There would be no true joy for me until I brought Serath and Romi home.

I WATCHED THE movie but didn't take anything in. My thoughts kept returning to Melanie and everything we'd learned, then skipping to Serath and Romi, wondering how they were faring. The graynites were probably hurting them. Torturing them. Serath was hanging on by a thread, and he'd been a captive for weeks while Romi...

No. I didn't want to think about that.

What was I doing? Sitting here relaxing when the people I loved were in danger. Hurting. This was all wrong. My mouth was too dry. My throat suddenly parched. The damn tincture to stave off the needing seemed to have side effects. I slipped off the sofa and climbed over Touron's legs to get to the kitchen.

Derek looked across at me, his diamond eyes darkening in

concern, but I shook my head, letting him know I was all right.

I crossed to the sink and filled a glass with water, then downed it.

"Hey..." Levi came up behind me. "You want to talk?"

I licked my lips to absorb all the moisture and refilled the glass. "No. I want to get the elite exam over and get out there. I want to punch a hole in the graynite wards and get Serath and Romi back. I can't sit here anymore. I can't pretend that everything is normal when it so obviously isn't."

"This will be normal for you as an elite," Levi said. "Seeing terrible things, knowing terrible things, being helpless sometimes. It will be the norm to come back here and watch a movie or eat a meal with your team because if you don't do those things, if you don't decompress and allow a little levity, then you will drown beneath the weight of all the responsibility. Our world is a dark and dangerous place most of the time, Cam, and this..." He looked back at the lounge area, at my goyle buddies chuckling over something happening on screen. "This is what makes it worthwhile. This is what we fight to come home to."

"When did you get so smart? You're not even an elite yet."

"You don't need to be an elite to know that to be an effective warrior, you need something to fight for." His eyes darkened. "I'll be fighting for you and them." He looked back at the others. "I'll be fighting to put a real smile back on your lips and light in your eyes. Cameron...I'll be fighting to bring your mate home."

My throat pinched. "Thank you."

He was about to say more when the entrance bell buzzed loudly.

Orix stood with a frown. "Anyone expecting visitors?"

He was met with a chorus of nos as he headed for the exit.

I drank my water and rinsed out the glass. Everyone who mattered to me that could be here was already here.

The sound of the door opening was followed by a tap on my shoulder. "Cameron..." Levi said. "It's for you."

"Me?" I turned to find Lionel Basque standing in the doorway.

He looked around and dropped the others a nod before focusing on me. "Cameron, can we talk...in private?"

I LED MY sire to the sixth floor and into the lounge I shared with Curi and Shar. I wasn't sure what to say. We hadn't been alone since my time in the infirmary, and now he was here. In the tower, in my lounge.

I cleared my throat. "Can I get you something? Coffee? Tea? Water?"

His eyes crinkled slightly at the corners. "No, Cameron. I'm good. Please, have a seat. I wanted to talk to you."

"About the trial tomorrow?"

"No, about what might happen after." He swept his arm toward the sofa. "Please." He took the armchair, filling it with his frame, and waited until I'd perched on the edge of the three-seater.

"You're making me nervous." I hadn't meant to say it.

"That isn't my intention, but...it's good that you are. Nerves keep us sharp. Never get complacent." He sighed and leaned forward, resting his elbows on his thighs and clasping his hands loosely between them. "When I asked you to take on the challenge of elite, I told you it was to bring back Romi. That I believed him to be alive."

"Yes." Where was he going with this?

"I do believe that...believe that he's still breathing. Hope that he's still...him, but I would be remiss in my duty, not only as your sire but his, if I did not consider the possibility that Romi may already be—"

"No. Don't say it." I'd avoided thinking about this. Avoided contemplating it, and I didn't want him saying it now. Didn't want to turn the thought over and examine it and the implications.

"Cameron, look at me."

I exhaled and lifted my gaze to his. "Please, don't say it."

"I have to. We must accept that Romi may already be a

graynite."

I bit the insides of my cheeks. "He's strong. He's fighting."

"Maybe. But he's been gone a long time, and graynites need sustenance...they need numbers." He sat up straighter. "If he's gone...if he's one of them, then you must promise me that you'll end him."

"You...you want me to kill him?" My voice went up a notch.

"Cameron, if he's a graynite, then he's already dead."

CHAPTER 33

Cameron

If he's a graynite, he's already dead.

Already dead.

Kill him.

End him.

I tossed and turned, my skin prickling, despite the fucking tincture. My throat was dry and arid. I needed sleep. Fuck. I needed to sleep. I needed Serath.

Please.

Please just shut up, brain, and let me go.

Let me sleep.

"My Cameron..." Derek materialized by the side of my bed and crouched. His hand was cool on my fevered brow. "You take the tincture?"

"I did, but I feel...odd, so fucking thirsty. Must be a side effect."

"Maybe," he said. "Or maybe you need to drink."

"I have been drinking. I had four glasses of water before bed."

"Maybe it's not water you need," Derek said. "Maybe you need blood."

An image filled my mind of thick crimson fluid, and my mouth flooded with saliva.

I bolted up in bed, chest heaving, and licked my lips. "No..."

"Mirrowind said—"

"I know what she said but no. I'm fine. I just...I need to sleep."

Derek looked like he wanted to argue but thought better of it and nodded. "Sleep, and I will watch over you."

My vision blurred. "It's been a while since you did that."

"It's been a while since you needed it, but my Cameron, I am always here for you if you need me."

"I know." I turned on my side to face him, and he stroked my hair.

"Close your eyes. You are safe. You are home."

Serath waits for me by the lake, and I run into his arms, pressing myself to his chest as he holds me tight.

"Cameron, what is it? What's wrong?"

"Nothing now that I'm here with you." I don't want to talk about the outside world. I don't want to waste the precious time we have here with my doubts and concerns.

He strokes my hair, and I allow my body a reprieve, a moment to simply be and forget about the weight of tasks that wait for me outside this haven.

"Cameron, look at me," he says.

I reluctantly tip my head back, gaze grazing his jaw and roving over his beautifully brutal features. "I wish I could stay here with you."

He cups my face, callused fingers grazing my cheeks as his gaze darkens with concern. "What's happening out there? Tell me."

I can't hide from him. Can never mask my true emotions, so I don't try. Instead, I turn my head to kiss his palm and give him half the truth. "Nothing. Really. It's the night before the trial, and I'm nervous is all. But then...then I'll be coming for you." The corners of his eyes tighten, and my stomach dips. "What is it? What's wrong?"

His lips brush my forehead, hands sliding down to my shoulders and resting there. "Nothing. Just the thought of you walking into danger. The fact that you must save me." His mouth turned down in disgust. "It makes me sick to know that I can't protect my mate."

"We protect each other, Serath, and—"

He breaks eye contact to look over my head, his body tensing.

"What is it?" I try to turn to track his gaze, but he quickly cups my face and crushes his mouth to mine.

Sparks ignite inside me, embers rising from the pit of my belly to fill my chest. I breathe him in, infected by his urgency, and the need to be beneath his skin, to be one, overwhelms me.

He breaks the kiss roughly, breathing raggedly, eyes dark and filled with a tumult of emotions as they meet mine. "I love you, Cameron. Not because you're my mate, but because you're you. Always, unabashedly you."

I blink back tears because this feels wrong. This feels like goodbye. "I love you, too, so fucking much."

His throat bobs. "Enough to let me go, if it comes to that?"

"I know we can't be together out there. I know one of us will have to leave, and I've made peace with that."

"No, Cameron, that's not what I'm referring to."

Wait, what was he... "No..."

He exhales against my lips. "I need you to promise. If I fail to hold on to my body, if they succeed in tearing me from it, if I become one of them, then you'll end me. Promise me."

First Lionel, then him...I don't want to think about this. "You're not going to fail. You can hold on. I know you can. This place will keep you safe, and I'll find you. I'll stop whatever they're doing to you, and we will fix you."

His gaze flicks over my shoulder again, and this time, he isn't quick enough to stop me following his gaze to a large shadowy mass on the edge of the water.

"Don't!" Serath grips my chin and forces me to look at him. "Don't look at it. Don't think about it."

But it is all I can think about now. "What is it?"

He shakes his head. "Nothing."

But the knots in my gut say otherwise. They tell me that we're running out of time.

He glances over my head again, nostrils flaring before kissing me hard on the mouth and whispering against my lips, "Promise me, Cameron. I need you to fucking promise me. Don't let them use me."

Heat gathers behind my eyes. I want to argue with him, to tell him to stop thinking this way, but I give him what he needs instead. I give him my word. "I promise."

He kisses me again, hungry, biting, and desperate, sending me spiraling into darkness and into the chaotic world of fragmented dreams and illusion.

Back to the real world, where the trial that will determine so many fates waits.

CHAPTER 34

CAMERON

The sun had barely broken the horizon when we gathered by the academy gates to take the port to the location where the trial would take place. The world was gray and dreary, echoing my mood because the dream with Serath lingered like a storm cloud overhead. Dread lurked deep in my belly, worming its way around and leaving me slightly nauseated. I needed this day done. I needed a victory.

Touron and the twins had been up to send us off, Touron with breakfast sandwiches and Palia and Ginia with huge mugs of coffee and words of encouragement and confidence, so despite the pit in my belly, I was more than ready to get this trial over with so I could get my ass into graynite territory.

The port to our location was set into the stone wall beside the main gates of the academy, and a middle-aged man stood beside it, dressed in a woollen coat and a beanie hat. He had the kind of face that smiled easily and eyes that spoke of wisdom and kindness. He didn't shy away from meeting our eyes.

"My name's Doran," he said, offering us a warm smile. "I'm with port management. We're a small team responsible for managing and testing the ports for council members."

"You're not a witch, though," Curi said. "What are you?"

"Witches aren't the only beings able to create portals, although they do it with innate talent, which, admittedly, is enviable..." He shrugged. "I don't have that kind of skill, but I can create stable portals given enough time."

"That did not answer his question," Derek said.

"No, I suppose not. I'm magi, or part magi."

The mageri could mostly be found in the domed city, but I'd heard a few lived out here in the rims. "So, you created this port?"

"I did. It's sound. You'll be met by your test master on the other side."

"I'll be waiting for you back at the tower when you're done," Orix said.

I looked across at him in surprise. "You're not coming?"

"The elite trials are a closed event, Cameron. I've already taken them."

And forgotten what they entail, which meant that whoever was testing us also had the skill to make us forget.

"I'll go first," Levi said.

Not that it mattered, because if this was a trap, there was no way for him to come back and tell us. Ports were usually one way.

Curi went next, followed by Shar, then I stepped forward with Derek in tow.

The blue light swallowed me and tipped me out onto wooden floors. I stumbled, but Derek steadied me.

We were in a small room with gray walls and a door leading off it. Two windows looked out onto a vast expanse of barren land. There was no furniture. Nothing to make it stand out, except the woman with the sleek bob standing by the door.

"Mother?" Levi looked stunned. "What are you doing here?"

But it was obvious to me. "She's the test master."

"You didn't know?" Curi looked suspicious.

"No, he didn't," Adaline said. "And when you're done, none of you will remember this."

"I don't like the sound of that," Sharniza said.

Neither did I, but if it got us closer to our goal, then so be it.

"What is this place? Where are we?"

"A secure location," she said. "Part of an estate owned by the five bloodlines. I believe it's a safe house, a bunker maybe, although none of that has ever been confirmed. What I do know is that only the heads of the elite bloodlines know of its existence, which is why, bearing in mind the recent attacks, it was chosen as the location for your test today."

The test would take place here? "I thought we needed an orb to get to the test site."

She smiled thinly. "In a manner of speaking." She drew an orb from her cloak and raised it in the air. "Best of luck." She dropped it, and smoke filled my vision.

THE SMOKE CLEARED, and I was alone in the room, but the windows were gone. The door that Adaline had been standing beside was now open, a dark aperture that dared me to enter.

"Hello?"

Nothing.

Great. Okay. Through the door it was, then.

Darkness swallowed me and spat me out into a space that felt like it had no end. No walls, no ceiling, the edges of the world shrouded in shadow, leaving me feeling small and exposed in the silvery light that illuminated the space around me.

"Hello? Is anybody there?" My voice echoed back at me, the cadence off, almost mocking. "Hello?" Once again, the echo came back sounding wrong, and the hairs on my arms stood to attention because that was no echo. "Show yourself!"

A figure emerged from the darkness, tall and regal, golden hair pinned up in a messy bun, gray eyes glittering where they caught the silvery light, and a jolt of recognition shot through me followed by unease, because the figure was me. Or a copy of me.

She tipped her head slightly to the side to study me, and her lip curled. "You're a pathetic thing, aren't you? We'll have to fix that if you're going to pass this trial."

"She's not pathetic." Another figure hurried out of the darkness. "You leave her alone." It was me again, but a softer version, hair unbound and flowing gently down my back. She looked over at me with a shy smile. "Hi."

My gaze bounced between them. "What the fuck is going on?"

CHAPTER 35

SERATH

It's back and getting closer. I can hear its breath, smell it, a faint scent like burning wood and kindling. "This is my domain. You can't have it."

It moves to my left, hovering there, waiting.

Because that is all it needs to do.

Wait.

I can feel my grip on this place fading as my strength wanes. If I allow it, I can hear the hum of voices, and if I tune in, I can make out words.

"The connection is made."

"Is it secure?"

"Yes."

"So if we administer it now?"

"It should work."

"Then do it."

The shadow moves closer, but there's no threat in the motion. Instead, I sense...fear?

I turn to face it, but it melts away, and cold fire rushes over my skin. It coalesces at the base of my spine, pulsing and circling my hips to collect in my groin.

A moan slips from my lips as hands skim up my back.

"I'm here," Cameron says. "I'm so here for this."

I turn to face her, my body rippling with need. She's naked and glorious in the moonlight, her gray eyes filled with stars as she reaches for me, mouth parting in carnal hunger.

My need is almost painful as I attempt to push her away. "We can't...Cameron, you know we can't."

"Yes, we can. It's safe here. It's just a dream, remember?"

I want her so fucking badly it's a clawing beneath my skin.

She runs her hand down her abdomen to the apex of her thighs and touches herself, eyes drifting closed as she tips back her head with a moan and a gasp. I can smell her, fuck...I can—

My beast surges to the surface, and I'm on her, pressing her into the grass, hips between her thighs, cock pushing against her.

"Yes!" She bends her knees and brings her legs up. "Fuck me. Do it now."

Her eyes flash an eerie silver. No. This isn't Cameron. This is—

Bright lights sear my vision, and a shadow moves above me, feminine gasps of pleasure filling the room.

The woman looks down at me with eyes as dark as the depths of the ocean, red mouth parted as she pants, moving up and down.

No...My body tightens, aching for release.

No. This is wrong, this isn't—

Heat floods my veins, need tearing away all thought, allowing my primal beast to take over completely.

The gathering shadows close in, ripping the memory from my mind and leaving me in darkness.

Emptiness.

I am nothing.

Gone.

CHAPTER 36

SELAS

I'm glad I can't see the skin on my leg. I know it's bad because of the soft gasp the medic made when he removed the cast earlier. I know it's bad because I can feel the scar tissue from the claw wounds. Areas that will never heal fully.

I take a turn around my room, wincing in pain with each step. I can do this. I will get stronger. I won't let this beat me. I'll go back to the academy and train the cadets like Farnell. Life doesn't need to be over. I can still shift and fly. The injury might make me slow on my feet but not in the air. I can be of use.

There's hope.

But I won't go back until Touron has moved on. I can't bear to see him day in, day out and not be with him. I planned for a tryst or two, but the damn goyle stole my heart, and now that's another part of me that's broken.

I make a fifth circuit past the balcony and slow at the sound of voices. My father must be on the veranda below, but who is he speaking to?

"No. I don't think so...Hmmm...if you say so..."

He's on the phone, and it's none of my business. I'm about to limp away when I hear something that stalls my step.

"Without the elites, they can't do a thing..."

I limp onto the balcony and tune in.

"No, I did my part, and it cost me...Yes, my daughter...I know it will be worth it...Once they're all dead...That's right...I know... It'll be over soon..."

My blood freezes in my veins as I piece together what he's saying. The implications...No. It can't be. Not my father. There must be some mistake.

I grab my gown and head downstairs.

I FIND MY father standing by the hearth, whiskey in hand. His aura is muddy, an aura of conflict, but it brightens when I enter the room, warm and loving, and my heart hurts because I don't want what I suspect to be true.

"Selas, sweetheart, you shouldn't be exerting yourself so soon. The medic said to take turns about your room for the next few days."

"I was taking a turn, and I ended up on the balcony."

He stills, his aura shifting to muddy once more. "Oh?"

"I heard you on the phone."

"What did you hear?" His tone is relaxed, but his aura darkens.

"You were talking about the elites, about them dying."

"Sweetheart, I was talking about the elite exam. It's happening as we speak."

"You said, '*Once they're all dead.*' Why would you say that? What's happening? Tell me!" There's a part of me that warns me not to push. Warns me to shut up and back off. Warns me to be afraid, but this is my father. He's never given me reason to fear him. He loves me. He would never hurt me.

His aura confirms it now, brightening to tell me that all he wants to do is protect. "This is my fault," he says finally. "I'm so sorry, sweetheart."

A shadow rushes me from my left, and pain explodes in my head.

The world goes dark.

CHAPTER 37

CAMERON

My two doppelgangers approached, and I resisted the urge to step back. One was taller than the other. Athletically built, her body was honed for a brawl, but the other was softer, her body more suited to an omega or a human, but they were still both me.

Suddenly I knew what this was. "I'm in a mind walk, aren't I?"

"In a manner of speaking," the tougher version of me said. "We're here to help guide you."

Her companion nodded. "Yes, if you'll let us."

"I have a choice?"

The one with the bun—version one—rolled her eyes. "There are always choices. That's how life works."

"Will you let us walk with you?" version two said.

I mean, what did I have to lose? "Sure."

She took my hand, and it was the strangest sensation, like holding my own hand, or something, but then she was guiding me forward while version one strode ahead, out of the silvery gloom and deeper into the darkness.

Soft amber light bloomed around us, and a path materialized underfoot. Images rolled past me, memories from my childhood—baking with my mother, being pushed on a swing, nighttime hugs and being read stories. Longing filled me with each. If only I could stay there, safe and protected, but the memories turned to gray skies above the cemetery where my mother was laid to rest.

I stood alone at her graveside, maybe about sixteen at the time, the rain masking my tears.

"Do you remember this day?" version two asked softly.

Version one made a sound of exasperation. "Let's show her." She shoved me into the memory, into the body of my sixteen-year-old self. My chest felt like it was being crushed, a weight sitting on it that made it hard to breathe, but the sobs kept coming anyway.

Why? Why did you leave me? I'm so alone, mum, I can't do this. I need you. I need you so badly.

"Jason Darcy broke up with you that day," version two said. "Even after you had sex with him."

"You gave it up so he wouldn't leave you," version one pointed out. "Pathetic. Look at you, crying to your dead mommy over a fucking twit of a boy."

My face burned with shame beneath the tears. Yes. Being with Jason had made me feel wanted. I'd known deep down saying no to him would mean losing him. I'd known deep down what kind of boy he was, but I'd been afraid of him breaking up with me. Afraid to be unseen once more, and so...Yeah, I'd agreed to sleep with him. He left me anyway.

"Stop it!" version two said. "She was sixteen. He was her first love."

"She knew better," version one retorted. "She knew he just wanted in her panties. She wasn't ready, but she did it just to try and keep him."

I remembered the ache of loneliness afterward. Seeing Jason with Clarissa Morton. The rumors he'd spread about me being a slut. The propositions from other boys. The shame and isolation. I'd never told Romi, too embarrassed, too scared that he'd be disgusted with me and stop coming to see me.

"You used your brother as a crutch," version one said. "And then he was taken, too, and look at you. You threw yourself into danger because you couldn't bear to let go."

"She needed closure," version two said.

"No, she needed a distraction from the fact that she was alone once more." She grabbed my shoulder and pulled me from my sixteen-year-old body and back into the dark. "You're pathetic, Cameron. You're desperate to connect. To belong, and it weakens you. People leave, they die, and every time that happens, it breaks you."

"That's not true," version two said. "Connections make us stronger!"

"Really?" version one sneered. "Let's see, shall we?" Light bloomed, clinical and bright as the infirmary bloomed around us. "A recent memory, perhaps?" She crossed her arms and arched a brow. "Take a look."

Heartbreaking sobs filled the room coming from the bed where I lay on my side, curled up in a fetal position. I closed my eyes to block out the scene, not wanting to feel that pain again.

"You see what connections can do?" version one said. "You wasted so much time grieving something you couldn't have had anyway. Even if you save him, you'll be forced to say goodbye all over again. How is that sane, *hmmm*?"

"It's called love!" version two said, hands fisted at her sides. "And it's what makes us—"

"Human?" version one taunted. "But we're *not* human, are we? And the sooner she accepts that, the sooner she can move on and pass this fucking trial."

The infirmary melted away, but we didn't go back into the dark place; instead, we materialized on a platform that extended partway across an abyss, and dangling from chains in the center was Derek's shadowy form. His head lolled onto his chest, body loose and limp in unconsciousness.

"Derek!" I rushed to the edge of the platform. "Derek! Can you hear me?"

"I'm afraid he can't," version one said. "And he never will if you don't make the right choice now."

Choice? "What do you mean?"

"Stop it, you're scaring her," version two said.

"She should be scared. The wrong choice now could mean she loses everything. Her shield. Her mate. Her brother, and her life."

My pulse raced. "What do I have to do?"

"Pick one of us," version one said.

"What?" I looked between them.

Version two stepped in front of me. "We are you, Cameron. Potential versions of you. And to pass the trial, you must choose one of us and kill the other."

"What the fuck? I'm not killing anyone."

"And therein lies your problem," version one drawled. "You're weak." She pointed at version two. "*She* makes you weak. Get rid of her, and we can claim our shield and pass to the next stage of this trial."

Once again, my gaze bounced between them.

"It's all right," version two said. "We don't feel pain, and we want what's best for you." She glanced at version one. "In our own way, of course."

"Just pick already," version one said.

They weren't real, and if I had to eliminate one to save Derek and move on with this test, then so be it.

"That's the spirit," version one said. "Maybe there's hope for you yet. You know what you need to do. You know which version of yourself you need to be to achieve your goals."

My goal was to save the people I loved, and no doubt the warrior version could help me do that, but she was cold, selfish, and kind of an ass. Version two was sweet and kind, but sweet and kind wouldn't help me fight graynites. She'd be plagued by doubts and indecision.

Chains rattled, and Derek dropped a foot closer to the abyss. "What's happening?"

"You're running out of time," version two said. "You have to choose. Now. Who do you want to be? Me..." She smiled sweetly.

"Or her."

Version one stood tall, her eyes cold, flat, and ready to take on anything. With her on my side, I could defeat the graynites. I could have the kind of grit needed to make the decisions that could save lives, but...would I care about those lives anymore? And version two would help me nurture the connections I'd made, be part of a family and care enough to keep them safe, but...would I be strong enough to do so?

They were two sides of a coin that I'd spent my whole life attempting to balance on the edge of, and up until now I'd thought I was doing pretty well.

Were they here to tell me otherwise or to test my conviction?

The chains rattled again, and Derek dropped another foot.

"Tick-tock, Cameron," version one said. "You know what you have to do."

A blade appeared in my hand, the hilt cold and hard against my palm. "I have to kill one of you."

"Doubts will cripple you," version one said. "Those feelings of abandonment, the need to belong, to connect, they will make you weak. Kill her and remove those fears."

"Fear keeps us safe," version two said. "The desire to belong gives us family."

Version one tutted. "Family who will hold you back and act like a noose stopping you from rising. Stopping you from making the decisions that will give you the things you want. Family stops you being invincible."

Invincible...Palia's words filled my mind... "*If we felt invincible, truly invincible all the time, then the world would be filled with egomaniacs with superiority complexes and no fear. Doubts keep us on our toes, they make us think and question before making decisions. They keep us safe...surely...*"

My doubts forced me to think through plans, and my fear of loneliness forced me to make connections and value them. My fear of abandonment made me a better friend. I had turned my weaknesses into strengths, and I suddenly knew what I had to do.

I turned to version two. "I'm sorry." I stabbed her in the heart, and she disintegrated, a smile on her face.

"Perfect," version one said. "Now we can—"

I stabbed her in the chest too.

"What..." She looked down at the blade in shock.

I released the hilt and stepped back. "I don't need either of you. I'm good just the way I am."

She vanished in a blaze of cinders, and I was alone on the platform with Derek suspended out of reach. What now?

"Hey! Come on! I made my choice." Unless I'd fucked up. What if I had to pick one of them to stay? What if by eliminating them both, I'd messed up the test?

No. This was right. I was right. I didn't want to become either of those versions. This version of me was who I wanted to be. It was who I'd worked hard to become, and up until now I'd doubted that. Not any longer.

The platform rumbled and began to move forward.

Yes! I reached for Derek as I got closer. "I'm coming, buddy. I'm coming." The platform stopped abreast of him. I was high enough to be able to wrap my arms around his neck if I wanted, but not high enough to get to the pulley system on the chains that held him suspended. I could try climbing up, but what if the weight dragged us down?

"Shit." I cuddled his waist and dragged him onto the platform as well as I could. He was still held up by chains, but I had him. "Let him go. Get the chains off him!" There had to be an architect here. Someone pulling the strings of this test. No one answered, though.

Derek groaned, his diamond eyes cracking open to focus on me. "My Cameron."

I kissed his cheek and hugged him tightly. "I'm here, buddy. I've got you."

The chains rattled, releasing him just as the platform dropped out from under us.

I held on to him, secure and safe as we fell into the abyss together.

CHAPTER 38

CURI

Her body burns with need, pressed against me, hips rolling against my groin as I thrust my fingers deep into her wet heat. Her moans make me ache to bury myself in her.

Do it.

Take her.

Disembodied voices fill my head.

She wants you.

She needs you.

You need her.

Take what she's offering.

I bite back a groan and squeeze my eyes shut, fighting the urge to replace my fingers with my cock.

You can fill her, stretch her, be hugged by her as you give her the release she deserves and claim the release you deserve too.

You're worthy, Curi. She knows it too. She just needs you to show her.

I want her. I want her so badly it hurts, but I need her to want me just as much. I can't take what she isn't freely offering. I can't take her if she can't give me her heart.

Then you'll remain worthless, just like your father always said.

A worthless, pathetic, useless—

No! I push away the memory, eyes snapping open to gloom lit only by silvery light that seems to come from nowhere.

"You could have taken her that night," Selas says from the shadows. "You could have claimed her. Made her yours. She wouldn't have gone back to Serath after that. She can't be with him anyway. You could have made it easier for her by taking the step her body wanted you to take."

She's not saying anything I don't already know; after all, she's in my head. "I know."

"Then why didn't you?"

I swallow the lump in my throat because this part, this part I've kept even from myself.

"Answer me, Curi. Why didn't you?"

I release the words on an exhale. "Because...because I love her."

Fuck, it feels good to finally admit it. To say the words out loud, even if they are only in my head.

"Finally," Selas says. "Maybe now that you've admitted that, you can finally accept that you're worthy of the same. Now for the next phase."

Bright light blinds me.

CHAPTER 39

SHARNIZA

"What is this?" My father holds up the glittery silver bow I've had hidden in my dresser for the past month. "Why do you have it?"

Because I bought it, and it's mine. "I...I found it."

His eyes narrow. "You found it? So, why did you keep it? Why hide it like a treasure? Is this what you want? To be a shiny, glittery thing?" He closes his fist around the bow, crushing it. "You think bows and bangles will make you a good warrior?"

The maid stands in a corner of the room—the culprit who obviously found the bow and gave it to my father. I shoot her a glare, and she meets it with sad, mournful eyes filled with remorse.

The wave of rage aimed toward her dies. She's a prisoner just like me. A woman in a household ruled by males. An omega who's served her purpose and now services my father when it suits him.

She's the closest thing to a mother I have here, but now I know that she's also his spy.

Fuck, my father is still speaking.

"You think that your enemy will quake in his boots at the sight of your sequins and chiffon?"

Part of me wonders how he knows about chiffon, and the other hopes the floor can open and swallow me.

"Why do you have it? Answer me!"

"Because it makes me feel pretty!" The words are out before I can stop them, and twin spots of color stain his cheeks.

"Pretty? You think *pretty* will help you become a guardian?"

I'm overcome by a rare wave of defiance. "What if I don't want to be a guardian?"

I know as soon as I say it that I've made a grave mistake. His face goes blank, and the rage in his eyes dims to something flat and cold. He drops the bow on the ground and walks out of my room, closing the door behind him.

Do you remember... my guide's voice asks. *Do you remember what happens next?*

There's a pit in my belly. "Yes."

Do you want to see?

"Do I have a choice?"

Look in the mirror.

A mirror appears in front of me, and I see myself, aged fifteen, wide-eyed and teary, long, dark waves cascading down my back.

You loved your hair.

I turn away from the mirror. "I did."

And he took it from you...

"I know all this. He had the maid chop it all off while I slept. What's the point of all this anyway?"

You stopped loving the things that made you happy. You became what he wanted you to be. You denied yourself...your true self. Look at the mirror, Sharniza, look at who you could have been...who you can still be.

I can't help myself. I stare at the woman in the looking glass—tall and powerful with thigh-high boots and long wavy hair pulled up in a ponytail and braided down her back. Her eyes are rimmed in kohl, and her lips are rouged. She looks badass, and she's me.

The image melts away. "I don't need makeup and fancy clothes to be me."

This isn't about the material things, Sharniza. But maybe you need to see more to understand.

The room melts away, and darkness swallows me...

CHAPTER 40

CAMERON

The abyss swallowed Derek and me, then spat us out in a room housing a huge gilded mirror. There were no windows, no doors, just the mirror.

"What happened?" Derek asked me.

"We're in a mind walk. I had to pick between two versions of me to free you. What happened to you?"

"All I remember is the orb and smoke, then I was dangling over a pit, and my Cameron, you were there."

And now we were here. "I'm not sure what we're meant to do now. I think I may have killed both of my guides."

"We don't need guides," Derek said. "We can figure this out together."

He took my hand, and we laced fingers before approaching the mirror. Our reflections stared back at us, my five seven dwarfed by Derek's towering frame. The image rippled, and the mirror went dark.

An androgynous voice filled the room. "You've made your choice, cadet, and now the strength of that choice will be tested. The five bloodlines have been gifted with chimeras, but not every gargoyle born to those bloodlines can access their second form. As an elite, your chimera will be your secret weapon, the form you can call upon when all else fails. Your chimera is a part of you, but it is also its own beast, and when we awaken it now, it will choose whether you are a worthy host."

Choice. Once again. I was sensing a theme here. "And what happens if it finds me unsuitable?"

"Then it will kill you."

"No!" Derek growled. "You're not touching her."

"You are right, shield," the voice said. "I will not be touching. But you will."

"What?"

"A chimera is fueled by a gargoyle's shield, and since you have made your shield sentient, you have also separated your chimera from your body. It is your shield that will now turn. It is your shield that will test if you are worthy."

"She is worthy," Derek said. "My Cameron is the most—"

He doubled over with a bellow of pain.

No! "Stop it! You're hurting him."

"The first shift is always painful," the voice said. "But it will get easier...*if* you survive. But if you don't, then you will both cease to exist."

Derek thrashed and slammed his body into the wall. "No. I won't...I won't let it hurt you."

"The more you resist, the more pain you will feel," the voice said dispassionately.

He was afraid of what the chimera would do, afraid that it would hurt me.

"Derek!" I put my arm around his waist. "Don't fight it. Let it out."

He shook his head. "My Cameron, I can't risk you being hurt. I must protect."

I cupped his face. "Do you believe that I'm worthy?"

His bright eyes flared brighter. "Yes, my Cameron, with every fiber of my being."

"Then there's nothing to fear. Let it out. Just...let go." I stepped back with a smile and a nod.

Derek clenched his teeth, then let out a drawn-out roar. His body expanded, rippling and morphing into something twice its size with claws, wings, and huge, curved horns. Chimeras were supposed to be a mishmash of different creatures, but this didn't look like anything I'd ever seen.

Behind me, the mirror flared bright, then dimmed. "This is...is...this is...is..." A sharp cracking sound resounded, and the mirror shattered.

I twisted away, holding up my arm to shield myself from the shards shooting off its surface, stone skin activating, but my chimera stepped forward, one wing flaring out to shield me from the glass, leaving me with no need for my stone skin.

Soft clinks followed as the fragments hit the ground, and I slowly lowered my arm to look up into this new monster's face. I'd seen pictures of demons in old graphic novels, and this thing... it looked just like that. Hooved with large muscle-rounded shoulders, it exhaled mist from its nostrils with each breath, but its eyes...its eyes were bright like diamonds.

Derek's eyes.

"Derek?"

"Yes," he said. "It is me, my Cameron."

I reached out to touch his wing, leathery but smooth. "How... Does it hurt?"

"No. I feel...whole." He lifted his huge head. "Something is wrong."

The ground trembled a moment later, and a band wrapped around the top of my arm, squeezing painfully. "Ouch." The lights began to flicker, and heat bloomed across my cheek as if...as if I'd been slapped. "Something's wrong. Derek, something is—"

I sat up gasping for breath with Adaline leaning over me. "Oh, thank the earth."

The ground rumbled. Someone screamed.

Adaline's head whipped toward the window. "Levi!"

I was back. On the floor. Awake. "What's happening?" My gaze went to the window as something dark hurtled toward it, then smashed through, hitting the ground and sliding across the floor.

A goyle.

"Curi!" I scrambled up. "What the fuck is going on?"

Derek materialized by the window, back in his usual shadow form. "We're under graynite attack!"

CHAPTER 41

CAMERON

"Three graynites," Derek said. "More on the horizon. We have to go."

I helped Curi to his feet, and he shook his head to clear it. "Fucking bastards." His voice was a bestial rumble in goyle form. "We fight them. Kill them." His tone deepened, body expanding.

Adaline grabbed my arm and pulled me back in time to avoid getting trampled on as Curi barreled forward, shifting into his chimera as he went—head morphing into a pantherine form, body leonine so that he was all muscle and bulk when he leaped out of the smashed window and into the night.

Adaline grabbed my shoulders. "This is bad. This is an ambush. They must know how vulnerable you are right now."

"What are you talking about?"

"It takes several days for an elite to adjust to their chimera. Several days for full assimilation; until then, the chimera form is unpredictable. It takes and it drains. You'll fight hard, but you'll fall harder. You must stop your friends. Tell them to subdue their chimeras and get back inside here. I can put up a barrier with Levi's help and hold it until the port reappears in fifteen minutes."

Fifteen minutes didn't sound long, but it would be an eternity when fighting off graynites. "I'm on it."

She grabbed my arm. "Don't let your chimera out. It'll want to break free when surrounded by the graynites, but you must subdue it."

But Derek *was* my chimera. "Derek, you'd best stay in here."

"I'm not letting you go out there alone," Derek said.

"You've got to. We can't risk the chimera emerging."

He clenched his jaw, clearly conflicted, but there was no time. "I've got this. Trust me."

Without him, I had no protection except my stone skin, which would probably be worth nothing against the graynites. I needed him out there with me as my shield while I warned the others. But he was more than a shield right now; he was also a chimera, and if he lost control out there, it would drain both our batteries, leaving us useless.

Outside, several huge forms collided, chimera on graynite, battling for dominance, and in the sky, dark shadows flew closer. More incoming. My gut contracted, heat flooding my veins and threatening to cripple me with adrenaline. I breathed slowly and evenly to calm the tremble in my veins because it wasn't brute force I needed out there, it was agility and precision, and for that, I needed to be calm and focused.

"Get to Levi first," Adaline said as I reached the window. "As a halfblood, he'll weaken the fastest. Get him back here. He has no goyle form, just the chimera, and when it drops, he'll be defenseless."

"On it." I took a deep breath, then climbed out the window and into the chaos of the night.

LEVI

We use our tail to knock a graynite down and our talons to shred its side. It twists and breaks free, jaws snapping at our face before punching us in the chest. We sail through the air and land in a crouch, ready to rebound and attack again.

"Levi!"

What is that? A small thing. A woman. Cameron?

She runs fast and low, keeping to the pockets of shadows, but her golden hair catches the moonlight.

Kill the graynite.

The thought eclipses everything.

"Levi, no! Get inside before the chimera drains you. You need to help your mother put up a shield."

The graynite sees her and rushes toward her.

"No!" We bound toward it on all fours and collide with it, wrapping our jaws around its neck and twisting to snap.

It goes limp. Dead.

Good.

"Levi, please. The chimera will drain you. We need you inside." So many words, too many for us to focus on when there is blood. "Portal...mother...More coming."

The part of me that is Levi pushes to the surface.

Hands touch my face. "Come back. Please. Levi, come back."

The chimera growls, attempting to push me into the background again, but I hold on to the image of her face, staring deep into her gray eyes, and emerge.

"Oh, thank fuck," she says. "Get inside. Get the shield ready. I'll get the others."

"I'm not leaving you!"

"If you don't, then we all die. Now *Go*!"

SHARNIZA

I'M IN THE back seat as my chimera attacks a graynite, swiping at it with huge paws tipped with five-inch talons. Sparks fly where our claws glance off its stone skin. We need to punch holes, hit harder to hurt it. We spin to evade a slash of its claws and barrel back, hitting it with our shoulder, lifting it off the ground, then slamming it into earth before smashing our heavy paw onto its chest.

"Shar, watch out!"

Cameron?

Another graynite hits us from the side, throwing us off our target. We slide across the ground with the thing on top of us. We twist and slash, and for a moment, the world fades away, and there is nothing but talons and claws, screeches and roars. Its hands are on our neck, pinning us, but we have reach. We have a beak. We rear up and stab it in the throat. It convulses, weakening enough for us to take control and roll it under us. Our vision goes red as we maul, taking chunks out of its body.

Hot blood spatters our face.

Don't swallow.

Spit it out.

Venom.

Bad.

Graynite dead.

More to kill.

We leap up, wings flaring, ready to fly at the next one when a small form dashes up alongside us.

"Get inside! Now!" Cameron cries. "You have to drop the chimera and get inside, or it will drain you."

A warning. I need to listen, but the chimera is too strong; it wants to fight. It wants to rage.

"Sharniza, no!"

There is no Sharniza, only the beast.

CAMERON

SHARNIZA WAS TOO far gone. All I could do was hope I could get her into the building once her chimera blipped out. I made a dash toward Curi several yards away, grappling with a graynite. Until he wasn't. He hit the ground, his body morphing to human form. The graynite raised a claw, ready to rip out his throat, and I was too far away.

A scream lodged in my throat, terror racing through me and freezing my limbs.

I was about to watch him die.

A dark figure materialized beside him, and in the next instant, Curi was gone.

Derek had him.

He was safe. My paralysis broke, and I altered my trajectory to aim for the building. Sharniza? Where was she? If I could grab her along the way, then—

A gust of air threw back my hair, and a gigantic form landed in my path, cutting me off.

I'd seen graynites before, been surrounded by them, but this thing was several feet larger, so bulky that his shoulder muscles had swallowed his neck. But it was his bright blue eyes that held me captive, eyes I'd looked into more times than I could remember. Eyes that had smiled at me, laughed with me.

My stomach dropped, hope leaching from my body. "Romi?"

The graynite roared, spraying saliva, but I was frozen in place, my body humming with recognition, stomach trembling with the horror of it. Powerless to do anything but stare at the monster that had once been my brother.

Romi snapped his jaws shut, lowered his head, and attacked.

CHAPTER 42

CURI

One moment we're grappling a graynite, and the next our body loses all power. I hit the ground, chimera slipping away, and the graynite looms over me, larger than life. My vision darkens. I can barely see its claws coming for my face. Arms materialize around me, and the world shatters and reconstructs itself into the testing room.

Is this a test? Am I dreaming?

Someone slaps my cheek. "Curi, hey, are you with me?" Levi says.

"I need to get my Cameron," Derek says. "Put up the shields and I will bring her."

"Teleport her?" Levi asks. "How the fuck did you do that?"

"Not sure. Don't care, as long as I can do it again."

Cameron? "She's out there?" I try to stand, but my limbs refuse to cooperate. "Dammit!" I'm wiped. No use. Cameron... fuck...

"Levi, the shields!" Adaline orders.

"The others are still out there," Levi counters.

"Then we'll drop it for them."

"We'll only get one shot," Levi says.

"Then we'll have to make it count," his mother replies.

A hum fills the air as the druid raises the shield. I drag myself to the window, barely feeling the slice of glass on my palms as I pull myself up to look out.

Blocks of ice form in my gut at the sight that greets me.

CHAPTER 43

Cameron

I was going to die. Romi was about to kill me.

"*No*!" Derek materialized in front of me, power radiating off his frame, blasting into Romi and knocking him back.

The ground shook as several more ginormous graynites landed around us. Derek stood over me, his hands up against the air, which shimmered with the power of a protective dome. But how long would this shield last against four uber graynites? Against Romi?

I was too late.

They'd turned him.

They'd taken his soul, and now he was here to kill me.

He was back on his feet now, ambling forward to join his comrades as they circled us.

An unearthly roar split the night as Sharniza appeared to our left, running at the nearest graynite.

"*No*!" Derek boomed.

A graynite backhanded her, sending her spinning through the air toward the building where the shadowy forms of the others were barely visible through the window.

Derek turned and wrapped his arms around me. The world fractured and materialized again a moment later, but we were now a few yards away from the building, next to Sharniza's prone form.

With the graynites rushing toward us, there was no time to ask how he'd teleported us. Derek threw the dome back up, while I crouched to check Shar's pulse. "It's steady. She's alive."

"Get inside!" Curi beckoned from the building. "Move!"

The soft blue shimmer around the building told me that they had a shield up. "Derek. Can you teleport us again?"

He shook his head. "Not both of you."

The graynites surrounded us, slamming fists into the shield to test it. Derek roared, holding firm as they battered his defenses.

I scrambled up and wrapped my arms around him, as if that would help, as if I could loan him more power somehow.

The hammering stopped, and the ground ceased shaking.

I slowly raised my head, searching for Romi, and our gazes locked—his cold, alien, and unfeeling, as if he didn't see me or know me.

"Romi. Please. If you're in there, please." But even as I said it, I knew it was pointless. Knew how it worked. If he was a graynite, then it meant they'd taken his soul. It meant he was gone.

He canted his head and slow-blinked. "Romi? Yes, this body belonged to a Romi once. But Romi is dead, and now this body is mine."

My heart fractured all over again.

"Come out and die gracefully, Basque," he said. "Do so, and the others can live. Resist and when your shields fail, then you shall all die."

My gaze flicked between him and the other three, then beyond, where two more regular-sized graynites stood awaiting instructions, before returning to Romi again.

No. This wasn't Romi. Not any longer.

Romi was gone, and there was nothing left that I could do for him now.

I had to focus on what was left. On Serath and my friends.

Being the last Basque meant nothing if it meant risking their lives. "How do I know you'll keep your word?"

"You don't," the thing in Romi's skin growled.

I'd give my life in a heartbeat to protect my friends, but then what? They'd be defenseless against the graynites. I was the last Basque. The last hope to take down the bastard who'd killed my brother. Like fuck was I going to roll over and die.

If I was going down, it wouldn't be without a fight.

I looked back at the building, at the blue shimmer that kept my friends safe. The portal would open in a few minutes. I just needed to buy them some time, but I knew in my gut that Derek's shield wouldn't last that long.

I had a plan.

"I need...I need a moment..." I ducked my head, feigning defeat, feigning the form of someone grappling with their upcoming demise.

"Take your moment, then," the graynite growled.

I grasped for the connection that Derek and I had cultivated over the past few weeks and spoke into his mind.

I have a plan. We're gonna use the element of surprise and make a run for it. I'll start talking and agree to their terms, and when I say "drop the shield," I need you to scoop up Sharniza and teleport her. I'll be right behind you. There's a break in their defenses to the left. You can drop her and then come back for me.

I don't like this.

It's the only way. We have to try.

Then I teleport you first, my Cameron.

My heart swelled with love for him. *If you do that, they'll kill Sharniza. She won't be able to run to get away from them. I can. Derek, please, I need you to do this for me.*

He was silent for several beats, wrestling with the decision. Turning it over no doubt to find a flaw, another way, but there was none. Finally, he spoke, his tone tight, demanding. *You run fast, my Cameron. You run like the wind, and I will come for you.*

I promise.

I raised my head and looked up at the graynite who now owned my brother's skin. "I agree to your terms. My life for theirs."

The air vibrated with the purrs of approval, and my insides twisted in terror. I let it wash over me. Let the adrenaline flood me, because I was going to flee, and I needed it.

I fixed my gaze on the break between the two graynites farthest to my right. "Derek, drop the shields."

The air crackled, the shields dropped, and I spun on my heel and launched myself at the breach between the graynites, breaking into a sprint. The building rushed toward me, and I spotted the others inside, jumping up and down, their voices screaming at me to hurry a moment before Derek appeared, running toward me.

If he was running, it meant he was out of juice. It meant... My stride slowed, weakness infusing my limbs, the beat of wings behind me growing louder.

"My Cameron, *No*!" Derek burst out of his skin, morphing into chimera form with a terrifying roar before misting into nothing.

He was out of power. Completely, utterly depleted.

"Cameron, come on!" Curi stood at the window, his hand reaching for me.

A fresh wave of adrenaline gave me a second wind, pushing me forward. I was almost there. Just a few more yards and—

The moon winked out, and the ground shook as a graynite landed in my path, his body folded into a crouch. It rose slowly, unfurling its stony, scaled frame as if it had all the time in the world to make its entrance.

Shimmering gray bony spikes jutted off its shoulders and ran down its arms. Its wings splayed, then snapped tight as it deliberately raised its head to reveal its grotesque face, lips pulled back against ivory fangs.

Something inside my chest tugged, and my gaze whipped up to meet its pale blue irises ringed in indigo. The tug inside me bloomed to a familiar heat.

No...

It couldn't be.

"Serath?" His name was a whisper sitting on my lips because it couldn't be so. This creature couldn't be my mate.

But it stared at me with Serath's eyes. Eyes that had flared with passion for me and softened with tender love. They studied me clinically now, as if I was a specimen on a petri dish.

The other graynites landed around us, but I couldn't tear my attention from my mate. "Serath, it's me. It's Cameron." I blinked against the sting of tears. "Please...please tell me you're in there." His eyes twitched, gaze flicking over my shoulder, then down to his hand. "You promised...You promised to hold on."

He was in there. He had to be, because I could *feel* him, feel our connection, low-grade but present. He slow-blinked, and his pupils dilated a fraction.

My heart leaped. "I know you can hear me. Dammit, Serath, fight it. You fight whatever they've done to you."

For a moment, it felt like I was reaching him. For a moment, I could almost believe that there was life behind his dead eyes, but then the graynite who owned Romi's body spoke, his grating grumble breaking the spell.

"There is no Serath," Romi said. "Not anymore." He jerked his chin up. "Finish her, Ubron."

Serath inclined his head. "Yes, General."

He grabbed me by the throat and hauled me off my feet so I was eye to eye with him. But he didn't squeeze. Didn't crush. He just held me, staring at me with darkening and dilating pupils that threatened to consume me.

He was in there. I fucking knew it. He was in there, but he wasn't in control, and he was about to watch me die. I couldn't let him bear that guilt.

I reached up to grip his wrist, running my thumb back and forth over his skin. "I love you, Serath. It's okay. This is not your fault. It's okay." I let my love shine out of my eyes. Let it rise and seep from my skin. Giving it all to him, one last time.

A low growl vibrated his chest.

"Ubron. End her now!" the general ordered.

Serath's grip on me tightened, and then his teeth rushed at my face.

CHAPTER 44

SERATH

I'm lost.

Trapped in the forever dark with an expanse of gray above me that's out of reach.

The darkness tries to pull me down, away from the gray, but I'm tethered. Somehow, Cameron tethered me. Her essence. Her power. Her love holds me here.

They can't evict me.

My body.

Mine.

If I can gather my strength. If I can just—

"Serath, it's me. It's Cameron."

Her voice filters into the darkness saturated with hope and... fear.

"Please...please tell me you're in there. You promised...you promised to hold on."

Cameron! Panic fuels me, pushing me up toward the gray. I must surface. I must see. A pinprick of light blooms, and her face appears, misty-eyed, mouth parted in a plea.

Beyond her, lethal threats loom. Graynites. I glance down at my hand, but it's no longer my hand. It belongs to a monster. To one of them.

I've changed, and I'm here, which means—

"I know you can hear me, dammit," Cameron says. "Serath, fight it. You fight whatever they've done to you."

Yes. I must fight. I need to protect her. I can't let them—

The darkness heaves, wrapping its arms around me, trying to pull me down. My hand wraps around her throat, and I can feel the softness of her skin and the thrum of her pulse against my palm. Her thumb strokes my wrist, and my chest aches as I fight the force trying to pull me away from her, because if I let go, she's doomed. If I slip now, then she's dead. I can feel the muscles in my arms tensing, and the thing that has control of me prepares to crush her windpipe.

"I love you, Serath," she says, absolving me of what I'm about to do. "It's okay. This is not your fault. It's okay."

Her face rushes toward mine, and a lance of pure energy shoots into me. Not mine. Cameron's. It rockets through my soul and connects to my power, and the shackles holding me in the darkness are burned away. It blazes, engulfing my veins. *My* fucking veins, in *my* fucking body.

"*No*!" The voice of the entity that houses my skin reverberates in my head. "This is my body now."

Fury floods me, a foghorn to my beast and chimera buried in the abyss. They shake themselves out of forced dormancy and rush up to meet me.

"No!" the entity cries. "You can't do this. You can't."

I fill my body with *my* essence and power, cutting off the bastard's voice.

"Fuck you. This is my body. *Mine*!"

CHAPTER 45

CAMERON

I closed my eyes and waited for the bite of Serath's teeth, but long seconds passed, and it didn't come.

I cracked open an eyelid and stared into his graynite eyes.

"Ubron? What is the meaning of this?" the general demanded.

Serath's left eye twitched, and a low, menacing growl rolled up his throat to blast me in the face. He drew me close, his words barely a whisper. "I'm going to throw you. Get ready to roll when you land. Then run."

My heart leaped into my mouth, pulse stalling only to kick into a canter. He was back. Serath was—

He swung back his arm, with me dangling from it, and I let go of him in time to go sailing through the air. I landed in a roll that jarred my bones before coming up and sprinting for the building.

"Now!" Curi bellowed.

The blue shimmer parted to let me past, and I dove through the busted window and straight into Curi's arms.

He gathered me to his chest for a moment, but I twisted back to the window. "Serath is out there! He's in control." He was in battle now. One against six. "He saved me, and we're taking him back with us. How long till the port opens?"

"It should be here already," Adaline said.

"It's not coming," Shar groaned. "Someone fucked us over. The fact that the graynites found this place..."

Fuck! "Then we get Serath in here, and we hold out until we can recharge and fight." I looked from Adaline to Levi. "Can you hold the shield?"

"We can," Levi said. "But we can't open it again. Letting you in was a one-shot deal."

Wait, that meant that letting me back out wasn't an option either. It meant Serath was on his own.

"No!" I rushed for the window, but Curi snagged me around the waist and hugged me to his chest. "Let me go! I have to help. I need to help." Tears blurred my vision.

"Dammit. Cameron, stop and think. If we drop the shield, we all die," Curi bit out. "I don't know how he managed to stay tethered to his body when they turned him, but it must have taken everything he had to surface and save you. Don't let it be for nothing."

His words were logical. They made sense. But the clawing desperation inside me to protect my mate wouldn't be denied. It seared up my throat, spilling from my lips in a roar of pain as Serath took a blow that knocked him to his knees.

He leaped up and countered an attack, using his body as a battering ram to break free of his attackers, but the general managed to get a hit on his skull. Serath swayed and went down.

He stayed down.

"No!"

The graynites flew at the building and smashed into the wards.

Adaline cried out against the assault. "Hold it, Levi. We must hold it."

The world was thunder and roars, ground trembling beneath my feet, but none of that mattered. All that mattered was out there on the dusty ground. Serath pulled himself up slowly, his huge frame heaving with each breath. He let out a bellow and launched himself into the air toward us.

The graynites, distracted by Serath, left the shields alone and zoomed back toward him to take him down again.

"He's buying us time," Curi said. "Fuck, he's buying us time, but he doesn't know there's no port."

"We need to recharge," Sharniza said. "We need to fight!"

But even as she said it, the mood dipped because we all knew that there wasn't enough time. I was tapped out, my body aching, limbs shaking with exhaustion.

Derek was gone.

There was no port.

There was no hope.

We were going to die here.

"What's that?" Sharniza rushed forward and pointed up at the sky.

There were more shapes in the sky. Large, bulky shapes with wings. "No...Not more. Please."

But as they got closer, there was no doubt that they were indeed more graynites. With that many bodies testing the wards, there was no way Levi and his mother would be able to keep them up.

In short, we were fucked.

Sharniza slipped her hand into mine and squeezed. "I love you, Cameron."

I squeezed back. "I love you too."

Out on the battlefield, Serath continued to fight. To go down and get back up, over and over, against all odds. My beautiful mate kept the graynites' attention on him with bellowed taunts every time they lost interest, every time they thought he was down. And as the fresh wave descended from the sky, I knew that if I was going to die today, then there was only one place I wanted to be.

"Drop the shields."

"What?" Levi said.

I turned on him, eyes blazing, voice deepening with the ire of my beast. My goyle was back. Awake. "We're dead anyway, and I won't let him die alone." I flicked my wrist and released my talons. "Drop them now!"

Sharniza squeezed my hand. "I can feel my goyle. We do this. We fight with what we have. Until the end."

"Till the end," Curi said, voice deepening.

We weren't fully recovered, but enough to put up a fight.

"No!" Adaline said.

"I'm sorry, Mother," Levi said. "If I'm going to die today, then I want to do it fighting alongside my team."

He dropped the shield, and with a unified roar, we rushed at the windows, shattering the unbroken ones and feeling nothing as we burst out into the night.

Serath spun toward me, sensing me, but the rest of the grounded graynites broke their attack to look up at the sky.

"Evacuate!" the general ordered.

They took to the air, flying away from the incoming graynite influx.

I kept running toward Serath, ignoring the confusion, ignoring everything because he was on his knees, his huge body swaying with the effort of trying to remain upright. I caught him before he could fall, clutching him to my chest and staggering beneath his weight.

"Serath, oh God. Serath."

"Cameron..." His eyes slipped closed, and I buckled beneath his full weight.

"I've got you!" Curi appeared beside me, helping me to hold Serath up.

"They're running," Levi said, confused.

"What are those?" Curi pointed at the green balloons hurtling toward us.

No, not balloons, orbs. Why were they—

"Take cover!" Shar threw herself over us as the sound of shattering glass filled the night.

The world turned green.

The air bitter.

And then nothing.

CHAPTER 46

CAMERON

I woke with the taste of ash and blood in my mouth, my throat so dry I was instantly coughing.

"Drink this." A bottle of water was thrust into my hand, and it was only when I'd drained it that my brain came fully online, asking me if it was safe to drink. But Sharniza was patting my back. She'd given me the water, so it had to be safe, and where the fuck were we?

Stone floors and iron bars for walls spoke of a prison cell. Curi was across the corridor in another cell with Levi. He hurried toward the bars but stopped a foot away from them. "You okay, Cameron?"

Was I? "What the fuck happened? Where's Serath?"

"I don't know," Curi said. "We woke up a little while ago. They left water for us."

"Who?"

"Whoever took us," Shar said. "The bars are charged with a paralyzing ward. Don't touch them. Curi spent fifteen minutes crumpled on the ground, unable to move."

I looked back at him, noting the dark smudges beneath his eyes. His skin was streaked with dirt, and so was Levi's and Shar's. I doubted I looked any better.

I took in our prison—stone walls, stone floor, no window. Weak light filtered in from somewhere by the corridor. "It has to be graynites. One of the two groups at war with each other."

"They drugged us," Curi said. "I didn't even know it was possible to knock out a goyle."

"They have my mother and Serath," Levi added.

Serath had been in my arms when the drug hit. "We have to get out of here and find them." We needed Derek. "Derek? Derek, can you hear me? I need you."

"If he could be here, he would be," Shar said.

"I know. I just...fuck. What are we gonna—"

The clang of metal on stone froze the words on my lips.

"Someone's coming," Curi hissed. "Get back from the bars. Just in case."

We all complied, pressing our bodies to the stone wall at the back of our cells.

Bootfalls approached, and a figure finally came into view.

"Hello, Cameron," Ignus said. "It's so good to see you again."

"You!" I GLARED at Ignus, incensed but strangely relieved also.

Ignus looked me up and down. "Yes, me. It seems I'm making a habit of saving your life."

"*This* is Ignus?" Curi raked him over, clearly unimpressed.

Ignus offered him a mock bow. "The one and only. And just in case you missed it, I saved your lives."

"Doesn't make you a good guy," Curi countered.

"No," Ignus said. "It doesn't. But where you're all concerned, I'm the best guy. The guy that is here to lift the veil from your pretty eyes and reveal the truth about what you've gotten yourselves into."

"I'll settle for you revealing what you've done with my mother and Serath," Levi said.

I took a step forward. "Where are they?"

He held up a hand. "All in due course."

"If you've hurt them..." Levi left the threat hanging, but Ignus's attention was on me.

"Do you believe I would hurt them, Cameron?"

The first time I'd met him, he'd tried to kidnap me. He'd used an invasive power to try to subdue me, and I'd been terrified, but the next time, he'd saved me, and now there was no malice or threat radiating off him. I had to admit it seemed his motives aligned with keeping me alive.

"I don't think you'd hurt them, Ignus, but keeping us locked up in cells hardly gives a good impression."

"It's a precautionary measure until you've learned and accepted the truth."

"And you're going to tell us that truth?" Sharniza asked.

"Some of it. The rest will be imparted to you...later."

"So, what can you tell us now?"

"I can tell you that we are not your enemy, and I can tell you that the true enemy is hidden in the gargoyle ranks. They call themselves the faction. I can also tell you that the graynites that attacked you were created by the faction."

Levi made a soft sound of disbelief, but Curi hushed him.

"What do you mean *created*?" he asked.

I answered for Ignus. "He's saying that this *faction* of graynites devoured my brother's soul and turned him into a monster?"

My team knew the truth about how graynites were made. I'd insisted that fact be shared with them as soon as they enlisted for elite.

Ignus rolled his eyes. "The faction isn't run by graynites, and even if it was, graynites *don't* feed on souls."

That wasn't what we'd been told. "Then how are graynites made?"

"Graynites were created by a curse," Ignus said. "They can't be *made*. They're born—either with the curse dormant in their blood, or as halfbloods like me." He grinned, showcasing even white teeth.

None of this aligned with anything I'd been told. "I don't understand. I thought graynites couldn't procreate with humans."

"They can't. They don't." He winked. "The boss will explain it all soon."

"Your graynite leader?"

"Yep."

"But the faction *doesn't* have a graynite leader?"

"Correct."

So non-graynites using graynites? "But they have graynites working for them..."

"See, you're picking it all up perfectly."

"What did you mean about the curse being dormant in their blood?" Sharniza asked my next question.

"Ah, yes. You see, there is only one kind of gargoyle that carries the curse." He smiled, but it didn't quite reach his eyes. "A sigma gargoyle."

STUNNED SILENCE MET Ignus's revelation, and suddenly everything began to make sense to me. Pieces of the puzzle fell into place as he continued to explain.

"The curse is ancient," Ignus said. "The story is long, boring, and something the boss will tell best, but this whole thing that your council has about sigmas being forbidden to consummate with their fated mates is wrapped up in the curse."

I licked my lips and said the words floating in my head. "Consummation activates the curse, doesn't it?"

"Yes. It activates the curse, and it kills the sigma's mate."

Shar exhaled sharply. "So, all this time when sigmas slipped up and the council took them away..."

"The curse had been activated," Curi said.

"Turning them into graynites," Levi said.

"Not exactly," Ignus said. "There's more to the change than simply activating the curse, but boss will be pissed if I tell you *everything.* He wants to speak to you himself. What I *can* tell you is that now that your fated mate has had his curse activated by artificial means, you're safe. You can consummate to your heart's content." He shrugged. "I suppose something positive has come out of everything, after all."

But how had this faction activated his curse artificially?

"Why should we believe anything you say?" Levi asked. "You could be playing us."

"True. But I'm not, and I think deep down you can sense that. Look, we have a common enemy. All these years we've been fighting the same fight. The graynite attacks you've fended off have come from the faction. They've dedicated their lives to finding sigmas and either forcing them to activate their curse or taking the sigmas that accidentally activate it and turning them into graynites."

But he was forgetting something. Something that refuted what he was saying. "Romi wasn't a sigma."

He arched a brow. "Wasn't he?"

The smug look on his face annoyed me. "He wasn't. He would have told me. Serath would have said."

"If he's a graynite, then it means he was a sigma. Lionel probably hid the fact. Not difficult for a man of his power." His eyes hardened, and his jaw clenched. "I'm sure he's used his influence many times to get what he wants."

A flicker of anger flared inside me. "Hey, that's my father you're talking about."

He blinked sharply. "Hmmm..."

"What is that supposed to mean?"

"It means that the problem is hiding in the gargoyle ranks."

"But why?" Curi asked. "Why would the gargoyles create this faction and do any of this?"

Ignus smiled a thin-lipped smile. "You'll get a story time off the boss later, but for now you have a choice—trust me and join me in more hospitable chambers, or don't and continue to languish here." His eyes narrowed, and he wagged a finger at us. "If you're thinking you can trick me into letting you out so you can make a break for it, think again. You won't get far. The complex is heavily warded and filled with...you guessed it, graynites."

I exchanged glances with the others, seeing my thoughts reflected in their eyes. After everything we'd seen and been through, it wasn't too far-fetched to believe that Ignus was telling the truth. That this faction was the real danger and the real home of the alpha.

I needed to know more, but first, "We want to see Serath and Adaline."

"Of course," Ignus said. "Adaline has been of great help to us looking over Serath. We needed to make sure that the entity inhabiting his body was gone."

Romi had called Serath Ubron. "What was it? What was inside him?"

"An infernal, but that's all I can tell you for now," Ignus said. "Serath is the first graynite that the faction has turned that we've managed to get our hands on. But he has very little recollection of what was done to him aside from the pain. He was able to carve out an anchor in his mind. A difficult feat. Very impressive."

My stomach twisted at the memory of the last time I'd seen Serath, the dark circles around his eyes, the gaunt look on his face...drawn with pain. They'd hurt him. Tortured him while I'd been free, doing pathetic, mundane things. He'd been hurting, and I hadn't known...not for weeks. And the shadow...there'd been a shadow by the lake...Had that been Ubron?

Ignus's jaw hardened. "Trust me, we will make them pay."

"Is that the curse?" Curi said. "Something takes over a sigma's body?"

"It's a little more complex than that," Ignus said. "But essentially, yes. Serath has been cleared, and we removed a tracker from his neck. He's already been debriefed and is eager to see you. I left Adaline in the guest quarters where I can take you all now, if you wish."

This was real.

It was all fucking real.

Serath was safe. He was free of the entity. He was whole again. "Please, take me to him."

CHAPTER 47

CAMERON

Splitting up in a strange underground bunker run by graynites was probably a bad idea, but in that moment, I was ruled by my primal emotions, by the need to see my mate and hold him, my ear to his chest so I could listen to the steady beat of his heart.

Ignus instructed one of the guards, another halfblood graynite like him, to take the others to the residences where he claimed Adaline was waiting.

There was no prickle of unease, no scent of deception in his tone, but was that because I wanted to believe him?

Their hideout was all gray and beige walls and floors, bleak corridors that connected to create a complex maze. I had no idea how Ignus navigated this place. There were no landmarks—nothing to indicate where we were or where we were going, but he took each turn with confidence.

I lengthened my stride to keep up. "This place must be big to house graynites."

"I suppose so."

"How many graynites live here?"

"Enough."

"You're not giving much away."

The corner of his mouth turned up. "I know."

What if I'd walked right into some kind of elaborate trap? No, he could have killed us while we were unconscious. There was no need for spinning a story unless he was trying to trick us and get us on side...The wrong side? Even if that were true, it hardly mattered if we went along with it and faked our belief in him. If it got us out of here safe and sound, then so be it.

We would have died in the barren lands if not for his intervention, which made me wonder how long we'd been unconscious. Orix would be going nuts by now. The academy, the council, they'd all realize something had gone wrong.

"Relax," Ignus said. "You've gone all tense and thoughtful. I don't plan to hurt you. We're on the same side. You'll learn to trust me."

"So, why did you try to kidnap me when we first met?"

"*Kidnap* is such a strong word. I'd call it extraction. Look, I was trying to save you from getting embroiled in whatever scheme the faction had set up."

"You knew who I was, and who Romi was?"

"Yes."

"You told me you could take me to him."

"I did, and I could have...back then..." He stopped outside a door and turned to face me. "I'm sorry for all the pain you've been forced to endure. For all the uncertainty. I probably could have handled that first assignment better, but...believe me, Cameron, you're in the right place now. We can keep you safe. You, Serath, and your friends."

My pulse jumped. "You want us to stay?"

He pressed his lips together. "If it were up to me, I'd *make* you stay, but the boss doesn't believe in enforced alliances. Once he's spoken to you all, you can make up your minds about whether you stay or go." He pressed his palm to a panel by the door. "In the meantime, how about some quality time with your mate." The door beeped, and he pushed it open and stepped aside to let me in.

I probably should have checked to make sure Serath was indeed inside before barging in, but the tug inside my chest and the heat that followed told me he was close.

I stepped into the room furnished in soft beige and brown that housed a bed and a couple of sofas. Serath stood in the center of it, his hands fists at his sides, and his face a mask of uncertainty and hope.

"Cameron..." His throat bobbed.

I made to cross the room, but Ignus grabbed my arm.

Serath growled low and menacing, and Ignus threw him a flat look.

"Calm down, big guy. I'm simply explaining the rules."

Serath exhaled and pressed his lips together. "I can do that."

"I'd feel better if I did it. Protocol and all." Ignus released me and pointed at the ground where a yellow line bisected the room. "Your mate can't cross that line. The bracelet we put on him stops him from doing so. It also stops him shifting."

"What? Why? I thought you said he was clean. That the entity was gone?"

"I did, and as far as we know it is, but we need to run some more tests. Who knows what else the faction might have done to him?"

"He's right," Serath said. "It's safer this way. If I start acting odd, you get across that line." Then to Ignus, "And if you touch my mate again, I'll tear off your hand, line or not."

"Noted," Ignus said with a concessionary smile. "Now, I shall leave you to it." He stepped outside. "I'm sure you're dying to be properly reunited. I'll be back for you once the boss returns," he said to me. "A few hours at least." He winked. "Enjoy."

He closed the door behind me, and I threw myself across the yellow line and into Serath's arms.

He rained kisses on my face, finally finding my lips and lingering there. I sank into him, body melting against the hard planes of his torso, fingers sinking into his luscious locks. I kissed him until my lips were swollen and throbbing before coming up for air.

He nuzzled my throat, inhaling me. "You smell so good." His

voice was a delicious abrasion against my sensitized skin. I rubbed against him, gasping as sharp shocks of pleasure tightened my nipples. "We should talk..."

He nipped my earlobe, then kissed the spot beneath, sending a shiver down my neck. "Yes. We should."

I found his lips again, sucking on the full bottom one before losing myself in my hunger for his mouth. He lifted me up and carried me to his bed, where I was enveloped in his scent. He hovered over me, eyes dark with desire and a tumult of emotions that echoed the swell and ebb of sensations inside me.

"I've dreamed about this moment so many times," he said. "Being alone like this with you, with no fear, no barriers. Being able to be here with you...to feel this with you...it makes everything worthwhile."

Everything he'd been through...the pain and goodness knows what else. Things his mind had forgotten to protect him from. Things that had happened to him while he protected his soul in the tethered place.

My stomach hollowed. We were alone. We were together. But at what price? "Serath..." I reached up to run my fingers along his jaw. "We don't have to do this right now. There's time." My beast pushed beneath my skin, begging for his touch, begging us to claim what we'd denied ourselves for too long, but I pushed her down. "We should talk. Really. Just talk."

He sighed and closed his eyes. "What if I don't want to talk? What if I simply want to feel?" He ran his hand down my body, starting at my collarbones and ending at my pubic bone. Heat bloomed in the wake of his touch, and my body arched beneath it.

"Fuck..."

"Yes, Cameron. I want to. I really fucking want to." He reached over his shoulder and yanked off his shirt. My breath snagged in my throat, my hot gaze feasting on the wide muscled expanse of his chest and every plane and ridge of his cobbled abdomen and thick muscular waist, then lower to his Adonis belt, partially visible above his waistband. I flexed my fingers, clutching at the sheets to stop myself from touching him, because if I started, I wouldn't be able to stop, and I needed this moment to take him in, to simply drink in every inch of the body I'd craved for too long.

He stepped away from the bed and hooked a thumb into the waistband of his trousers, slowly drawing them down. I'd seen him before, taken him into my mouth and savored him, but the memory was nothing compared to the reality before me. He was huge, ridged, perfect, and my body reacted, softening and tensing in all the right places while the pulse between my thighs deepened with need.

"Now you," he said.

I licked my lips, and he tracked the motion, a low purr vibrating his chest. It deepened as I pulled off my shirt and shucked off my pants, eagerly and nowhere near as sexily as he had.

My pulse raced, my heart beating so fast that all I could hear was the whoosh of blood in my head. Each breath felt like a chore without his mouth on mine. I needed him, skin on skin. I needed to feel him all over me. But he continued to worship me with his gaze.

I reached for him. "Serath."

He let loose a ragged exhale. "You're so fucking beautiful. And you're mine." The bed dipped as he climbed up, body eclipsing mine. My stomach dipped beneath the raw power he exuded, knowing he belonged to me.

That this...I ran my hands up his biceps, reveling in the sensation of taut, slightly silken skin against my palms. His muscles jumped beneath my touch, flexing as I gripped and dug my fingers in. This was mine. I gripped his nape with both hands, offering him my mouth, which he claimed without hesitation.

Our bodies settled, coming together as they were meant to, fitting perfectly against each other, skin to skin, igniting a fresh heat inside the pit of my belly that connected to my core. He fit between my thighs, his arousal thick and heavy against me as I coated him in my need. His growl of pleasure vibrated through me, and he broke the kiss, pulling away enough to make eye contact and hold me there, trapped in his pale blue gaze as he reached down between us to touch me.

"I don't want to hurt you." His tone was thick and deep. "I need you to be ready."

But I could barely focus on what he was saying, my body focused on the spiral of sensation he was creating between my thighs, on the stretch and invasion of each digit as he thrust into me, curling his fingers up to reach the spot that had my hips bucking up to meet his hand over and over.

"Fuck..."

"Yes." He gripped my jaw and claimed my mouth, swallowing my cries of release, a wave that seemed to keep hitting, getting higher each time.

He replaced his fingers with his cock, the pressure bigger, the stretch a burn. I cried out, eyes burning, tears leaking down the sides of my face as he entered me.

"Tell me if it hurts," he said thickly. "Just...tell me to stop," he panted.

But my body was still in the grip of an orgasm, sucking at him, drawing him in as he circled my clit with his thumb. I needed him to fill me, didn't care about the burn, the pain. I needed him. "No. Don't stop. Please don't."

He rocked his hips against mine, entering me inch by inch, and when my body met his ridges, light exploded behind my eyes, stealing my vision, stealing my breath, so all I could manage was a drawn-out, strangled moan that shuddered through my body.

"Fuck. Cameron. Fuck." His body locked against mine for a delicious beat before he drew out and thrust deep, slamming me into the bed. Our cries rose as one, again and again with each thrust.

I was broken, unmade, and unraveled. His to claim. His to own.

We came together, and in that moment, I was no longer in my body but above it looking down at myself, trapped beneath the monolith that was my mate as he drove into me with brutal abandon—the powerful muscles rippling across his back and shoulders, his ass tensing with each thrust. Rivulets of blood trickled down his sides where my talons sank into his skin. And as the sounds of our rutting created a delicious mating symphony, a silvery glow rose up out of our bodies—tendrils that became thick ropes that entwined, but what was that dark thread amidst it all? What was—

A force pulled me back into my body, and I was swept into a vortex of feelings as release ripped through me. Serath's essence wrapped around me, tight, cocooning.

Home.

THE BUNKER HAD decent water pressure and hot water enough for us to take a quick shower together before falling into bed again.

I'd ached for this, to be wrapped in his arms, skin to skin, no barriers, no rules. I'd ached for it, but now that I had it, there was a pit of foreboding inside me. What if it was taken from me? What if he was taken from me again?

To prevent that, we needed to understand what was happening with the faction and figure out what their goal was. He'd already relayed what little he remembered to Ignus, but why did I feel as if he were holding back? "Serath, you know you can talk to me if you want...about what happened. About what they did to you..."

His throat bobbed. "I know."

There was more to it. More to what had happened with him. "Ignus said that consummation is what activates the curse... Serath...What did they do to you?" My pulse thudded hard in my throat because I could feel his tension, sense the darkness that came over him when I asked this question.

"I think they injected me with something that heightened arousal. It made me see you at the lake, and I wanted you. I wanted you so fucking badly." He covered my hand on his chest. "My beast came out and took what it needed."

They made him imagine he was having sex with me? "They triggered the curse by deception? I don't understand...If the curse could be activated by simply *thinking* that you were having sex with your mate, then any sigma who dreamed of sex with their mate would have activated it."

He was silent for several seconds before replying. "I could smell you, Cameron. Your true scent, and I heard them mention pheromones at one point. I think they had yours."

"But how? How could they...Prasan?"

"It wouldn't have been difficult for him to take samples of sweat from your clothes. DNA from your hairbrush, your toothbrush even. Whatever they did worked and activated this curse, and then...then I was trapped in darkness, and something else was in control."

"Ubron?"

His body rippled with tension. "Was that its name?"

"That's what the general called you." I refused to think of the graynite as Romi. "But Ubron's gone now, right?"

"I believe so. I can't feel him." He turned his head to look at me. "But I felt our bond solidify. They may have mimicked a consummation and activated the curse, but what just happened here, that was real."

"I felt it too." But there was more. Something I'd seen...Fuck, I was overthinking.

Nothing else mattered right now except the fact that he was here. He was safe. I kissed him, a brush of the lips. Just a taste. "You fought, and you came back to me. You saved me."

"*You* saved me." He raked his gaze over my face. "I'd be lost without you. You tethered me, Cameron." He cradled the back of my head and pressed his lips to my forehead. "I thought I'd never see you again. Feel you again. But you're here. You're here." His voice cracked, and he gathered me to his chest, holding me as if I were the most precious, fragile thing, and he was afraid he'd crush me.

Heat bloomed behind my eyes. "I'm never leaving you. We're

never going to be apart again." I pushed up on one elbow to look down into his beautiful face. "No more running from this." I cupped his jaw and ran my thumb across his bottom lip. "We can have it now. All of it. Us."

His eyes darkened. "We will. We'll have it all, and we'll bring down the faction in the process. I'm not sure what they're planning, but when that thing was inside my body, I felt its intent, its excitement. Whatever is coming, it's close. We can't get complacent. We can't back down. We've got to do everything within our power to stop them."

My gums ached where I ground my teeth. "They killed Romi. I'm going to make them pay."

"We'll make them pay together," Serath growled. "Whatever comes our way now, we will face together."

"Yes, we can—" My skin prickled with a familiar heat, and I stilled.

"Cameron? What's wrong?" His nostrils flared, chest vibrating in a purr of pleasure. "You smell...so fucking good." He buried his nose in the crook of my shoulder, inhaling me.

My pussy throbbed at the contact, swelling as his mouth parted over my skin to taste me.

Fuck. I didn't have the tincture, hadn't taken it since before the trial. All the activity must have burned it out of my system faster than usual, and—

He pinched my waist, then slid his hand down to grab my ass, hauling me closer while he sucked on my neck. "Fuck, Cameron." He kissed his way up to my earlobe and across my jaw toward my mouth. "I want inside you. Now."

My eyes rolled back, and I moaned into his mouth, surrendering to the kiss that promised so much more. I wanted his cock deep inside me. Needed it. I could have it.

Like you had Curi's fingers in you?

Ice crystalized in my gut. Oh, fuck, how could I have forgotten about that? I pulled away. I needed to tell him about Curi, had to confess before the needing hit hard and took my senses.

He'd gone still, too, watching me. Waiting. He knew something was wrong, of course he did. He could probably sense it through our bond.

"It's all right, Cameron," he said. "You can tell me anything."

I breathed past the twisted ache in my chest. "Remember they said I had fae blood?"

He kissed my jaw, his lips coasting across to my mouth so his words hummed against my lips. "I do, yes."

I wanted to kiss him so badly. "Well, we figured out what it means, but before that..." I gently pushed him back so I could meet his gaze. "But before that, the needing hit hard. It was painful, and I couldn't assuage it."

His nostrils flared, eyes narrowing. "Go on..."

Spit it out, Cameron. I exhaled the words. "Curi helped me."

He froze, every muscle in his body gripped tight. "*Helped* you?"

I swallowed past the dryness in my throat. "He had to help me orgasm and—"

His roar shattered my ear drums, and he reared away from me, coming to stand across the room with his back to me. His shoulders rose and fell with heavy breaths.

My scalp prickled as I sat up. I could sense his beast close to the surface, but it wasn't fighting to be free, merely present. Listening? The bracelet was obviously subduing it.

Several seconds passed, and I waited for Serath's breath to calm before speaking. "We didn't have sex. It wasn't like that."

His growl made the hairs on my body stand to attention. "I need...I need a moment."

I waited some more, sheets clutched to my chest. He finally turned to face me, his form draped in shadow.

"Would you have let him touch you otherwise?" he asked. "If you'd been in control? In your senses?"

"No." The answer came easy. "I was desperate. In pain. I needed help, and I trusted him not to take advantage."

"Then I understand."

I exhaled on a shudder, blinking back a fresh wave of tears. "You do?" My lips trembled. "You forgive me for—"

He crossed the room and cut off my words with his mouth. "There's nothing to forgive." He kissed my throat. "I'm sorry I wasn't there. That you were forced to make such a decision. But I'm here now, and every desire"—he cupped my breast and squeezed gently, pinching my nipple so a line of pleasure shot down to my core—"every fucking aching need"—he slipped down my body and parted my thighs, his breath hot on my pussy—"I'll satisfy."

"Yes...Yes, please."

"What do you want, Cameron? My tongue or my cock?"

"Both."

He chuckled, raw and dirty. "Your wish is my command."

He started gently, lapping and sucking, circling my clit with his tongue, but the needing grew, filling me with a burning ache.

"Please, Serath. Please..."

He gave me his tongue, entering me deep and pushing up against the sweet spot to unleash a guttural cry of release.

I milked him as I came, thighs flexing, hips pressed to his face. He held me tightly, feasting on me as I rode the wave.

The needing ebbed to a simmer, and Serath raised his head to look up my body at me, his pupils blown, his nostrils flaring with each deep breath.

"My turn," he growled.

He flipped me onto my front and pressed my head into the pillow before hooking an arm around my waist with an impatient growl. There was no time to brace myself before he was inside me, driving into me hard and fast, burning me with his claiming as he held me in place. This was punishment for Curi. Penance. I'd take it. I'd take whatever he had to give because he was mine, and I was his.

Finally.

CHAPTER 48

Cameron

"Oh, Cameron...Wakey, wakey." Ignus stood by the door.

I sat up, clutching the sheet to my chest, but beside me, Serath continued to sleep.

"Don't wake him," Ignus said. "He's been through a lot. Best to let him recuperate. He's going to need his strength for what's to come." He glanced at the puddle of clothes by the bed. "Get dressed and meet me in the corridor. The boss is here, and he wants to speak to you."

"The others?"

"Them too, but you first." He left the room, closing the door softly behind him. This time it didn't beep, telling me it was unlocked. Had he locked me in here before?

Curiosity warred with a twinge of unease, but I slipped from the bed, dressed quickly, and hurried out to find Ignus waiting on the opposite side of the corridor, arms crossed.

He pushed off the wall and set off. "Follow me."

Once again, we navigated a network of corridors, and the lack of windows and view to the outside made my skin itch. "How do you do it? Live underground?"

"Needs must," Ignus said. "It's safest here."

"And where is here?"

He gave me a knowing smile and a wag of his finger. "Naughty, naughty. I'm not giving anything away until the boss says it's all right."

We took a flight of stairs, the space so narrow I couldn't help but wonder how a graynite would navigate it. It opened onto another corridor that ended in a door. Ignus knocked, and a deep muffled voice instructed us to enter.

"In you go," Ignus said. "I'll be waiting out here to escort you back to your mate once you're done."

I eyed the door. There was a graynite on the other side. The leader of this group. "You're not coming in?"

He leaned in with a smirk. "Why, do you need me to hold your hand?"

"Only if you want Serath to rip it off." I smirked back.

He stepped away from me with an exaggerated wince. "Good point."

If this graynite leader wanted me dead, I'd be dead already. There was nothing to worry about. I took a deep breath and pushed open the door.

The scent of peppermint hit me before I had time to register anything else. Everything was brown leather and old-school antique furniture. The lighting was soft and warm, giving the space a cozy feel. It was obvious this was a study, but the only occupant was a man standing by one of the bookcases.

I stared at him in shock. I knew him. We'd met in Mistlegate at Calista's place. "Ivor, what are you doing here?"

He exhaled, simply staring at me for several seconds before smiling. "It's so good to see you again...properly."

"I don't understand...Who are you?"

He smiled, open and welcoming. "I've been thinking about how to do this part. How to answer that question. Whether to start at the beginning and talk until we come to the end, or whether to drop the bombshell and clean up the mess a little at a time. I think...I think I should simply rip off the Band-Aid." He walked into the center of the room and tucked his hands into his pockets, looking down at me with bright eyes. "My name is Ivor Basque, and I am your biological father."

UBRON

THIS IS NOT how it was meant to be. This body is a gift to me. Mine, and yet he has claimed it back. How? How is this possible? I need to understand this strange tether that exists inside him. The inky ropes of power that hold me captive are threaded with crimson. They pulse with a strange heat that is almost...pleasant.

I can't break free, and so I wait. I gather my strength, and although time has no meaning here, I still feel its passage until something changes. The dark ropes of power trapping me slacken, and I rise toward the gray, toward a pinprick of light.

Oh...his presence is heavy here.

Saturating this body.

Filling it so that I have no space but this narrow tunnel to squeeze through.

No matter. It is enough. A space to hide and a route to the surface while his defenses are down.

Like now.

He slumbers.

Oblivious. Unaware. I push forward and gently steal control of his body.

He is not the only one that can hide, and while he sleeps, I will live...

Cameron and Serath's story continues in

The Stone Survival.

ALSO BY DEBBIE CASSIDY

The Veritas Legacy
Wicked Onyx

Gargoyles of Stonehaven
The Stone Initiation
The Stone Secret
The Stone Curse
The Stone Survival

Labyrinth of Gods
Lost and Stolen Gods
Damned and Broken Gods
Restless and Insurgent Gods
Wrathful and Avenging Gods

ABOUT THE AUTHOR

Deviyanee Cassidy is a *USA Today* Bestselling Author of Paranormal and Fantasy Novels. She writes under the pen name Debbie Cassidy. Born in the UK, and raised in a small town, she spent most of her time reading and dreaming up stories. After studying psychology at university, she worked various jobs before finally pursuing her passion for writing full time.

Deviyanee has drawn upon her cultural experiences, and Indian Mythology when creating some of her worlds. Her books are filled with action, vivid descriptions, multi-layered plots, and heart stopping romance. They feature strong female protagonists who find themselves drawn into supernatural worlds filled with magic, danger, and romance.

Deviyanee explores themes of personal growth, redemption, and the struggle between good and evil. She's been praised for her engaging characters, intricate world building, and emotionally resonant storytelling.

Learn more at: debbiecassidyauthor.com